SHADOWS AT THE WINDOW

Mack looked at her in the dimly lit hotel room. "You're only human after all. And here I thought I was being protected by Superwoman."

"Only human, Pulaski," she agreed, sliding her long bare legs across the bed toward him. The ancient springs sagged beneath her weight as she reached him. "And don't call me paranoid," she said in a husky murmur, "but someone is outside our window."

"You wanna convince them that we're really lovers?"

"No, but maybe you'd better kiss me while I figure out what we're going to do."

For a moment she wished she could just lie back and enjoy it. He was kissing her with a cheerful abandon that seemed to suggest he'd forgotten all about any enemies skulking around outside. And then his mouth moved away from hers, trailing a warm, wet path to her earlobe. She moaned and his raspy voice said, "Got any ideas yet?"

*Don't miss the next MAGGIE BENNETT Novel
by Anne Stuart.*

DARKNESS BEFORE THE DAWN

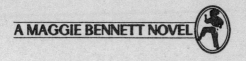

A MAGGIE BENNETT NOVEL

ESCAPE
out of
DARKNESS

Anne Stuart

A DELL BOOK

Published by
Dell Publishing Co., Inc.
1 Dag Hammarskjold Plaza
New York, N.Y. 10017

Chapter One first appeared in *In Search of the Dove* © 1986 by Rebecca York.

Dell ® TM 681510, Dell Publishing Co., Inc.

ISBN: 0-440-10061-5

Printed in the United States of America

January 1987

10 9 8 7 6 5 4 3 2 1

DD

one

Peter Wallace was irritatingly vague when he met her at JFK Airport as she stumbled, still sleepy, off the plane from London. There was the obligatory touching of cheeks, the awkward concern of two people who were no longer lovers and didn't really know why. "You look wonderful, Maggie," he said, hustling her through the crowds of people with his usual aplomb. "I don't know how you do it."

Maggie Bennett took the compliment for its worth, which was well-meant but essentially empty. She knew what she looked like. She had inherited her height, which was just an inch short of six feet, and her rippling wheat-blond hair from her Danish father, her aquamarine eyes and delicate bones from her English mother, her generous mouth and small nose from no one in particular. The dexterity and power in her lithe, strong body she had put there by sheer determination and a self-discipline that made her work out when she would much rather lie in bed and eat nachos. There was strength and warmth in her eyes, the slight shadow behind that warmth an inheritance from thirty years of living a none-too-easy life. All in all it was a package that added up to Margrethe Elisa Bennett, divorcée, older sister extraordinaire, reluctantly dutiful daughter, and one of the best damned lawyers Peter Wallace had ever been fortunate enough to hire.

"Thank you, Peter," she murmured, shoving a neat folder into his reluctant hands. Well-shaped hands, she noticed with an absent sigh. Clever, experienced hands that knew just how to please a lady. But not for her. Not any longer. "Everything's taken care of in the Kenya case. The political prisoners will be released next week, the families will be compensated at twenty-eight cents on the dollar—"

"How the hell did you manage that? I wouldn't have thought N'Bombo would have gone any higher than twenty cents."

Maggie shook her head. "I tried to get them to go even higher, but it was hopeless. At least it's better than nothing. So tell me, Peter, why am I blessed with having you meet me? Surely the president of Third World Causes, Ltd. has better things to do than meet one of his lowly employees at the airport."

"Not lowly. Most trusted." He was guiding her down the crowded corridors of the Pan-Am terminal with his usual adroitness, but Maggie knew him too well not to be suspicious. Besides, it didn't take her long to realize he wasn't heading in the direction of the parking lot. "I don't know how we'd manage without you, Maggie. These last three years have been wonderful."

"Why do I get the unpleasant feeling you're about to fire me, Peter?" she questioned coolly, halting in the middle of the corridor. Busy travelers threaded around them, muttering their disapproval, but Maggie stood her ground, impervious to Peter's gentle tug. "And where exactly are you taking me?"

"I'm not firing you, Maggie. I'd sooner cut off my right arm," he said. "I've got a new job for you, and we don't really have any time to spare. I'm putting you on a flight for Washington to meet with Mike Jackson, and then we have you booked on a flight to Salt Lake City leaving Washington at two-thirty tomorrow morning."

"Peter!" she wailed. "I've been on the go since three this afternoon. It's already after nine at night, and I've got a case of jet lag you wouldn't believe. Surely you don't . . ." She looked at his determined face, and the last complaint vanished. "Okay," she said with a sigh. "Clearly you do. Lead on, Macduff. I am yours to command."

Once more they were hurrying through the maze of terminals. "I need you to go to Utah and pick up a client of ours named Mack Pulaski. You're to pose as a couple—I'll leave it up to you whether you want to be married or not. I need you to bring him down to Houston within the next three days without anyone following you. Got it?"

"Got it. Who's Mack Pulaski?"

"He's a producer over at Horizon Records. He saw something he wasn't supposed to see, and certain people are trying to shut him up. I've had him holed up at an abandoned ranch outside of Moab for the last two weeks, until you finished up the Kenya job."

"Couldn't someone else have taken care of it?"

"You're the best, Maggie. Besides, it didn't hurt Mack to stay on ice for a while, just until we find out who's after him."

"And who do you think is after him?" She switched her carry-on luggage to her other hand and hurried along, her long legs keeping pace with his hurried strides. "What did he see that he wasn't supposed to? Should I presume it has something to do with drugs?"

"No one ever said you couldn't add two and two and get four," Peter said. "As for who's after him, we're still not sure. Mafia, probably. He already had one run-in with them years ago. The CIA may or may not be involved. It was Jeff Van Zandt who first sent him to me, but he took off before he could fill me in."

"So why Houston in three days?" She shifted the bag back again. Peter reached out his hand, then pulled it back before she could notice. He'd learned a long time ago that she was measurably stronger than his over-forty, desk-bound body was.

"Van Zandt is supposed to meet us down there if he can with some answers. If not, at least I'll have a couple of possibilities. I've got a folder on Pulaski that you can read on the plane, and Mike Jackson in our Washington office is supposed to provide you with some help. New IDs, credit cards, etc." He stopped in front of a boarding gate for National Airport. "Will you do it, Maggie?"

She laughed then, a deep, throaty chuckle that had once enchanted him. "I hadn't realized you were giving me a choice, Peter. Of course I'll do it. But after Houston I'm taking a vacation. Two weeks in the L.A. sunshine with nothing to do but tan. Okay?"

"Okay. But if I know your family, I'd think Alaska would be more restful."

"You're probably right." She took the folder, the flight pass, and once more they brushed cheeks. "I presume I'll find out anything I need to know in here?" She flipped the folder at him.

"It's still pretty sketchy, but Mack will fill you in on the details." She turned to go, and he caught her arm, the professional mask dropping. "Take care of yourself, Maggie. I don't know how dangerous this is. Probably a piece of cake, but there are no guarantees. I don't want to have to tell your mother and those sisters of yours that anything happened to you."

"Coward," she laughed, giving him a politely affectionate hug. "Just for your sake, I'll stay in one piece." And she headed on to the next lap of her journey.

She slept the short hour to Washington, picked up the paraphernalia from the faithful Jackson, and didn't get a chance to crack the material till she was flying over Middle America in the dead of night. The contents in the folder didn't tell her much—only that Mack Pulaski, a record producer and vice president at Horizon Records, had stumbled into a drug deal and someone was after him.

She still couldn't quite figure out why Peter had taken the case. They seldom dealt with anything involving organized crime; the majority of their work was in mediating third world crises, springing political prisoners, finding homes for refugees from the constant wars that plagued their small planet. The matter of Mack Pulaski could have easily been passed on to someone with more expertise in that area.

Maybe it was just because Van Zandt had asked Peter for a

favor. Maggie had met Jeffrey Van Zandt only twice, and she hadn't liked him. He had Kennedyesque charm overlaying the instincts of a great white shark, and he made her own instincts cry out in protest. But Peter genuinely liked him and trusted him, and Maggie had no choice but to go along with Peter's judgment.

Still, it was surprising that she was being pulled into this affair. Her experience in drug-related cases was almost nil, her interest and sympathy equally minimal. It made traveling an extra three thousand miles less than appealing, and her bad temper stifled her curiosity as she drove the wide, deserted highways down from Salt Lake City. Even the magnificent geography failed to penetrate her determined brain. She needed every ounce of her concentration to stay awake and alert, and she couldn't afford to waste any of her attention on the magnificent archlike formations she passed.

So here she was, standing outside a seemingly deserted cabin that had taken her far too long to find, with her feet sweating, her head aching, and her usually even temper shredded. It was a hot, dry day just outside of Moab, Utah, and the red-hued sandstone radiated waves of heat like a furnace blast. There were no trees, and no shade from the midday sun, just baking, blinding heat ripping the moisture out of her skin without even pausing long enough to turn it to sweat. It was the kind of day that made you long for February blizzards, she thought, pushing her hair back from her forehead. And what the hell was she doing standing out in it, like a mad dog or an Englishman, and not knocking on the weather-beaten door of the deserted-looking cabin in front of her?

Maybe a last remnant of ESP or her long-dormant instincts were warning her? She couldn't rid herself of the feeling that once that door opened, nothing would ever be the same again. She found it seldom paid to listen to that little voice of hers, and it was the last thing she needed right now, when those edgy feelings were probably founded on nothing more than too much junk food and a bad night's sleep.

Well, the longer she put it off, the longer it would take to get to her mother's swimming pool in Laurel Canyon. She would drag Mack Pulaski down to Houston, dump him, and then she was free. Without another moment's hesitation she reached up and rapped sharply on the door.

There was no answer. Damn the man, she thought bitterly. He was told to stay put and wait to be rescued. So of course he's gone for a walk. She banged on the door, more loudly this time, and then pushed it open. "Pulaski?" she called out, her voice low and even. "Are you in there?"

It was pitch black inside the little cabin, the bright glare of the sun penetrating only a few feet into the dim interior. Of course Mack Pulaski might not have gone for a walk at all. His enemies might have caught up with him and left him here in this arid climate to rot away. She took a reluctant, tentative sniff of the air. Dryness, dust, and the lingering odor of . . . coffee, she recognized with a start. If Mack Pulaski had gone, he hadn't been gone long.

"Pulaski?" she called again. "Are you in there?" Steeling herself, she stepped inside, keeping her back straight and her eyes on the tiny pool of light from outside.

"Stop right there." A voice issued from the back of the cavernous room. Raspy, raw, hoarse, it held a curious depth and power. She stopped where she was, grateful not to have to immerse herself farther into the darkness.

She couldn't see a thing. She peered into the inky confines of the cabin, and as her eyes adjusted to the darkness she could see a faint chink of light from a shuttered window outlining a shadowy figure standing in one corner. The shape of the body radiated wariness, and Maggie found herself speaking in a low, soothing voice, as if to a cornered animal, ignoring her own irrational fears.

"Mr. Pulaski?" she said again. "I'm Maggie Bennett. I work for Peter Wallace. He sent me here to pick you up and take you to Houston."

"Did he?" The rusty voice was skeptical, and the figure made no move. "Close the door and come over here."

"No." She was grateful her voice sounded so calm and self-assured. "I don't like being in the dark. Why don't you come over here so I can see you?"

"Why?"

Maggie considered controlling her temper, then gave up the effort. "Because I'm hot, tired, and hungry, and I don't want to play games."

"Okay, no games, but why the hell would I go to Houston?" Some of the wariness faded, and he moved closer. Not into the light, but close enough so that she could vaguely make out some of his features.

"Peter wants us to meet him there and I'm not exactly sure why. I'm just following orders, and my orders are to bring you to Houston." She allowed the full irritation she was feeling to show in her voice. "Do you want identification? I've got plenty—"

"Hand it over. And move into the light," that raw voice ordered, and she complied, tossing her open wallet at his feet. He bent down to scoop it up, and all she could see was his rumpled hair, his face still hidden in the shadows. "All right, I trust you," he said finally, moving closer. "I can see you aren't carrying a gun."

"You can't see any such thing," Maggie said. "I'm wearing a loose shirt. I could easily have a gun tucked in the back of my pants. The pants legs are loose too. I could be wearing an ankle holster, pretend I needed to tie my shoe, and a moment later you'd be history. I own guns small enough to fit in the palm of my hand that you wouldn't even notice until you had a bullet between the eyes. Don't be so damned sure of yourself, Mr. Pulaski."

He laughed then, a carefree sound in that ruined voice of his, and moved out of the shadows so that she could get her first good look at him. "What do you want, a strip search?"

"I want you to be careful. Your life and mine might depend

on it." He didn't look much like the grainy photograph Peter had provided her with. The shaggy blond hair was shorter now and mixed with gray. He had several weeks' growth of beard, a nose that had been broken at least once, and the warmest eyes she'd ever seen in her entire life. They were at complete variance with the rest of him—the rough-and-tumble clothing that had clearly been slept in, the tough-looking body that was maybe an inch taller than hers, the world-weary face and cynical mouth. His eyes were hazel and warm and lit with a sense of humor, and the effect was startling.

He was looking her up and down with those eyes, a curious, guarded expression on his face. "So you're my bodyguard—Maggie, is it? You don't look like you'll be much protection against the kind of people who are after me. Those wrists of yours look so delicate they might snap in a strong wind."

"Looks can be deceiving."

"I sure as hell hope so."

"I'll get you to Houston," she said, "if you follow me and do as I say."

"If I follow you and do as you say," he echoed thoughtfully. "Why did Wallace choose you for this?"

"Because a man and a woman traveling together are less conspicuous. And because I'm very good at what I do. Don't be sexist, Pulaski. I'm a lot stronger than I look." She turned back toward the welcoming light streaming from the doorway. "Let's go."

"Are you?" he said softly, almost to himself. A moment later she felt an arm swoop around her throat, cutting off her breath as she was yanked against a hard, implacable body.

She didn't waste a moment on useless struggling. She knew exactly how long it would take for her to pass out from lack of oxygen, and she also recognized that he wasn't using his full strength on her. She fought back, quickly, cleanly, efficiently, jabbing her elbow directly into his ribs, bringing her booted heel down on his instep, turning and raising her knee toward his groin and her freed hand toward his vulnerable throat.

But he was swiftly out of reach, far enough so that she had the time to recognize the attack for what it was, a test of her skills. "Satisfied?"

He nodded. "You're fast and good."

"And you pulled your punches. I could have taken you out even if you'd used all your strength."

His smile was no longer cynical; it matched the warmth in his eyes. "I'm sure you could. Maggie, my fate is in your hands. Let's go to Houston."

two

"You want me to drive?" Mack paused by the big white American car parked down below the cabin.

"Later. Driving will keep me awake long enough to get out of here. Once we've been on the road for a few hundred miles and I'm sure we're not being followed, I'll let you take over." She gave him a disparaging glance. "Maybe."

"Do I get the impression your heart isn't in this particular job?" He climbed in beside her, tossing his battered leather suitcase behind them and leaning back with a weary sigh. He'd grabbed a pair of mirrored sunglasses on the way out and a battered old hat, and he looked tired, grubby, and dangerous. "Or is my paranoia acting up?"

"You're right. I don't like drug cases, and I don't really know what I'm doing here. I can't imagine you're in any danger—Peter doesn't do anything halfway. He wouldn't have left you out there if it wasn't safe. If anyone has the faintest idea where you are, it would surprise me greatly. I think I'm doing makework when I've more than earned a vacation, and I . . ." She let her voice trail off, flushing slightly. "I'm sorry," she said, her voice more composed. "I don't usually whine. I'm just damned tired."

Mack pushed his shades down on his imposing broken nose, peering at her over them. There was no disapproval, no judgment in his hazel eyes. "No offense taken," he said in his sexy rough voice.

Silence reigned in the air-conditioned confines of the rental car as Maggie piloted it down out of the hills and into the scraggly town of Moab. But it was a comfortable silence. Maybe the trip to Houston wouldn't be as awful as she'd imagined.

They were heading out Route 191 when she spoke again. "Do you want to tell me about it?"

"About what?"

"About why you're on the run. The details in the folder Peter gave me are sketchy, to say the least, and my contact in Washington wasn't much help either."

"What do you know? I'll fill in the gaps."

"You're a record producer in New York, with Horizon Records. You were working on a recording session with a rock group when you went outside during a break and walked in on a drug deal. Am I right so far?"

"Completely."

"Okay. So you recognized someone you shouldn't, and you took off. That leaves a lot of holes."

Mack slid down farther in the seat, stretching his legs out in front of him. "So ask me some questions."

"How long have you been in the recording business?"

The rusty sound coming from him might have been a laugh. "About eighteen years."

Maggie took her gaze off the road for a moment to stare at him in surprise. "Well, then, you must have been around drugs before. You couldn't have been in the business all those years without bumping into drug deals."

"Sure, I've bumped into drug deals before."

"Maybe been involved in a few yourself?" she hazarded.

There was a long, dead silence. "Maybe been involved in a few myself," he agreed finally, his ragged voice flat and unemotional.

"Then what makes this so different? Who did you see, the President deliver coke or something?"

His mouth curved in a grim smile. "Something like that. I better explain something, Maggie. In my past I had more than a passing acquaintance with drugs. That was a lifetime ago, and

15

I've been clean for a long time. The people I work with know I don't like drugs, and they keep them out of my sight. There's no way I can stop someone from getting high during a session, but I don't want to witness it. I figure what I don't know won't hurt me."

He reached forward and turned the blasting air-conditioning down a notch before continuing. "Three weeks ago I went outside during a break in a recording session and saw one of the musicians, a guy I used to work with, buying a very large quantity of cocaine. He was buying it from someone I'd run into years ago, a man who's become very powerful in organized crime. At first I couldn't believe Mancini would be there doing the actual dirty work until I recognized who was with him. I'd seen the second man on Dan Rather just three weeks ago. He was one of the leaders of the rebels fighting the leftist government down there. The U.S.-backed rebels, I might add. It appeared they'd found a new way of financing their revolution."

"Not a good idea," Maggie said mildly.

Mack grinned. "Not a good idea at all. Mancini recognized me immediately, of course. He's got a good memory, and I played a pivotal part in his rise to power in the early seventies. I took off, planning to hide out until I decided what to do about the situation. I spent the night with a friend, and when I got back to my apartment the next day a bomb had removed the top floor of my building. It also removed three people living in the other apartments."

"And that's when you went to Peter?"

"That's when I went to find the musician who was the buyer in the drug deal. There wasn't much left of him, I'm afraid. It was pretty effective as far as warnings go."

"So you went to Peter?" she persisted.

"I went to Jeffrey Van Zandt."

"Not everyone knows a friendly neighborhood CIA agent."

"I know a lot of people," Mack said. "Van Zandt put me in touch with Wallace and Third World Causes. He thought you guys might be interested because of the rebel connection."

"He was right. That explains a great deal. So you've got the Mafia after you and the rebels. Not good, Pulaski."

"Add the CIA to your list. They've been turning a blind eye to the rebels' fund-raising efforts, what with Congress being so close-fisted about supporting them. According to Van Zandt, the Company wouldn't mind if a little accident happened to me along the way. I'm something of an embarrassment. Every way I look I see trouble."

"What do you want to do?"

"I'm not interested in heroics. I want to go back to work and be left alone. There's no way I'm going to stop the drug traffic between here and Latin America, and I'm damned if I'm going to risk my butt trying. People can stuff whatever they want up their noses as long as they don't involve me. Unfortunately, no one seems to believe that. Everyone wants to shut me up when I have no interest in opening my mouth in the first place."

Maggie's lip curled in disgust. "I guess you're not out to save the world."

"And I guess you are. Third World Causes, Ltd. sounds pretty damned noble. Do you get off on being a lady bountiful?"

She couldn't see behind the glasses, but she could guess that those warm hazel eyes were now cold and hard. He hadn't liked her judgmental tone, and while she couldn't blame him, some little devil prodded her onward.

"I get off on making a difference," she snapped back. "I think looking out for number one gets a little old after a while. But hey, it's your life. You can live in a little bubble, and Peter and I will do our best to make sure that bubble is safe and no bad guys will get you."

"You're so goddamn smug, lady. You think you're the expert on life?"

"I think . . ." She took a deep, calming breath. "I think we'd better not fight all the way to Houston. It's about fifteen hundred miles, and we're supposed to be a newly married couple on our first vacation. There are papers in the glove compartment. Credit cards, driver's license, the works. You're Jack

Portman, forty-one years old, an advertising executive from Phoenix. I'm Maggie Portman, your wife of two years. I'm in corporate law, working for an oil company."

"Sounds repulsive."

Her strong, slender hands clenched the white leather-covered steering wheel for a moment, then she relaxed them. "Sorry, you're stuck with me. Have you been married before or am I your first?"

"You're my third, and I hope to God you aren't going to cost me as much as the first two."

"You can count on that."

"But I bet you're going to be just as much trouble," he muttered direly. "Listen, Maggie Whoever, I'm going to sleep. Wake me up when you want me to drive." He began to slide down in the seat, the battered hat pulled down over his eyes.

Maggie casually checked her rearview mirror again. "You're going to miss all the fun," she murmured.

He straightened up. "Do I want to know what you're talking about?"

"Not if you want to keep living in your safe little bubble," she said sweetly. "I think we're being followed. For Christ's sake, don't turn around, you idiot! You can see them in the rearview mirror, two cars back. It's the requisite black sedan, two anonymous-looking men driving. They've been following us since we reached the paved road more than twenty miles back."

"Maybe they're just going in the same direction we are. This is the main route out of town."

Maggie shook her head in disgust. "Do you want me to stop and ask?"

"I want you to drive like a bat out of hell. Better yet, let me drive."

She grinned at him, the adrenaline pumping through her veins and temporarily wiping out the jet lag. "I don't think we should stop long enough to change drivers. Granted they're probably CIA rather than Mafia or the rebels, but I still haven't got a lot of faith in their sense of fair play. I think we're better off outrunning them."

"In this white elephant?" he groaned in disbelief.

"In this white elephant. It's got a V-eight engine the size of Greater Miami, enough horses for the Russian Cavalry, and it'll outrun any piece of garbage the CIA can come up with. The question is, can we take a chance in outmaneuvering them? I don't know whether they saw us, whether they can put out the word and have someone a little more talented catch up with us. Maybe we can just keep driving, looking real innocent and . . ." She let the words trail off as she looked once more in the rearview mirror.

The black sedan had passed the two intervening cars and was now riding close enough on their trail for Maggie to see the expressions on the men's faces. "Hell and damnation. They've made us."

"So it seems," Mack said mildly. "What are you going to do about it?"

"You're pretty damned casual, considering it's you they're after," Maggie snapped, keeping her hands resting lightly on the steering wheel.

"I have complete faith in you, Maggie," he said, leaning back in the seat and pulling the hat down over his face. "Peter Wallace wouldn't have sent you after me if you weren't the best. Wake me when it's over."

Maggie allowed herself a brief, exasperated glance at his recumbent figure. "Some help you are," she muttered.

"How could I help?" he mumbled from under the hat.

"What about moral support?" She took one last look in the rearview mirror, at the black sedan about to climb up on her tail. The stretch of highway wound straight ahead of them, dotted with RVs and trailers lumbering along like prehistoric animals looking for a place to die. "Forget it, Pulaski. We're out of here." And she shoved her narrow, high-heeled foot down on the accelerator.

As the speedometer climbed from fifty to seventy to ninety,

Maggie kept her eyes glued to the road. The RVs were looming up on her, but the sedan proved to have a bigger engine than she'd expected. Leaning forward, she pressed one of the switches on the dashboard and lowered the driver's window. Reaching into the map compartment in the door, she flung out a handful of stuff and quickly ran the window up again.

"What the hell was that, Maggie?" Mack demanded, raising the hat an inch and trying to look unperturbed.

"Nails. It's not foolproof, but a blowout would slow them down considerably."

"Nails? I thought it was going to be something more exciting, like tiny explosives or an oil slick."

"I'm not James Bond. Just a poor working girl, doing my best with everyday household objects. You'd be surprised what I can do with a can of tuna fish."

"I'm beginning to think nothing about you would surprise me. Do you mind if I ask how you happened to come equipped with nails?"

"A friend of mine named Jackson suggested I buy some on my way out here. Just in case of unpleasant possibilities."

Mack looked in the rearview mirror. "By the way, the nails seem to have worked. They're slowing down."

Maggie allowed herself a sigh of relief as she passed two huge Winnebagos and pulled back in line just in time to miss an oncoming BMW. "Thank God for that. A blowout might have killed them at that speed. A flat tire will just annoy the hell out of them."

"You ever kill anyone, Maggie?" he inquired pleasantly.

"Not yet, Pulaski." She smiled at him, a ravishing, delighted smile, and took great pleasure in his startled response. "But don't push me too far. There's a first time for everything." And slowing the car to a sedate fifty-five, she drove on.

"I know," Mack said five hours later. "You're not human, you're a new CIA secret weapon, and that scene outside of

Moab was just to curb my suspicions while you drive me straight into their clutches. Right?"

"What makes you say that?" The sun was sinking lower in the sky, casting ominous shadows that seemed to dart out at Maggie's exhausted eyes, and she couldn't even afford the energy to cast a glance at her previously silent companion.

"You don't stop to eat, to go to the bathroom, to walk around. The damned car doesn't even seem to need gas. I figure you've got to be the latest in advanced robotics. Or some sort of Superwoman."

Maggie ignored the shaft of irritation at the latter name. "I'm the latest in advanced exhaustion, I'm starving, my bladder is about to burst, and the car's on empty. According to my information, there's a sleazy little motel another ten miles down the road. With a sleazy little cafe right next to it. We'll stop there for the night."

"Sounds wonderful. Maybe I'll be able to get a sleazy little drink."

"I doubt it. We're still in Utah—the drinking laws are erratic to say the least."

"Maggie," he said, his low, rasping voice very steady, "I will kill for a drink. I have been living in a cabin that was little more than a cave for the last two weeks, eating canned chili and drinking warm bottled water with nothing for company but lizards and desert rats, and goddamn it, I need a drink. We can keep driving all night long until we get out of this state, but you're going to find me—"

"Will Jack Daniel's do?"

"Jack Daniel's will do just fine," he said with a grateful sigh. "Where?"

"In my suitcase in the backseat. You can wait till we get to our motel room. Another fifteen minutes won't kill you."

"It might," he said grimly. "Did you say motel room, singular?"

"Don't be coy. We're married, remember? You're not going to pull any nonsense about who's sleeping where, are you?"

"All I want is a bed, Maggie." He'd shoved the hat to the back of his head, but he still kept the sunglasses in place despite the twilight landscape. "I know better than to make a pass at Superwoman."

"Don't call me that," she said tightly.

He grinned then. "Listen, kid, it's a compliment. You leave me breathless and in awe."

"I'll leave you unconscious if you don't watch it," she warned. "I'm not in the mood to be teased."

"Maggie, you may look like Miss Sweden and act like Superwoman, but you've got the personality of a king cobra. Don't you ever lighten up?"

She thought about it for a moment. Every muscle in her body ached, her eyes were gritty and stinging, and she would have given anything to be able to dump Mack Pulaski at the nearest airport. But it wasn't his fault, and normally she would have responded to his teasing with better temper. But she was too damned tired to make the effort.

"Pulaski, if anyone could ever die of jet lag, I'm going to be the one. I was in London twenty-four hours ago, and I didn't get more than three or four hours of sleep a night while I was over there. I am so tired I could cry, and I'm sorry if I've been less than gracious, but that's life and you're going to have to put up with it. I'll keep you safe but I'm not going to flirt with you. And it's Denmark."

"What?"

"I'd be Miss Denmark. My father's Danish." She pulled off the road in front of a low, rambling motel that had clearly seen better days. "You stay put—I'll go register."

His hand reached out and caught her arm, and she noted its strength with absent relief. He'd be able to hold his own if it came to that. "You stay put," he said. "When married couples travel it's the husband who registers, not the little woman."

"Little woman!" she roused herself enough to snap.

"A definite misnomer in this case, but the idea's the same. I'll be right back."

She watched him go with her mind in a fog. Someone could leap out of the bushes, shoot him in the back, and she'd just be sitting in the car like a zombie. Well, too bad. Until she got a few hours of sleep he was going to have to fend for himself. He was strong, so surely he could manage for just a few minutes while she sat here and closed her eyes. . . .

three

"Hawkeye, incoming wounded . . ." The voice blared into her unconsciousness, and she burrowed deeper, away from the sound. "Hawkeye . . ." Maggie rolled over, away from the noise, and then suddenly her eyes shot open, all her senses alert.

"Not Superwoman after all," Mack's raw skeleton of a voice came from a few feet away. "Have you decided to join the living again, Maggie?"

Maggie raised her head, looking around her in complete disorientation. She was lying on a double bed in a motel room that had clearly seen better days. The paint was peeling, the color scheme was mud, the air-conditioning was complaining loudly enough to be heard over the black-and-white television with its interminable *M*A*S*H* reruns, and the bed beneath her closely resembled a sack of potatoes. Mack was lying stretched out on the second double bed, which filled the small room to bursting. He'd taken a shower, and drops of water still beaded his shaggy blond hair. The two weeks' growth of beard was scraped clean from his chin, the sunglasses were reposing on the bedside table, and he was lying there in faded jeans, a black T-shirt, and bare feet. There was a very dark amber glass of Jack Daniel's in his hand and an amused smile lingering around his mouth and lighting those warm hazel eyes of his.

"Wake up, little Maggie. I've got a sandwich for you from the sleazy little cafe. You won't like it much, but I don't think it'll kill you. But I'm not sure if I'll survive their chili."

"Why did you eat chili? I would have thought you'd be sick

of it by now," she said wearily, pulling herself into a sitting position on the lumpy bed.

"I'm a glutton for punishment. Do you always sleep like the dead?"

"Not usually. What'd you tell the motel manager?"

"That we were on our second honeymoon and I was going to carry you across the threshold. I don't think he even bothered to look." He reached down on the floor beside him and tossed her a paper bag. "Eat hearty, and don't ask me what's in it. Figure it's just one more price you have to pay."

Maggie swallowed the mystery sandwich dutifully, washing it down with the glass of whiskey Mack provided. "You want to call a truce?" she said when she'd finished.

"I was never fighting, Maggie," he said. "You must be feeling more human after your nap."

"I am," she said, leaning back against the headboard. "And more observant too. Who are you, Pulaski?"

"I've already told you who I am."

"I don't mean now. I haven't gotten a really good look at you until now, and you look strangely familiar. I can't get over the feeling I've seen you before."

"You may have," he said casually, draining his glass and pouring himself a healthy second dose. "Were you into rock 'n' roll in the late sixties, early seventies?"

"Who wasn't? Even in my early teens I had a thing for Jim Morrison. Not to mention—oh, my God."

He grinned. "You do have good powers of observation, don't you? I don't think I've been recognized in years."

"Snake," she breathed. "You were the lead singer of the Why, weren't you? With that glorious blond hair down to your hips. God, you were every teenybopper's dream of heaven, in your leather pants and no shirt, leaping all over the stage. And that wonderful . . . voice . . ." She let it trail off, her enthusiasm draining. "Good God, what happened to you?"

"My run-in with friend Mancini," he said with a shrug. "And don't look at me with that shocked expression, Maggie. You know as well as I do that things were pretty wild back then, and I was whacked-out. Different woman every night, different drug every hour. Or maybe it was the other way around. I was an arrogant bastard, and I thought people like Mancini couldn't touch me if I decided what they provided wasn't the proper quality. A couple of his goons taught me otherwise. A kick in the throat can put quite a dent in a singing career." He took another sip of his whiskey, and Maggie stared at him, unbelieving.

"And you don't want to kill him?" she demanded. "You're in a position for revenge, and you don't want to take it?"

"It happened more than fourteen years ago, Maggie May. I've had a lot of time to come to terms with it. Mick Jagger might be able to shake his ass all over the stage at age forty, but I haven't got his stamina. I was all set to burn out early and, in a way, Mancini gave me a second chance. You can't do illicit drugs when you're in intensive care for a month."

"But Mancini must think you want to crucify him."

"Don't get me wrong. I'd love for people like Mancini to be run out of business. I'm just not about to offer my aging body as a sacrifice in the cause. You can be Superwoman. I'm only a mere mortal who'd like to make it to the other side of forty."

"Pulaski, I'll ask you nicely. Please don't call me Superwoman," she said.

"Since you ask me nicely, I'll do my best. But it's tempting. You want to tell me why you don't like it?"

"Maybe when you know me better."

"Am I going to get to know you better?" It was an idle question.

"Maybe," she said. "Maybe not."

She let Mack drive the next day. He'd been almost docile the night before, remaining in his own bed without a single suggestive remark escaping that remarkably sexy mouth of his. He hadn't even objected when she insisted on leaving the bedside light on. He'd merely slouched down in the bed and covered his face with his hat. A few moments later he was snoring quietly.

She hadn't expected to sleep so well. She wasn't used to sharing a room, particularly with a healthy, attractive member of the opposite sex, and she was still keyed up and almost too tired from the last forty-eight hours to sleep.

For some reason Peter Wallace kept creeping into her mind. It had been months since their affair had faded away from lack of interest, and its end had been so subtle she'd hardly noticed it. That was what bothered her the most, she thought, punching the lumpy pillow. Maybe she wasn't able to fall in love, maybe her emotions had been so wrung out years ago that she had none left to give. The thought was depressing, and Mack's sleeping body in the bed next to hers didn't help matters. But his gentle snoring proved soporific, and the unexpected revelation of his past career faded out of her consciousness and into her dreams. Suddenly there he was, a long-distance kinescope of a sixties rock star, whirling, dancing, posturing, and prancing, that mane of thick blond hair flying around him, that glorious voice of his singing, howling, screaming, and crooning into the microphone. Until even that dream faded into a deep sleep that lasted until six the next morning.

The arid land of the Navajo reservation seemed endless as they drove from Utah into Arizona. The radio picked up nothing but static and Barry Manilow, the artificial climate produced by the air conditioner made Maggie's eyes itch, and there wasn't a fast-food joint in sight.

But at least there was no black sedan in sight either. The roads were filled with the requisite pickups that seemed the major form of transportation in that part of the world, interspersed with the omnipresent Winnebagos.

"I like the name of that one," Mack said out of the blue. "The Snow Princess out of Fairbanks, Alaska. You'd think if they lived in a place that pretty, they wouldn't bother to travel."

Maggie was instantly alert. "Don't you think that's sort of a suspicious name? I mean, isn't snow another word for cocaine? Or is it heroin?"

Mack gave her an amused glance. "Are you seriously going to tell me that Mancini and his boys would advertise if they went undercover? Or the CIA? Or the rebels?"

"Hell, Pulaski, you have too damned many enemies," Maggie said, leaning back. "You're right of course. You didn't happen to get a look at who was driving?"

He grinned. "A very large, very cheerful-looking lady well past sixty years old. Her equally large, equally cheerful spouse was beside her."

"How do you know they're married? You shouldn't jump to such conclusions. If they were both looking cheerful, they are probably living in sin."

Mack gave her a brief, curious glance. "I take it you've been married too."

"Not on your scale. Just once, for a very short time," she said, looking back at the Snow Princess with not much more than idle curiosity. It lumbered along in serene innocence. "We both knew it was a mistake, and fortunately neither of us was so egocentric that we couldn't admit it. I was on the rebound, and I should have known better. Did you ever marry on the rebound?"

"Maybe number two, but I don't really remember. I stopped marrying them a while before I lost my voice, and most of that time is a little vague." He smiled at her, that curiously seductive smile that she wasn't sure she trusted. "So who were you rebounding from?"

"A man. And a way of life," she said repressively. "And that's all I care to say about it. You want to tell me about your love life?"

"We've got only two days to Houston, Maggie May. I don't think I'd get past age twenty."

He managed to get a laugh out of her. "You're a con artist. I bet you played havoc with all the groupies' hearts."

"Groupies don't have hearts. Besides, I've learned my lesson.

I'm now down to one woman at a time. Quality wears a lot better than quantity."

"I imagine it does." She sat back, remembering for a moment. Quality and quantity. When it came right down to it, her past had been sorely lacking in both. Of course there was more than one kind of quality. There was breathless, mesmerizing, addictive passion that left you stupid and vulnerable and in so much pain it took years to recover. And then there was the quality that came with a good man trying his best, with her doing everything she could to love him back and, ultimately, failing. She'd known that with Will, her husband of eight short months, and she'd known it with Peter Wallace. The sense of emptiness and failure that had been nagging at her for the past few months came back full force.

Maybe it was bad blood. Maybe she was doomed to follow in her mother's footsteps, always falling in love with the wrong man, never being able to love the right one. Her sisters hadn't been blessed with any more luck than she had. Kate was on the verge of a divorce, Holly seemed to go through men like Kleenex, and Jilly kept away from them altogether. They were a sorry lot, the four of them.

"Penny for your thoughts," Mack's voice rasped beside her, and she looked up, startled.

"I was thinking about my family. You got any brothers or sisters?"

"One brother. He lives in Seattle, drives a car very much like this one, and totally disapproves of me. Loves me, but thinks I have a helluva life-style."

"So you do."

Mack shrugged. "I like it when I'm not being gunned down. It's not for Alan, but then I'd suffocate if I had to live his life. He's a stockbroker, with a socially ambitious wife, socially ambitious children, even socially ambitious dogs. I think their image is more real to them than what's behind it."

"What is behind it?"

"Basically good people but lacking in depth. Do you have brothers and sisters, Maggie May?"

"Three sisters. Half sisters, to be exact." She wrinkled her forehead. "Actually, I guess I have more than that. My mother had four daughters, my father had me and then three sons by his second wife. I tend to think of my half brothers as more like cousins. It's odd, because they're just as closely related as Kate or Holly." She shook her head.

"So what were you thinking about your family?" It was a casual question, one to wile away the long hours of Arizona flatland, but Maggie wasn't in the mood to spill her soul.

"Just that I missed them," she said evasively. She could see by the look he gave her that he wasn't fooled, but he dropped the subject. She was learning he had a way of doing that, pushing just a little bit, then pulling back when she got uncomfortable. She sort of liked that about him. She sort of liked a lot of things about him, even though she still wasn't quite sure she trusted him.

"Do you have any more of those nails you threw on the road yesterday?" he asked in a tone of no more than casual curiosity.

She looked at him, as she had many times during the morning, trying to superimpose her memory of the legendary Snake on the rumpled, world-weary, very real man beside her. He had the mirrored sunglasses perched on his nose and his hands were resting with casual competence on the leather-covered steering wheel. Big hands, strong hands, she noticed.

And then his words penetrated her abstraction and Maggie was instantly alert. "I threw them all. Why?"

"Because while I think the Snow Princess is completely innocent, I'm not too sure about the Little Hustler from Mobile, Alabama. Vern and Donna Jean and Jennifer and Tommy are supposed to be inside. Instead, they look like Juan and Carlos and Manuel. And I don't think they're here to see the sights."

"The men in the car yesterday weren't Hispanic."

"So we've traded one set for another. Great." Mack straightened in his seat, just marginally, and she could see those strong, broad hands of his flex experimentally around the steering wheel. "Where's the Snow Princess?"

"I can't see it but I guess it's behind the Little Hustler. Do you want me to drive?"

"I thought we already agreed that in these circumstances we didn't have time to stop and switch drivers?" His voice was still casual. "You're going to have to leave it up to me. Fasten your seat belt."

At least he'd stopped calling her Superwoman, she thought gratefully. "Are you sure you can handle it?"

"We don't have much choice, now do we? If it's any consolation, I can tell you that I managed to survive two Ferraris, a Corvette, and a Jaguar XKE in my misspent youth. I can assure you I did not drive slowly."

"This thing doesn't handle like an XKE."

"No, it handles like a goddamn tank. But at least it's fast." He cast a calm glance into the rearview mirror. "And I think it's about time for it to prove its stuff."

The Little Hustler had been gaining steadily. Mack had been accelerating, pushing the speedometer up and up, but the RV had managed to keep pace, even move closer. The Snow Princess was left far behind in the summer dust, but things were still overtly polite between the white sedan and the Winnebago. Maggie huddled down in the seat, her eyes trained on the side mirror.

"I think you're right," she said. "I don't think our friends from Mobile, Alabama, want to talk." Close up, their faces looked frighteningly implacable. "Why don't you step on it?"

"I'm afraid I have. Does this thing go much faster than ninety?"

"You mean to tell me the Little Hustler is following that fast? The damned thing must be all engine!"

"Enough engine to keep pace with us, not enough to pass us. They're going to realize that sooner or later, and we're going to have to hope they don't have guns. I don't suppose . . . ?"

"Nope. I came straight from London. Even with a permit it's

too much trouble to carry weapons around the various airports of the world." She allowed herself the luxury of swiveling around in her seat to get a good look at their pursuers. At speeds of ninety plus there was no longer any pretense they weren't in an automotive duel to the death. She swung back quickly, not even wasting her breath enough to swear. "They have guns."

Mack shrugged. "Got any suggestions? You're supposed to be protecting me."

"Don't remind me." Suddenly she undid her seat belt and dove over into the backseat, almost kicking him as she went.

"What the hell are you doing?" His imperturbable calm had begun to shred. "It's just slightly distracting to have you bouncing around the backseat. If you can't come up with a rescue, you could at least hold my hand."

"Shut up," she muttered under her breath, ripping open her suitcase and tossing clothes all over the car. "I've just had a brainstorm. Where the hell is the Jack Daniel's?" She pulled it out with a cry of triumph. It was half empty, which suited her purposes even better. She paused long enough to take a long pull off it, and then set to work with feverish haste.

"I hate to be touchy, Maggie, but this is no time for a drink." Mack yelled. "The Little Hustler is getting impatient."

As if to emphasize his point, the big RV crept up on them, tapping them lightly on the fender. The car lurched forward, and it took all of Mack's professed expertise to keep it on the road. "Maggie!"

"Shut up, Pulaski. I'm making a Molotov cocktail and it's tricky business."

"I don't care how tricky it is. If you don't speed it up, we're not going to need it."

"Damn, I wish I had something a little more . . . I've got it." She rummaged back into her suitcase, holding on tightly as their car was once more rammed from the rear. Grabbing her nail polish remover, she soaked her favorite pair of silk panties, poured the rest of the contents into the whiskey, and stuffed the underwear in the top. "Got a match?"

"Christ, no!" He was sounding definitely ragged at this point. "I gave up smoking years ago."

"Hell and damnation! Plug in the lighter."

"The lighter! You've got to be out of your mind—" Once more they were rammed, and Mack's language grew colorful indeed. Enough so that Maggie stopped a moment to listen respectfully.

"You've got a way with words, Pulaski," she said coolly. "Hand me the lighter."

She finally got the panties to light. "When I count to three I'm going to open the rear window. You just drive like hell. Ready?"

"Okay, Maggie. Do it."

She was both amazed and awed. To her Molotov cocktails were only theory, and the real thing was impressive indeed. The front of the Winnebago was coated in a sheet of flame. It fell back immediately, veered off the road, rolled over twice, and came to a stop in a forest of flames by the side of the road. Maggie watched long enough to see three figures scramble away before it blew up.

"Very satisfying," she murmured, neatly folding her clothes with shaking hands. "Just like television. No one gets hurt but the bad guys get vanquished."

"It would be nice if it always worked like that," Mack said from the front seat. "You okay, Maggie?"

She met his eyes in the rearview mirror. "I'm just fine." She kept the shaking hands out of sight. "I do this all the time."

"Sure you do, Maggie. Sure you do." And he drove on down the road.

four

"Chicken-fried steak?" Mack's voice was thick with loathing disbelief. "Are you seriously intending to eat chicken-fried steak?"

Maggie ignored him, flashing her brilliant smile at the tired waitress. "And a glass of red wine and a large Tab," she added.

"You're a barbarian," he said the moment the waitress was out of earshot. "No one in their right mind would order chicken-fried steak."

"I would. We're in a diner in rural Texas, and I intend to immerse myself in the experience." She cast a deceptively casual glance around the diner, at the flat, twilight landscape outside the dirty windows. "I've read about chicken-fried steak for years, and now's a fine time to try it."

"Read about it? What the hell kind of books do you read?" He took a healthy swig out of the coffee that every self-respecting Western waitress served first.

"Anything and everything. Mysteries, romances, science fiction. Everything but spy books." She ran a casual finger through the layer of grease coating the gray Formica tabletop.

"Why not spy books?"

She grinned at him. "I'm afraid they'll give me bad ideas."

He shook his head, and Maggie watched in interest as the fading sunlight played over his face. She was getting used to that face beside her day and night. Hell, she might as well admit it. She was getting to like it. Those hazel eyes of his were a peculiar combination of cynicism and warmth, as if he knew just how rotten life could be but still liked it immensely. His mouth was turned up in a half-smile more often than not, and the broken nose added character to a face that Maggie remembered as being almost angelically beautiful when he was younger. He could no longer be called angelic. If anything, there was a devilish streak about him that Maggie was finding more and more attractive. And she was old enough and smart enough to know better.

"Just because you grew up in Texas and take things like chicken-fried steak for granted," she said, her wayward thoughts completely hidden, "doesn't mean I can't enjoy the exotic local cuisine."

"What makes you think I grew up in Texas?" The waitress had placed a dark glass of bourbon in front of him, and he took a slow, appreciative sip, his eyes never leaving her.

"I'm good at accents. You must have left Texas early, because there's some California overlaying it."

"Good God," he said disgustedly. "Just what I always wanted to hear."

"Not too much though. I grew up in California so I'm sensitive to the accent."

"Well, your ear has let you down this time. I never lived in Texas. I did, however, have a best friend who came from Port Arthur—maybe I picked it up from her."

"Her?"

"Her." He didn't elaborate. "And the time I spent in California was when I was with the Why, and most of us were so stoned we didn't talk much. Guess again."

She took a sip of her warm, vinegary wine. "Not the East Coast, definitely. You don't really look rural, though that may be the result of the last few years. But I'd guess you were from a city. A big, nasty city like Chicago. You have the look of a street fighter about you."

"Right the third time. I grew up in the inner city. I think I joined my first gang when I was eight years old. Problem was, I always picked the wrong gangs. We kept getting the shit beat out of us." He laughed his raw, sexy laugh.

"What were you doing in Chicago in the first place?"

"My father dragged the family there after the war, looking for work. He found it for a while, but by the time I was a kid he'd left us. My mother always said either Alan or I was bound to go to hell—we couldn't both make it."

"And which of you made it?"

Mack grinned. "Who do you think, Maggie May?"

"I think I made a big mistake."

He looked startled. "Why?"

Maggie stared in shock at the platter of chicken-fried steak. "I should never have ordered this."

He laughed again, and she found she was liking that laugh more and more. "What did you think you were getting?"

"A nice chicken cutlet." She eyed Mack's thick, red steak with longing.

"I tried to tell you. With chicken-fried steak they take the oldest, ugliest piece of steak, coat it in flour, and slap it in old grease till it's the texture of shoe leather. Then they pour white gravy that's not quite as tasty as library paste on top of everything. The biscuits look good, though."

Maggie poked at the mess on the chipped china platter. "You wouldn't want to trade?" she said in a properly wistful voice.

"Immerse yourself in the experience, Maggie," he said cheerfully. "I'll save you a bite of the real thing."

"Thanks," she said sarcastically. She picked up her fork, put it down again, and leaned across the narrow table. She reached out, gently stroking the side of Pulaski's momentarily startled face. She liked the feel of his skin, warm and smooth, with character lines. She smiled up at him, a tremulous loving smile. "Darling," she said in a barely audible voice, "we're being watched."

He didn't move, didn't swivel around, as the realization darkened his eyes. And then he grinned back at her, a sexy grin promising all sorts of things a lover would promise. He moved his head to kiss her hand, his mouth hot and damp against her palm. "I still won't trade you my dinner," he whispered.

"I'm going to be sick."

"You didn't have to eat all that chicken-fried steak, Maggie." Mack's hands were relaxed on the steering wheel as they moved out along Route 10. "As a matter of fact, you didn't have to eat any of it. We could have ordered another steak for you."

"I didn't want to call attention to us."

"Maggie, you're getting paranoid. Those men weren't after us, they didn't even look up when we left. They were probably just some sort of sales reps for a gas company."

"You'll be glad I'm paranoid, Pulaski," she muttered darkly. "Just because they didn't leap up and follow us doesn't mean they aren't after us. They didn't look like sales reps to me, they looked like CIA."

"They looked like DEA to me," he drawled. "That's Drug Enforcement Agency, my innocent one. But I'm not about to let paranoia take over. I'm not the only wanted man in the Southwest, you know. I don't even know for sure who wants me." He cast Maggie an appraising glance in the dusk-darkened car. "I don't suppose you do?"

It sounded almost wistful, but Maggie decided it had to be an illusion in his ravaged voice. "Now isn't the time for fooling around," she said in her most severe, schoolmarmish voice. A voice that was at odds with her long, tanned legs, the rough cotton shorts and shirt, the tousle of thick blond hair wisping around her perspiring face. "In case you haven't noticed, I'm trying to save your butt. I would appreciate it if, in the meantime, you wouldn't covet mine."

Mack let out a burst of laughter. "Sorry, babe, but you have an eminently covetable butt."

"I'm not one of your groupies, Pulaski."

"Hell, Maggie, I haven't had a groupie in years. I've told you before, I think quality's a hell of a lot more important than quantity. Though I must admit," he added, his eyes sweeping over her six-foot length, "that you'd provide both."

"Cut it out. My only interest is getting you safely to Houston."

"Sure it is, Maggie May," he said genially, drumming his long fingers on the steering wheel. That wry half-smile of his broadened into a grin, and he began to whistle.

"You may be right," she said after a while, her voice sounding disgruntled. "There's no sign of anyone following us."

"Does that mean we can stop for the night?"

"That means we can stop for the night." She cast him a covert glance beneath her heavy eyelids. He was entirely at ease and relaxed. For all the sudden, unexpected verbal flirtation, there wasn't even the hint of sexual threat from him. She had no worries that he was going to jump her when they got into whatever dingy little motel room they'd be sharing. They'd spent two amiable nights together, and Maggie had no doubt they'd spend their last night on the road equally comfortably. Unless he was becoming as aware of her as she was of him.

The Lone Star Bide-a-Wee Motel sat alongside a deserted stretch of county highway, bypassed a decade ago by the interstate. Maggie chose it at random, Mack was amenable, and by ten o'clock she was standing in the rust-stained shower stall letting the hot streams of water wash away the grit and tension of the last three days. She could hear the sounds of the television through the pulsating shower and she smiled. It was a good thing she and Mack were going their separate ways tomorrow. If she had to room with him for one more day, she'd put her foot through the television screen.

"I don't suppose you'd feel like turning that off?" She ran the threadbare white towel through her sopping mass of hair as she paused in the bathroom door. Mack was lying on his double bed, his bare feet on the pillow, his head at the foot, staring with great fascination at an old Sybil Bennett movie.

He didn't bother to look back to her. "No way. I love old movies."

He'd taken his shower first, and was lying there in his favorite black T-shirt, khakis, a glass of whiskey in his hand, totally absorbed in the very bad drama on the grainy color TV.

"Maybe something better is on," she suggested.

"Forget it. I've always had the hots for Sybil Bennett, and I intend to enjoy every moment of this."

"She dies at the end."

"Thanks a lot," he growled, rolling over to glare at her.

"Don't worry, it has a great love scene," she assured him, moving past him to her own bed. She was dressed in running shorts and a sleeveless T-shirt, a good compromise for coeducational sleeping arrangements, but she could feel Mack's eyes run over the solid length of her legs. She dropped down on the bed, tossing the wet towel at Pulaski's head. "Maybe there are *Family Feud* reruns."

"Listen, Maggie May, let me have my erotic fantasies in peace," he grumbled, but he was watching her, not the television screen. He paused, staring at her for a long moment. "Did you know you look like her?"

"You've had too much Jack Daniel's, Pulaski."

"No, you do."

"Sybil Bennett is five feet two with jet-black hair and perfect features."

"Yeah, but still, there's something about your expression. Especially when you're giving me that go-to-hell look. You look just like Sybil Bennett telling off some pirate king."

"Sybil Bennett should have told off a few more pirate kings in her time."

"What do you mean?"

"She's my mother, Pulaski. And there were a few too many pirate kings in my childhood. Not to mention desert sheikhs, handsome princes, thirties gangsters, and the like. Sybil's very sentimental—she can't live without being in love."

He'd taken her announcement with his usual imperturbable calm. "Sounds like my kind of woman. You wanna introduce me?"

"She's too old for you." She could hear the irritation in her voice, and she didn't bother to disguise it.

"No one's too old for me. I told you, I've had the hots for Sybil Bennett since I reached puberty. Probably before. If you won't have me, I may as well go for the closest thing."

"I have three younger half sisters, all by different stepfathers. You could take your pick of them."

He was looking at her with undisguised fascination. "She's really your mother?"

"She's really my mother. Come to think of it, you're probably too old for her. She'd been heading down toward the early thirties last time I met one of her lovers."

"You don't approve?"

Maggie smiled at him. "Pulaski, I do my absolute level best not to pass judgment on other people. Particularly on people I love. My mother has a certain weakness for men, and sometimes it does her more harm than good, but most of the time she just enjoys herself. And more power to her."

"And what about you?"

"What about me?"

"Do you have a weakness for men? Do you enjoy yourself?"

"No to the first question, yes to the second. I try very hard to have no weaknesses whatsoever." Her voice was self-mocking.

"And do you succeed?"

"No."

Mack looked at her, and in the dimly lit motel bedroom she could see the crinkles around his eyes as he smiled at her. "You're only human after all. And here I thought I was being protected by Superwoman."

"Only human, Pulaski," she agreed, sliding her long bare legs across the bed toward him. She crossed the space between the two beds, and the ancient springs sagged beneath her weight as she reached him. "And don't call me paranoid," she said in a husky murmur, "but someone is outside our window."

This time it didn't even faze him. He smiled up at her. "You wanna convince them that we're really lovers?"

"No, but maybe you'd better kiss me while I figure out what we're going to do."

"Well, if you insist," he said in a deliberately reluctant voice. "But I'd really rather save myself for your mother." And before she had a chance to reply his arm slid around her and pulled her down against the wiry strength of him, and he was kissing her with far too much enthusiasm for her peace of mind. Not to mention her ability to concentrate on how they were going to get out of the motel.

For a moment she wished she could just lie back on the sagging bed and enjoy it. He kissed well, and his arms were relaxed, strong, and knowing around her, his hands sensuously molding her to him. His hands were on her rear, his tongue was in her mouth, and he was kissing her with a cheerful abandon that seemed to suggest he'd forgotten all about any enemies skulking around outside their window. And then his mouth moved away from hers, trailing a warm, wet path to her earlobe, and his raspy voice was in her ear.

"Got any ideas?"

She had a great many ideas, most of them involved with the hard, male body she found herself wrapped around. But common sense reared its ugly head, and she forced herself to withdraw from the temptation of warm male flesh. "Turn off the lights." She said it aloud, in a convincing imitation of a sensual growl, and Mack's answering rumble of laughter helped douse the burning coals of passion that had built up against her will.

"Sure thing, babe," he said in a husky murmur pitched to reach the silent watcher outside their window. "But I'd rather be able to see you. You didn't used to be so shy." Without letting go of her, he reached across, turning off the low-wattage light bulb that the Lone Star Bide-a-Wee Motel thought would suffice for reading. Then they were alone, with only the quiet murmur of Sybil Bennett's cultured British tones warring with the sound of their mingled breathing and the flickering light from the television providing eerie illumination to the drab motel room.

"What next?" he mouthed silently against her ear. His body was still half on top of hers, but he held himself very still, doing nothing to increase the pressure of his hips against hers.

"Stay where you are." She slid from underneath him, off the bed with a fluid, silent grace, moving through the dimly lit motel room like a ghost, keeping well away from the windows. She edged over to the outside wall, pressed her back against the stained and scarred paneling, and moved her head a fraction of an inch, just far enough to get a tiny glimpse out into the scrubby bushes that lined the front of the motel.

"What are you doing?" Mack pitched his voice perfectly—it reached her on the breath of a sigh, going no farther than her ears. And then he raised it a few decibels. "Damn it, Maggie, are you laughing?"

She couldn't hold it back any longer. The amusement rippled out of her, a rich full laugh as she staggered back to her own bed. Only for a moment she considered rejoining him on his bed, considered and then wisely rejected the notion. She flopped down on her bed, still laughing. "You can turn on the light," she said in a normal voice. "And you can call me paranoid."

"Don't tell me there was no one out there. I heard them too." He switched on the light, squinting in the sudden brightness.

"Oh, there's someone out there, all right—three teenage boys! They've given up on us since we were unsporting enough to turn off the lights, and now they're peering in the window three doors down." She let a last chuckle fade away in a contented sigh. "I guess I have been too alarmist. I'll be glad when we get to Houston tomorrow and you're no longer my responsibility."

"Been that tough on you?" he drawled, turning his attention back to the television.

For the first time Maggie felt a moment's doubt. Surely Mack Pulaski couldn't have hurt feelings? Surely he wanted this small odyssey to be over with as much as she did. Didn't he? Didn't she?

"I'd like to deliver you in one piece, Pulaski," she said after a moment. "We can argue about it when I fix you up with my mother."

He grinned, and she decided she'd imagined that momentary reaction. But he said nothing, turning back to the ever-present din of the TV, and Maggie lay back on the bed, stretching her long legs out and closing her eyes. She wasn't lying when she said she'd be glad to pass him over to Peter Wallace. It had been years since her instincts had played her false. She could have sworn the men in the diner were far too interested in the two of them. She could have sworn someone had been watching them tonight, and not for the sake of vicarious thrills. When it came to a time that her reflexes were so far off, it was time for a long break. Whether she liked it or not, lives were depending on her. And she was beginning to doubt whether she could live up to the responsibility. This was still fairly new to her, this life-or-death situation. She'd managed so far, but there were no guarantees that she'd continue her lucky streak.

"Don't worry about it, Maggie May," Mack's raw voice came from the other bed. "A little paranoia can come in handy sometimes."

Maggie's eyes flew open. "How'd you know what I was thinking about?"

He grinned. "I know you better than you think, lady."

"Am I that transparent?"

"No, I'm that good," he said, reaching down beside his bed for his abandoned glass of whiskey. "I'll tell you something else, Superwoman."

She didn't even bother to snap at him for the nickname. "What?" she demanded warily.

"I don't think you'll be abandoning me in Houston. I think we've got more in store for us than a three-day trek across the Southwest."

"Oh, you do, do you?"

"Yup. And my instincts are seldom wrong."

Maggie opened her mouth to protest, to announce that her instincts didn't tell her any such thing. But she realized with a

43

sudden rush of indecipherable emotions that her instincts agreed with his. Their journey together was far from over. And she wished she could figure out whether the idea pleased or worried her.

But right now she was too tired to worry about it. With the sound of her mother's voice echoing in her ears, she willed herself into a deep, dreamless sleep.

f i v e

She was awake in an instant. The harsh blue fluorescent light from the bathroom provided a glaring pool against the darkness of the motel room. She squinted at the flat, thin Rolex that was her one concession to yuppie-dom. It was 4 A.M., and something wasn't right. The instincts that had been acting up for the past twenty-four hours, the instincts that she'd tried to ignore, that seemingly had been proven wrong, were now back in full force. And suddenly Maggie knew that the salesmen in the diner weren't salesmen, and even if the teenage boys lurking outside their window were harmless, there were other eyes watching, eyes that weren't quite so innocent.

She moved from her lumpy bed, edging next to Mack's sleeping body, over to the curtained window that let in the murky glare of streetlights through the shiny, threadbare material. She pushed the drape to one side and peered out into the darkness, and then swore.

Their big white rental car was still sitting outside beneath the streetlamp. From her vantage point Maggie could see that at least two of its tires were slashed and very flat indeed. And on either side, like dark, evil sentries, sat anonymous black sedans, hemming in their only means of escape.

The sedans were empty, and there was no one in sight, but Maggie knew they couldn't have gone very far. These people were frighteningly professional. She couldn't imagine how they had found the two of them, but find them they had, and she was going to have to be even more inventive. She could see something running underneath the picture window and she couldn't tell if it was a string that could be cut or a wire.

"What's up?" Mack's voice was a whisper of sound in her ear, and she jerked upright, slamming her head against his chin.

He didn't say a word, though she could see it cost him a great deal of effort. "Someone's here," she mouthed back at him, barely a sound escaping her lips.

"Are you sure?"

"Look for yourself. But don't open the door. I can't be certain, but I think they've got a wire or a string leading from our door to wherever they're hiding out. Probably in the room next door. All we have to do is open that door and they'll be on us like fleas on a dog."

"String sounds pretty basic to me. Aren't the people we're running from a little more into technology?"

"It's basic but effective. Besides, maybe it's a wire-tripped bomb. Would that satisfy your sense of propriety a little better?"

"What makes you think it isn't?"

"They've got cars hemming ours in. All three cars would go up if that string trips a bomb, and I don't think they'd be into needless waste. Not to mention all the noise it would make. I wouldn't think our friends, whoever they are, would want to call attention to themselves. Even the Mafia frowns on too much publicity."

"Unless it's the CIA. They've got the power to cover up our explosion with a logical explanation and they wouldn't give a damn how many cars they blew up. After all, our taxes would pay for it, and the government doesn't give a damn how much things cost."

"Don't you think this is a ridiculous time to discuss government overspending?" she hissed.

Mack shrugged. "What else are we going to do? It doesn't look as if we dare open that door."

"We go out another way, of course."

"What other way?"

"There's a small window in the bathroom that'll prove a tight squeeze. You might put some clothes on," she added dryly, casting a seemingly disinterested glance at his body, clad only in a pair of navy-blue Jockey shorts. "But we won't be able to take anything with us. Only what you can put in your pockets."

"What do we do once we get out the window?" he drawled, and there was a slight edge to his voice. "Not that I don't have complete faith in you, Maggie May, but I hate to go into anything blind."

"Don't bother me with details. I'm making this up as I go along."

She dressed more quickly than he did, pulling a pair of jeans over her running shorts and topping it with a cotton sweater against the early morning chill. She didn't bother with her purse, simply taking out the credit cards and money. Slipping into her Nikes, she was busy with the latch on the narrow window when he came up behind her.

"You really think we're going to fit through that?" He eyed it dubiously.

"If I can, you can," she muttered, pushing the rusty hinge open with what seemed a scream of metal to her sensitive ears. She stood motionless, waiting. No sound came from anywhere around them, and Maggie could guess that in a sleazy old motel such as the Lone Star Bide-a-Wee the soundproofing was almost nonexistent. Either they hadn't alerted their watchers or their enemies were as circumspect as they were. Whichever it was, Maggie didn't care to wait around to find out. "Follow me, Pulaski," she said, climbing up on the shaky toilet seat and scrambling out the window, landing on the ground with more silence than grace.

Mack landed with more of a thud, but he hit the ground running, and within moments they were a block and a half away, racing down the deserted sidewalks of the sleazy little border town. They didn't stop until they were winded, until Maggie fell against the side of a building, gasping for breath, holding the stitch in her side. And then she grinned up at him, immensely pleased with herself.

"Damn, we're good," she said, with almost a sense of wonder.

Mack took a little longer before he was able to speak. "You like this, don't you?" he wheezed.

"I haven't decided yet." Her breathing was slowing to normal. "But it sure is exhilarating."

"If you say so. I'll ask you again—what next?"

"I was thinking we might sneak back, reconnoiter a bit, and see if we can learn anything. If we're very careful—"

"Lady," Mack interrupted her in awesome tones, "you just dragged me at a dead run halfway across this miserable little town. Are you seriously suggesting we go back again, putting our lives in danger?"

"Who says our lives were in danger?" she shot back, stung. "They may have been just watching us. I want to see—" Whatever she wanted to see was lost in the sudden bright flash of light to the west of them, followed by a crack of thunder and a minor earthquake. Maggie was flung back against the building, but Mack maintained his balance, staring at the billowing black smoke that was filling the predawn sky.

"I guess the black sedans were expendable," he said grimly.

Maggie followed his gaze. There wouldn't be much left of the motel in an explosion of that size, and she ran a nervous tongue over suddenly parched lips. "As I was saying, the first thing we do is get the hell out of here," she said, her voice almost as raw and strained as Mack's permanently wrecked one. "We need transportation. I'm counting on you for that. Come on." She headed off at a brisk trot, and he followed.

"What the hell do you mean, you're counting on me?" he demanded, jogging beside her.

"You're the one who used to run with teenage gangs," she pointed out coolly. "Surely you remember how to steal a car."

"I should be offended."

"You should be flattered. I'm sure I could manage to steal a car if I had to, but I'm trusting your expertise. Is our best bet a private car or something on a car lot?"

Mack gave up arguing. "I always preferred car lots. That way you get your choice."

Maggie nodded. In the distance they could hear sirens, fire engines and, no doubt, police. "Be ready to duck if they come our way."

"Yes, ma'am," he said with spurious docility. "Anything you say."

She cast an apologetic glance back over her shoulder. "Sorry. I forget that you're more than capable of holding up your end of this situation. I think there were car dealerships somewhere in this area of town."

"Used car would be better."

"Used cars if we can find them," she agreed.

Her memory, thank heavens, hadn't failed her. As sirens screamed by on parallel streets she and Mack moved farther and farther away. Until they finally turned onto what passed for the local strip, the golden arches of McDonald's dim in the slowly lightening sky, the used-car lots lit by strings of brightly colored lights.

"How does O'Malley's Used Cars sound, Pulaski?" she asked.

"Sounds terrific as long as Mr. O'Malley doesn't have a night watchman or an unfriendly Doberman."

Maggie smiled at him sweetly. "I can't tell from here. We'll just have to live dangerously."

He just stared at her for a long moment, a bemused expression on his face. "I'm warning you, I'm out of practice. And I never was one of the experts. Fast Dougal was as good as they come, stealing a car in under a minute. The closest I came was three and a half minutes, and that was when I was in practice."

"I have faith in you. Take your pick."

He surveyed the unpromising landscape around them. "American cars are easier than foreign cars," he mused, half to himself. "But VW Bugs are the ones I had the most experience on. Why don't we go for that one?" He pointed out a bright orange monstrosity that had seen better years. Tattered yellow daisy decals dotted the hood, and a matching, wilted-looking plastic flower hung from the sagging antenna.

Maggie made a face. "Why couldn't you have been adept in Mercedes?" she moaned. "Go ahead, Pulaski."

For all his doubts, he made fast work of the car. The door wasn't locked, probably due to the fact that the driver's window was missing. Maggie watched with mingled amazement and respect as he deftly hot-wired the little vehicle, jumped in the driver's seat, and grinned up at her. "You ready, Maggie? Let's get the hell out of here."

She climbed in beside him, yanking the loosely hinged door shut behind her. Staring at the cramped, definitely smelly confines of the little car, she sighed. "Hit the road, Jack."

It hadn't been her best night's sleep, and no sooner had they put the little town behind them and headed back out on Route 10 than Maggie dozed in her seat. The old VW was surprisingly comfortable, and the cool breeze blowing in the missing driver's window was even better than air-conditioning. It was getting on toward midday when she finally awoke, the AM radio penetrating her determined sleep.

She turned to look at Mack. He was relaxed, an arm resting on the empty window frame as the little bug chugged along the wide highway. He had the beginnings of a beard again, and the chambray shirt he'd grabbed before their midnight dash was open to the midday heat. It was a nice chest, Maggie thought sleepily. In another place, another time, there would be nothing she'd like better than to reach out her hand and slide it inside that open shirt. . . .

But that wasn't exactly her style, even in the best possible of places and times. And besides, hadn't she just given up on ever finding a happy-ending kind of love? Still and all, Mack Pulaski, a.k.a. Snake, certainly looked as if he could provide a substantial temporary distraction, even if forever after wasn't in the cards.

"What're you looking at Maggie May?" His raw voice startled her. He kept his eyes straight ahead, but he must have been aware of her perusal the entire time. She had to remember not to underestimate him.

She yawned, sitting upright and running a hand through her tangled blond hair. "Your luscious body, Pulaski," she said. "Did you manage to bring a comb when we checked out?"

"Nope."

"Damn," she said genially. "By the way, does this car have license plates?"

"It's a little late to think of that, isn't it? I checked before I made my choice. We would have been stopped hours ago with no plates."

"Do you think Mr. O'Malley's discovered it's stolen yet?"

"I have my doubts. It was about the worst car on the lot. He's much more likely to have noticed if one of his Cadillacs had disappeared."

"Which reminds me," Maggie said, braiding her thick, tangled hair and wrapping a rubber band around the end. "Why in the world would you steal VWs in the first place? They wouldn't be worth much in resale—I thought car thieves usually went for the big-ticket items."

"That's why I was only a third-class car thief. I stole VWs because they were the easiest to steal. I didn't make a practice of it, you know. It was more a test of manhood in the gangs, not a major source of income."

"I don't think I want to know what the major source of income was," she said faintly.

"I don't think you do." He cast an enigmatic glance over at her disheveled figure. "There's Tab and peanut-butter cookies in the backseat if you want breakfast. It was the best I could do at the gas station, but with someone of your sophisticated palate I figured it would hit the spot."

"God, I didn't even realize you stopped."

"You were pretty tired." Still that distant expression, both on his face and in his voice. Maggie dived over the back, retrieved the goodies, and settled back down in the front seat for a feast.

"Okay, Pulaski," she said, taking her first swig of the soft drink. "What's bugging you?"

He didn't even bother to deny it. "How many people do you think were in that motel this morning?"

She put the cookie back down. "It wasn't your fault," she said in a gentle voice.

"How many?"

"Three other rooms were occupied when we went to bed last night. Probably six other people at the most. I don't think anyone registered late. I would have heard them."

"You didn't hear whoever set the bomb."

"No, I didn't," she agreed, waiting for his condemnation. He was suffering a near-terminal attack of guilt, and the only way to get rid of it was to heap some on her head. She expected it, didn't even mind it. She was used to dealing with guilt.

But once again Mack surprised her. "There were three people killed in New York," he said. "When they bombed my apartment building."

"Yes," she said, still not knowing what he wanted from her.

"And it's possible that you could get killed delivering me to Peter Wallace." He didn't look at her, his posture behind the small wheel of the bug was relaxed, but Maggie wasn't fooled. She could see a nerve jerking in his cheek, and his usually warm eyes looked bleak as they surveyed the Texas landscape ahead of them.

"It's possible," she allowed. "But not very likely. I'm good at what I do. Not good enough, or no one would have gotten killed at the motel, but good enough to protect both of us."

"I wasn't blaming you, Maggie," he said, and to her amazement she realized that he wasn't. "But I've got to figure out if my life is worth—what is it, nine lives already? And God knows how many more before they're through."

"What did you have in mind? Walking into their welcoming

arms next time they sneak up on us? I didn't know you had a martyr complex."

She was hoping to sting him. Instead, he just smiled. "I don't want to be the indirect or direct cause of anybody else getting blown away, Maggie. Particularly not you."

"Very noble. But even if you made the ultimate sacrifice, they'd probably do their damnedest to get to me, just in case I saw anything or you told me anything that might be incriminating. The people who are after you make a habit of killing innocent people. You included. And once they took care of you they'd be after someone else. There's no way you can win, you can only do what feels right." She knew she was preaching, but she couldn't help it.

"And what if I told you that letting them get me is what feels right?"

"Then I'd tell you you're full of shit. And you'll do it over my dead body."

"That's exactly what I'm trying to avoid."

"Do me a favor then," she said. "Don't give me any more problems with these sudden noble impulses. I've got all I can handle with the Mafia, the CIA, and the rebels after you."

"Don't forget the state police. We've stolen a car."

The tension had broken. "Heavens, let's not forget the state police," she said, popping a peanut-butter cookie in her mouth. "If anybody gets you, I'll have to take the rap alone for this little felony. You can't give up now, Pulaski. I need you."

He turned to look at her then. His hazel eyes were warm once more, his sexy mouth curled in a smile, and for the first time in days Maggie remembered his earlier incarnation as Snake, the sex god of the sixties. "Do you, Maggie May? I'll keep that in mind." And he turned his attention back to the highway.

s i x

"Okay, Maggie," Mack said, pushing the mirrored sunglasses down on his nose to peer at her. "We're approaching Houston, it's three-thirty in the afternoon, and you still haven't told me where the hell we're going."

Maggie shifted for the thousandth time in the cramped front seat of the noisy little VW. Beetles weren't made for anyone nearly six feet tall—she did far better in big American cars, she thought with a nostalgic sigh. It was lucky she had Third World Causes behind her, because she'd have a hard time explaining to Avis just what happened to her rental car. "We're meeting Peter Wallace," she said finally.

"You've already told me that much. You just haven't told me where or when. Or why, for that matter."

"We're meeting him at his offices at the Travers Hotel in downtown Houston. I don't know when—my orders were to check in sometime on Friday and he'd be in touch."

"Why?"

"He's supposed to have come up with some answers. Jeffrey Van Zandt might be there too. He always knows more than he should." Her neutral voice would have fooled most people, and she leaned back in the uncomfortable seat, pushing a hand through the wisps of blond hair that were escaping her braid.

"You don't like Van Zandt."

It was a statement, not a question, but Maggie answered nonetheless. "I don't like Van Zandt."

"You want to tell me why not?"

She considered it for a moment; discretion was second nature with her. But she had learned during the past three days that she could rely on Mack Pulaski more than she'd relied on anyone in years. "I don't trust him," she said finally. "He's a little too charming, a little too friendly, a little too knowledgeable."

"A little too handsome?" Mack suggested, and she looked at him in surprise.

"I suppose so. I don't find him particularly good-looking. I guess I see through that artificial smile to the snake inside."

"Watch who you're calling a snake."

"Sorry. There's really no comparison. The Why's Snake was an erotic fantasy of delicious temptation. Jeffrey Van Zandt is an oily sleazoid who's all the more disturbing because he fools so many people." She stopped for breath, disturbed by how vehement she'd become.

"You think Wallace is wrong to trust him?"

She shook her head. "I wouldn't go that far. We've been involved in a number of joint ventures in the three years I've worked for Third World Causes, and he's always been helpful. I just have a bad feeling about him, so I keep my distance whenever I can."

"Does he know you don't like him?"

"Of course. Jeffrey Van Zandt has to have everyone eating out of the palm of his hand. You should know that; you're his friend."

"Not his friend. An acquaintance. He was simply at the right place at the right time when I needed someone to turn to."

"Was he?" She slid up higher in her seat, shifting her long legs. "How coincidental."

"Stop being cryptic, Maggie. I thought you said you trusted him."

"You weren't listening. I said I didn't think Peter was wrong to trust him. I wouldn't trust him as far as I could throw him."

Mack cast an appraising glance over her lean, strong body. "Given the fact that Van Zandt is at least three inches shorter than you, that might be quite a ways indeed."

"Don't quibble. If I really thought he was a danger, I wouldn't take you anywhere near him. I'm sure he's just an oily, manipulative civil servant. As long as we're useful to him he'll be useful to us. When that time passes he'll be history, and we won't have to worry about it."

"Let's hope you're right. I don't like the idea of walking into a trap."

"You won't be. It's all very simple—we check in to the hotel and wait for Peter to be in touch. Only Peter and I know the names we're going to be registering under, only Peter and I know where we're planning to meet. We just sit and wait in our room, watch a little TV, order champagne from room service, use the sauna. Everything will be fine."

"Why does it sound like you're trying to convince yourself, Maggie May? I trust you."

"Yeah," she said gloomily, looking at the huge, sprawling city through the shimmering haze of heat surrounding them. "I just wish I could trust myself."

"Okay, Maggie." Mack dropped down on one of the two king-sized beds that took up only a quarter of the space of their hotel room. "What next?"

Maggie was staring out at the city around them, trying to ignore the shiver that ran up her backbone, telling herself it was only the air-conditioning. The Travers Hotel was one of the newer, fancier, larger buildings among a great many new, fancy, large buildings in downtown Houston. It combined a world-class hotel, the American headquarters of Travers Petroleum, and twelve floors rented at a phenomenal price to various corporations that could afford the prestige. One of those corporations was the nonprofit Third World Causes, Ltd., whose space was rent-free, a convenient tax write-off for Travers Petroleum that aided them in their quest to pay zero income tax. A quest that had met with success three out of the last four years.

She turned back to Mack. He looked hot and sweaty and

rumpled, but he also looked damned sexy, she had to admit. It was probably just as well this little excursion was almost over.

"What I want most of all is a bath and a change of clothes," she said. "And then a nap."

"Sounds good. Where are we going to find the clothes?"

"There are boutiques on the second and third balconies of this monstrosity of a hotel. You want me to find something for you too?" She grabbed her wallet and headed toward the door.

He made no move to get off the bed. "That'd be nice. I think I'll go for the nap first. Pants are thirty-two, thirty-four, shirt large, no polyester or double knit."

"Aw, c'mon, Pulaski. A powder-blue leisure suit would be just the ticket."

He raised his head long enough to glower at her. "You buy it, you wear it, Maggie May."

She stuck her tongue out at him, glanced at her watch, and grimaced. "It's a quarter of five. Don't answer the phone. I'll be back within an hour."

"I won't answer the phone," he replied sleepily, and she watched his eyes drift closed above his stubbled face. Very sexy indeed, she thought dismally. And she needed to run, as fast and as far as she could. She wasn't ready for this, for him, for the odd, tender, unexpected longings and emotions that were cropping up.

Of course he wouldn't have been half as sexy in a polyester leisure suit, if they even still made such things, but she couldn't bring herself to do it. It took her half an hour to buy him khakis, a field shirt, socks, and turquoise Calvin Klein briefs, another ten minutes for a beige cotton jumpsuit for herself and the toiletries they'd need to get them through the next twenty-four hours. Then she was off to Peter Wallace's office on the thirteenth floor.

It was almost six o'clock, and the long, wide hallways were deserted, the offices shut tight. No one worked late in Houston, at least not on a hot summer's evening. Third World Causes, Ltd. was at the end of the broad corridor, and Maggie moved with caution, her running shoes silent on the thick smoke-colored carpet that lined the hallway. She was being neurotic and paranoid, she told herself, clutching her noisy paper bags beneath her arm. And why the hell did she hate guns so much? She would have felt a lot happier having one tucked in her belt at that very moment.

There was nothing to worry about—Peter probably wasn't even in Houston yet. He'd call as soon as he got in, and then he'd tell her what to do with Mack. And she'd be able to turn her back and head to L.A. with a clear conscience, a sigh of relief, and more than a trace of regret.

The heavy oak door, with its raised brass lettering, was open just a tiny crack, and all Maggie's doubts rushed back tenfold. With as much stealth as she could manage, she pushed the door open. It moved back silently, on well-oiled hinges, displaying a tableau that would haunt her nightmares for years to come.

Peter Wallace was lying on the red carpet. Except that the carpet was pale beige—it was only red surrounding his body. Blood was everywhere, covering his torso, his arms and legs, his face. It even reached the man leaning over him, staining his hands and shirt.

Mack looked up into her horrified face. He had a gun in his hand, a large, nasty-looking thing, and there was blood on that too. The two of them stared at each other for a long, breathless moment, and Maggie wondered whether she should scream, run, or try to kick the gun out of his hand. She did none of the three. She just stood there, clutching the bags in her nerveless hands.

Mack sat back on his heels, reached a hand up to push his hair out of his face, and left a streak of blood across his forehead. "He's dead," he said in a flat voice.

Maggie opened her mouth, tried to speak, and then shut it again, swallowing back the nausea. "No kidding," she finally managed, moving into the room and shutting the door behind her with a silent click. "Did you do it?"

There was no feigning his astonishment. "Why the hell

would I kill him? He was supposed to be my ticket out of this mess."

"Maybe." She moved closer. She'd seen dead men before, far too many. People dead from violence, from starvation, from the ravages of illness. But she never got used to it. "How long have you been here?"

"Just a few minutes."

"And he was like this when you got here?"

"No."

"No?" She looked up, startled, into his bleak face.

"He was still alive. He tried to say something, but I couldn't quite get all of it."

"What did you get?"

"He thought I was Jeffrey Van Zandt."

"What makes you think that?"

"That's what he kept calling me," Mack snapped.

"Maybe he wasn't calling you that at all. Maybe he was telling you to find him. If Peter can't help us"—there was a catch to her voice—"then Van Zandt's our only other possibility. At least that I know of."

"Wallace wasn't in much shape to be cross-examined, Maggie," Mack said dryly, moving away from the body.

Maggie stared down at him for a moment longer. "Damn you, Pulaski," she said in a quiet, bitter voice without looking up. "You may not care that a man is dead, but I do. He was my boss, my lover, and my friend. And I haven't got enough of them to spare."

"Enough what? Lovers or friends?"

She turned to him, ready to do battle, when she realized that he'd said it on purpose, to jolt her from her grief. His next words verified it.

"Are you okay?" She looked at him, and his hazel eyes seemed more concerned with her than with their sudden, untenable situation.

"I'm okay. We've got to get the hell out of here." There was blood on her hands, and she wiped them on the carpet before rising on surprisingly steady feet.

"But the police . . ."

"Will probably be here any moment. And I don't think they're going to want to hear what we have to tell them. I think we've been set up. What the hell are you doing down here anyway? I thought you were taking a nap."

"I answered the phone," he admitted somewhat sheepishly. "It was Wallace, asking me to meet him here. What about you? I thought you were buying us some clothes."

"I got the clothes. I thought it might be worth checking in here in case Peter got here earlier. Apparently he did." She was suddenly very still. "Do you hear sirens?"

"I can't tell in this building," Mack said.

"They're probably already here," she said bitterly. "I think—" Her voice stopped as the shrill telephone broke through. They both turned to stare at it with a kind of repulsive fascination.

"Should I answer it?" Mack asked finally.

"No."

"But what if it's Van Zandt? What if it's someone with the answers?"

"We'll find out our own answers. Come on, Pulaski. We're out of here." She turned back toward the door, unable to give Peter's corpse even one last look. Three days ago he had been golden, handsome, and regretful in the New York airport. And now he was lying in a pool of his own blood, past regrets, and she didn't even have the time to mourn for him. Her energies had to be spent on the living, on Pulaski and herself. Later, when some of this began to make sense, she'd grieve for him.

"What about the gun?" He'd followed her example and tried to wipe some of the blood onto the carpet around his feet.

"Bring it," she said grimly. "It looks like we're going to need it."

The corridor was still deserted when they stepped out into it, closing the door on the office and its grisly occupant. Maggie

gave him a cursory glance. The blood could have been anything
—it was drying to a rusty brown, and if they both looked a little
the worse for wear someone would have to look twice to notice.

"Where are we going?" Mack murmured as she started off.

"Stairway. They'll be watching the elevators."

"Who will be?"

"Whoever killed Peter."

"I thought you weren't sure whether I killed him or not?"

"It was only a temporary thought. You didn't kill him. If you
had, you would have been long gone. And you're right, you
didn't have any reason to kill him. At least none that I know
of."

"So I'm not completely exonerated?"

"I don't trust anyone completely," she shot back over her
shoulder. "Come on." She kept moving until she heard the ominous sound of the arriving elevator pinging in the distance.
"Damn." She grabbed his wrist, the bulky bags still under her
arm. "Let's move it."

She raced back down the hallway, with Mack keeping up
with her. They rounded a corner, and she could hear the noise,
the voices, the ominously official sound of what was very likely
a large group of Houston police heading in their direction. They
hadn't seen them, but they were moving rapidly toward Peter's
office. By the time they reached it, Maggie and Mack would be
in plain sight.

"I hate to interfere," he wheezed behind her, "but do you
want to get caught?" He suddenly stopped, and she was jerked
back against him.

"Let go of me, you cretin," she railed at him in a barely
audible whisper.

"Sure thing. But you just raced past the fire exit."

"Why the hell didn't you say so?" She wheeled around, div-
ing through the door with Mack on her heels, and moments
later they were clattering down the stairs. Three flights down,
she flung her body against the wall, gesturing Mack to do the

same, and they stayed there, listening, for what seemed an eternity.

"They didn't see us," she gasped. "So far so good. Let's go."

"Won't I look a little odd carrying this?" Mack gestured with the gun.

Maggie opened one of the bags. "Toss it in here."

"And then what?"

"We find a way out of here without tripping an alarm. Then we find a car, a motel, and we find a way out of the country."

"You want to tell me where we're heading?"

She pushed herself away from the wall. "Honduras."

"Honduras?" He managed the semblance of a shriek.

"That's where we're most likely to find Van Zandt. He spends far too much of his time as a military adviser for various rebel groups. Last I heard he was stationed in Honduras. So that's where we're going. Any objections?"

"No. As long as we get there in one piece."

"I expect we will. We've been damned lucky so far." She started down the next flight of stairs at a more reasonable pace.

"Luck has a habit of changing," Mack said from above her.

She paused long enough to meet his troubled gaze fearlessly. "And some people make their own luck. Come on. I promised I'd get you out of this mess, and I'm going to. It's just going to take a little longer than I expected."

"That's all right, Maggie May. I've gotten used to having you around." And he caught up with her just as she was trying to decide whether she liked the sound of that or not. "Let's go steal another car."

"A Mercedes this time," she said.

"Maybe. More likely another Beetle."

"I won't be able to walk if my legs are cramped into another VW," she warned.

"I'll carry you."

And she was damned if she didn't like the sound of that, after all.

seven

"You sure know how to pick 'em, Maggie." Mack surveyed the shabby motel room with more curiosity than actual condemnation. "I think I preferred the Travers."

"Beggars can't be choosers. Jail would probably be more comfortable too." She dumped the much-abused shopping bags on the bed, then dropped her aching body beside them. It was the worst motel she'd come up with since they left Utah—even the late, unlamented Lone Star Bide-a-Wee was a model of cleanliness and luxury compared to their current quarters. There were two different patterns of paper on the water-stained walls—cabbage roses on the outside wall, green polka dots on the bathroom wall. The two narrow beds were covered with raveled chenille bedspreads, and the wall-to-wall carpeting showed the paths of a thousand weary feet.

But it was outside the sprawling city limits of Houston, ten miles from a small, run-down private airport, and for the moment they were safe.

Somehow, they had managed to escape the death trap in the Travers Hotel. Through a stroke of amazing good luck the stairway had ended in the basement garage of the huge building. It had taken five minutes to retrieve their aging VW, and then they were off, chugging past the police cars with their lights flashing into the early evening sky. Maggie had been right— someone had sent for the police, and she had no doubt at all that Peter's killer made the phone call. Mack had read the road atlas, directing her toward Simmons Airfield, and the Lazy

Cowboy Doze-Motel had loomed up out of the darkening sky like a beacon.

A somewhat dimmed beacon, Maggie had to admit. "I'm too dirty to sleep and too tired to move. All I want is a hot shower and twenty-four hours' sleep."

"Let me go first. There's a Laundromat two doors down—I can wash the clothes we're wearing while you're taking your shower."

"Suit yourself. Just don't take all the hot water." The words came out in a tired mumble as she turned and buried her face in the chenille bedspread. For a few blissful minutes all was silent —just the rustle of paper bags, the rainlike sound of the shower, the quiet little thuds and knocks as Mack undoubtedly tried to fit his large body into a small shower stall. She remembered the turquoise Jockey shorts, and she smiled in her sleep, waiting for his reaction.

The door to the bathroom opened quietly, and Maggie considered staying facedown. But curiosity got the better of her, and she rolled over to stare at him.

He was wearing nothing but the turquoise Jockey shorts. His blond hair was wet and hanging in tendrils around his freshly shaven face. A face that wore an expression of doubt and amusement as he met her gaze. "You've got to be kidding, Maggie May," he said after a long moment.

With great deliberation, she ran her eyes over his body. Hell, it was a great body. Long legs, flat stomach, broad, sort of bony shoulders, and not too much hair. She was tempted to ask him to turn around so she could check out his rear, but she didn't quite have the nerve. She smiled sweetly.

"I think you look adorable, Pulaski," she purred.

"Thank you for your thoughtful shopping." He quickly divested his new khakis of their various tags and pulled them on. Maggie watched the turquoise shorts disappear with a trace of regret. "Your turn at the shower. And believe it or not, there's plenty of hot water. Dump your clothes on the floor so I can wash 'em."

"You're very domestic," Maggie said as she stumbled toward the miniature bathroom. "Be careful out there." She couldn't keep the concern out of her voice.

He paused in the act of buttoning his shirt. "Don't worry, Maggie. Even if I prefer having you take care of me, I've been responsible for myself for years. I won't let the bad guys get me."

"Humph," she said, disappearing into the tiny bathroom.

He was right, there was plenty of hot water and she took full advantage of it, letting the shower scrape the sweat and dust and blood away from her. She heard Mack leave, and the sound of the front door made her nerves tighten in sudden anxiety. He would be okay, she reassured herself. He'd taken care of himself for probably forty years.

Besides, she was absolutely certain that no one had followed them. They were guaranteed a decent night's sleep, and then she had to get them out of the country. With Peter's murder, half of her sources had dried up. It was more than likely that someone at Third World Causes was linked up with their hunters—they'd been showing up far too regularly, just when she'd thought they were safe. She no longer knew whom to trust, and she wasn't about to take chances when it wasn't just her own life at stake.

She also wasn't going to worry about it right now. Tomorrow would be soon enough. Right now she was going to collapse on that singularly uncomfortable little bed and sleep the sleep of the dead.

Peter's blank, dead features suddenly shot into her mind, and a low, keening wail escaped from deep inside her. Quickly she shoved the wet washcloth into her mouth to try to stop the sounds of her sudden grief. And then she leaned against the rusting metal stall, beneath the steady beat of the hot shower, and wept.

She heard the sound of the key in the lock from a distance, hours later. Pulaski, she thought, not moving. The door opened, someone stepped inside and shut it behind him. She waited with sleep-drugged patience for the dim light to flood the room, but nothing happened. The figure moved stealthily across the room. Not to the television, which would have been Mack's first move. Not to his own bed. But straight toward hers. It couldn't be Pulaski.

She was suddenly alert, though she kept her body completely still, her breathing even. The small pool of light from the bathroom provided little illumination, and she didn't dare move her head. When she made her move it had to be fast and accurate. Doubtless it would be her only chance.

Her muscles bunched, ready to spring, as the dark, menacing figure paused above her. The menace was tangible in the air, a threat of death and violence that all the wishful thinking in the world wouldn't drive away. Why the hell had she left the gun on the dresser?

He bent over her. She could see the hand coming toward her through the shadows, holding something undoubtedly lethal. She held her breath, counted to five, and then spun around in the bed, leaping toward her attacker without another moment's hesitation.

Ten seconds is a long time when you're fighting for your life. It took twelve for Maggie to pin him flat on the floor, straddling him with her long legs, her knee at his vulnerable throat. She was barely breathing heavily. Unfortunately she couldn't say the same for Pulaski.

He lay there gasping for breath. "Not that this isn't erotic in a kinky sort of way," he managed to gasp, "but do you suppose we could use the bed instead?"

Maggie scrambled off him immediately, her hands quickly running over him, assessing the damage. There was little, except perhaps to his pride.

But thank God Mack's pride wasn't of the overly macho variety. "Are you okay?" he asked.

She found her hands were shaking. Perceptive of him to have noticed, considering he was the one who'd been decked. "I'm fine. Why the hell did you sneak up on me like that? If I'd had the gun, I could have killed you." Her voice was breathless and as shaky as her hands.

"Shoot first, ask questions later? I don't think so, Maggie May." He sat up, flexing his muscles a little gingerly. "I didn't want to wake you if I could help it."

"Then why didn't you just get in your own bed and be quiet?" she demanded. "Why did you come and stare at me like you were a . . . a . . ."

"I was staring at you like a red-blooded, healthy American male, Maggie," he drawled. "I wanted to see if you were sleeping in the raw."

"As you can see, I wasn't." The lace bra and bikini panties weren't much, but they were better than nothing. "What did you have in your hand?"

"Dinner," he said, with his first touch of irritation.

"For you?"

"For you. I brought you a corned-beef sandwich from the diner across the way. From the smell of it, I expect it's now decorating the wall."

Slowly Maggie moved away from him, climbing back onto her bed with more than a trace of embarrassment. "I'm sorry," she said finally. "I guess I'm a little jumpy."

He rose from the floor, groaning audibly and with a melodramatic flair that should have reassured her. "I guess you are. You want me to get you another sandwich?"

"I don't suppose you managed to come up with some Jack Daniel's?"

Mack's face split in a grin that lit the darkened room. "Someday you'll learn not to underestimate me, Superwoman," he replied. He retrieved a half-full bottle from the top of the television, switching it on before he turned back to her. As the sounds of *Dallas* filled the motel room Maggie took a good, healthy swig from the bottle.

"Did you drink this much already?" she questioned.

"Nope. I bought it from the owner of the Laundromat. Paid

twenty bucks for it too." He caught it from her hand and took an even healthier swig. "Worth every penny," he said reverently.

"I suppose. You'd better ration it, though," she warned, grabbing it back and matching his drink. "I don't know how long we'll be here."

"Till tomorrow at ten."

"What?" She wasn't sure if she heard him correctly.

"I said we'll be here till ten. At which point we will meet up with Jesse's friend Sam, who will take us to Chico, who will pass us on to Lonesome Fred."

"And who will Lonesome Fred pass us on to?"

"To Honduras, if all goes well. Lonesome Fred is a pilot. I gather it wouldn't be wise to ask how he usually earns his living in this part of the country. Suffice it to say he'll take any cargo anywhere, without the inconvenience of customs or rude questions. For a sizable sum of money, of course."

"How sizable? With Peter dead my resources are limited."

"I've got more than enough." He dropped down on the bed opposite her. "You don't approve of messing with smugglers?"

"I didn't say that. Dopers got us into this mess, they may as well help us get out. You've been very efficient." Her voice was flat.

"And you don't like it."

"Why shouldn't I like it?"

He shrugged. "Maybe you like being Superwoman all by yourself. Maybe you don't like anyone else saving the bacon."

"You can save all the bacon you want, Pulaski," she said wearily. "I'm going to sleep." She crawled beneath the covers, pulling them over her head to shut out the blue light from the television set.

"That's all right," he said softly beside her. "You can save the bacon next time."

With luck there wouldn't be a next time, she thought, turning her face away from him. With luck they'd find Van Zandt's rebel camp in Honduras and she could dump Mack back on him. The sooner that day came, the better.

She had to get away from him. He was having a terrible effect on her, challenging all her hard-won beliefs, seducing her with nothing more than those warm, laughing eyes of his.

He was probably right, she conceded, sinking down lower in the bed and shutting out the noise of the prime-time soap opera. She didn't like having anyone else take care of things, not unless she asked them to in the first place. But it wasn't overwhelming pride or the need to dominate. It was much more basic than that. If you had to rely on someone else for help, you were then in their debt and beholden to them. And if you had to rely on them, they would let you down, sooner or later, and break your heart. Far better to be beholden to no one, to be the one who made the decisions, who stayed in charge and kept things moving in the right direction.

She needed that control to feel safe within herself. And now Mack had taken it away from her, leaving her resentful, grateful, and unpleasantly helpless. Damn him.

She opened one eye, peering at him through the darkened room. He was stretched out on the twin bed, seemingly absorbed in J. R. Ewing, the bottle of Jack Daniel's by his side, his shoes off and his shirt open. He was entirely at ease, and she was lying there trying to recapture the blissful sleep she needed, feeling guilty and miserable.

He was right, she was wrong. He hadn't taken control away from her. He'd just done what any sensible person in danger would do—take the opportunity when it was offered. He'd found transportation in a far shorter time than she would have managed it. Damn it, she'd be grateful, and ignore her feelings of uneasiness. And if the chance came again, she'd welcome his taking control, just to show she could do it.

With that noble resolution, she fell back into a much-needed sleep that not even the torments of the Ewing clan could interfere with.

* * *

It was pitch black. The darkness, like a velvet shroud, pressed around her, weighed her down, smothering her in its evil grip. She felt the bed beneath her shoulder blades, felt the cold sweat covering her body, and she couldn't move. She was paralyzed, darkness all around her, holding her captive.

Desperately, she looked for light. There was none—all was blackness, stealing her breath, stealing her life, leaving her there helpless and alone on the bed. She could hear the air struggle in her lungs, feel her heart pounding so hard it shook the narrow bed. Tremors of panic swept over her, and she was cold, so cold, and so alone. Her mouth moved, but she could say nothing. She was alone with darkness and death, and a thousand hands were grabbing at her, pulling at her, pulling her down and down and down. . . .

She heard the scream from somewhere up above the pit she was sinking into. And then suddenly light flooded the room, and she was no longer alone in the darkness. Mack had grabbed her, wrapping himself around her, holding her shivering body tightly in a grip that was comfort and safety, his voice soothing, with meaningless, gentle words that were a litany of calm and quiet and clear white light.

Slowly the tremors faded from her body, slowly the tight, panicked muscles relaxed against him. A rasping, tearful sigh caught in her throat and then flowed from her, and she sank against him, against the strong body that was so warm.

His hands were tenderly brushing her tangled hair away from her tear-streaked face. "Are you okay?" he whispered in her ear.

Not quite trusting her voice, she nodded against him. She knew she should move away, say something light and amusing, laugh it off. But she couldn't move; she could only huddle closer for warmth and comfort and hope this wasn't as danger-ous as the darkness and the death.

He made no move to let her go. If he was wearing anything at all, it was only those absurd Jockey shorts, but there was nothing sexual in his embrace. "I'm sorry," he muttered against her hair. "I forgot about the damned light, tonight of all nights. Are you sure you're okay?"

She tested her voice. It came out raw and rusty, a perfect twin to Mack's ruined voice. "I'm sorry . . ." she whispered, but his hand moved and covered her mouth, gently.

"Shhh," he said. "It was my fault. I knew you were afraid of the dark, but I didn't know it was this bad. Like an idiot, I forgot."

"It's not usually this bad," she said slowly, pressing her face against the warmth of his arm. "At one point I had it beaten entirely. It must have been Peter that set it off."

His arm tightened imperceptibly. "Were you in love with him?"

She thought about it. Exhaustion had swept over her body in the wake of her panic, and she lay there, dreamy, comfortable. "No," she murmured. "What we had between us was over, and had been for a while. But we did love each other, as good, dear friends. Damn them."

"Damn who?"

"Whoever did that to him. Damn them to hell." She buried her face against him, snuggling closer. Never had she felt so safe, so protected.

"Are you going to be all right?" She could feel his muscles tense beneath her hands, feel his tentative withdrawal.

She raised her tear-streaked face for a moment. "Don't leave me," she said, for the second time in her life, and she hated herself for her weakness.

But Pulaski didn't take advantage of it. "I won't," he said simply, pulling her back against him. "Go to sleep, Maggie. Tomorrow you can be Superwoman again. Tonight you can ask for help."

With the cocoon of Mack's warm, strong body curled protectively around her, Maggie did as she was told.

eight

If Lonesome Fred was an unprepossessing sort of pilot, his twin-engine prop plane was even less encouraging. Both of them were beaten, battered, and had clearly seen better days. Lonesome Fred had a stubble of beard, mirrored sunglasses, and spoke in a laconic, stoned voice; his plane was decorated with decals, bullet holes, and the hardly reassuring painting of a mule on the fuselage.

She turned accusing eyes on Mack. "I can't say much for your transportation," she muttered under her breath as Lonesome Fred busied himself with a casual check of their flying machine.

He shrugged, his smile warm in the bright Texas sunlight. "What can I say? He assures me the plane flies like a dream and we'll be in Honduras in a matter of hours. Given the worth of his usual cargo, I'd expect it to be reliable. Come on, Maggie, you know you shouldn't judge a book by its cover. She's probably got the cleanest engine this side of a factory."

"I checked while you were busy giving Lonesome Fred his exorbitant fee. It's absolutely filthy, gunked up with oil and crud, and we're all going to die," she said prosaically.

Mack grinned at her. "At least we'll die together. Chin up, Maggie. We'll be safe enough."

"Sure we will," she said in a gloomy voice. "I think I'll walk."

She wasn't serious, but his sturdy hand beneath her elbow didn't leave her much choice. "All aboard, Maggie May." He pushed her up into the plane, shoving her butt with unnecessary force. She stumbled into one of the seats, grimacing at the smell of fuel and vegetation and stale beer. Mack took the seat behind her, leaning back with a casual air she envied.

The engines could have sounded smoother, but at least both were working. And despite Lonesome Fred's unpromising demeanor, he seemed to know what he was doing once he climbed into the cockpit of the plane, his sweat-stained Stetson pushed back on his lined forehead, his mirrored sunglasses balanced above the grubby, weak chin. He was smoking as the plane took off, roaring down the runway and bouncing over potholes, and Maggie turned away to stare fixedly out the greasy window.

"I didn't know you were afraid of flying, Maggie."

"Along with being scared of the dark?" she snapped back. "I'm not a bundle of neuroses, Pulaski."

"I didn't say you were. Are you afraid of flying?" he persisted.

"No. I'm just a few hours short of getting my license. I'm afraid of death traps and strange pilots and . . . oh, my God."

"What?"

"Lonesome Fred is smoking a joint the size of a cigar!"

Mack shrugged. "He says he flies better stoned."

"Hey, passengers," Fred's sleepy voice issued from the pilot's seat. "You guys know how to swim?"

"Why do you ask?" Maggie demanded in a dubious voice.

"I don't carry parachutes. I figure it shows a lack of basic trust in my baby." He patted the instrument panel and some of the ash fell from the thick joint. "So just in case we have any trouble, I like to fly over water."

"Do you often have any trouble?" Maggie had to ask.

Lonesome Fred shrugged, and the plane lurched as it continued its unsteady ascent into the bright Texas sky. "Now and then," he said dreamily. "Now and then." And he began to whistle the theme song from *The High and the Mighty*.

"Great," Maggie said, sinking back. "Pulaski, I'm too young to die."

"Don't worry, Maggie. He may not carry parachutes, but he has life preservers."

Maggie sneered, leaned back in her seat, and tried to ignore the rough-sounding engines, the inane whistling from their stoned pilot, and the man behind her. She traded one set of worries for another. Jeffrey Van Zandt would be somewhere in Honduras, most likely near the border. Someone had mentioned a little town, and if she had a moment of peace and quiet it might come back to her. Though how helpful Van Zandt would end up being was always questionable, unless he thought they might have something to offer in return.

No, she was being too harsh. Van Zandt was the one who'd brought Pulaski to Third World Causes, Ltd. in the first place. He had responsibilities, and an interest in the outcome. Besides, he'd know better than anyone how deep the rebels were involved in drug smuggling. And how tolerant the U.S. Government was of that involvement.

What if they didn't find Van Zandt? What if they ended up in a camp of rebels, all with a grudge against a man who'd seen more than he was supposed to have seen? A lot of people wanted Mack, and most of them wanted him dead. The CIA, the rebels, the Mafia, and now the Houston police. And the only chance they had of getting them all off their tail was to find out who was behind the drug deal and get him to call off his vultures.

That had to have been Peter's plan. As far as Maggie could see, there was no way out of the mess Mack had unwittingly landed himself in without very careful negotiations and access to the source of power behind it all. Peter had had access, and had died because of it. Van Zandt would have knowledge and access, and if he failed them she didn't know what else she could do. Except find some place to hole up with Mack until the heat died down.

Damn, she hated feeling so helpless. But Peter's death had thrown everything in an uproar, and she had to face the fact— even with Van Zandt's help her time with Mack was far from over. It was going to be a long time before she saw her mother's swimming pool in Laurel Canyon.

Not that a few weeks with her mother was the answer to her need for peace and quiet. Sybil Bennett wasn't a restful woman. Exuberant, loving, and imaginative, yes. Feckless, ruthlessly self-centered, and narcissistic, yes. But never restful.

And there was no way to tell who'd be in residence in the big white pseudo-Italian monstrosity of a house that Sybil had held onto through good times and bad. There'd be Queenie, of course, Sybil's devoted maid cum housekeeper cum nanny. For as long as Maggie could remember Queenie had been there, her ample bosom ready to be cried upon, her common sense ready to be leaned upon. Whatever failings Sybil had as a mother, Queenie had more than made up for them.

Any or all of her three sisters might be there. Jilly was still in college, and she spent most of her summers back in California. Holly was busy with her career as a model, but she and Sybil had always gotten along the best. Vanity was one trait Sybil could identify with. And Kate was commuting between Chicago and L.A., working with a small regional movie company based in the Midwest. With luck, Sybil might have a full house. Not to mention whatever young man was currently enjoying her favors.

No, it would be hectic, exhausting, and wonderfully innocuous after the past few days of blood and bullets. And within a week Mack Pulaski would be as much a part of her past as Randall Carter, albeit a less painful part. But it didn't look as if a trip to Laurel Canyon was anywhere in her near future.

She should never have bought him those damned Jockey shorts. It had been meant as a joke, and he'd taken it as such. But the sight of him in them had been unnerving to say the least. And if she was going to spend months, weeks, or even days hidden away with him, their involvement was going to change. And she didn't know if she was ready for that change.

Her love life, such as it was, had never been spectacularly successful. Granted, it had gotten off to a hideous start when she was sixteen. And her involvement with Randall hadn't been much of an improvement. Randall Carter had taken her trust, her ridiculous faith in human nature that even her stepfather hadn't managed to shake, and destroyed them, tossing away her love with a casual disregard, unlike the usual care he reserved for rare and precious things. But then her love hadn't been rare and precious to him, it had been a disposable commodity—useful for a time, but only temporary. It hadn't been temporary for her.

Her marriage had been doomed from the start—a rebound alliance to a terminally nice guy who was as far from Randall as she could get. And then a discreet couple of affairs, just to prove she was healthy, ending with Peter Wallace.

He was typical of the men she'd chosen since her eight-month marriage. Charming, gentle, undemanding, he, like all the others, had ended up backing away. She couldn't blame them. After her disastrous mistake with Randall, she kept all her passions carefully banked. She couldn't afford to let them flame out of control ever again.

Control. A nasty word. Maggie sighed, peering out the greasy window. They were heading over the ocean now, the greeny-blue of the Gulf a dubious safety net beneath them. The acrid scent of Lonesome Fred's marijuana cut through the gas and diesel fumes that filled the cabin, and she wrinkled her nose in distaste. She could swim, and swim well. She could only hope to God she wouldn't have the chance. Not unless it was in a nice big chlorinated pool in a Honduran Holiday Inn, if such a thing existed.

"Hey, passengers." Lonesome Fred had stopped his whistling, but his voice was still cheerfully stoned. "Where are we heading? Honduras is a small country, but I need to have some idea of the general area."

"By the Nicaraguan border. If you can find an airfield . . ."

"Lady, I don't need no airfield. Leave it to Lonesome Fred." And he leaned back and began to whistle again.

"Leave it to Lonesome Fred," Mack agreed behind her.

"Why don't you try to get some sleep, Maggie? You didn't sleep well last night."

"Maybe," she said dubiously. "But I have the feeling that as long as I'm awake and paying attention, this thing will keep flying. Ridiculous, I know."

"Ridiculous," he agreed. She could feel his hand toying with the rough braid she'd fashioned. It felt suspiciously like a caress, but that was unlikely. He'd been paternal, calm, and almost businesslike that morning. No sexual tension whatsoever, all day long, and she was missing it.

Brooding on whether Mack wanted her or not was a good enough diversion. She needed to get her mind off the mess they were in, to stop going back and forth between possibilities and impossibilities. Sexual fantasies and frustrations could keep her mind off the pilot at least. With a sigh, she sank back down in the cracked leather seat and shut her eyes.

"Maybe not so ridiculous after all," Mack's voice rumbled in her ear. She opened her eyes with a start, looking up into his grim face. There was no laughing warmth in his hazel eyes. Something was wrong.

"What?" she murmured groggily, pulling herself up. The seat belt held her back, and she suddenly remembered where she was. "What's happened?"

"We've lost the engines, man," Lonesome Fred called out from the cockpit, sounding completely unruffled. "Looks like you're gonna get your chance to swim." And he lit another joint.

With a shriek of rage, Maggie leapt for the front of the plane, but the seat belt jerked her back. She struggled with it, slapping away Mack's restraining hands. "Leave me alone, Pulaski," she snarled. "I know how to fly, better than that idiot at least. Maybe I can get them started again."

"No time, Maggie. Grab this pillow and put your head down. Now, goddamn it!" he added at her mutinous expression.

She could feel the plane gather speed as it hurtled toward the ocean. "Take your own seat, too, then," she snapped.

"It doesn't have a seat belt."

"Oh, my God," she moaned. "Then hold on to me."

"I think your chances would be better if—"

"I don't give a damn what my chances are. Hold on to me or I'll unfasten the seat belt and beat Lonesome Fred into a pulp as we drop into the ocean."

He laughed, and if the sound was slightly forced, his hazel eyes warmed for a second. "You're a hell of a woman, Maggie May," he said.

"I know." She smoothed the pillow in her lap. "Put your arms around me and your face on the pillow. Who knows, maybe we'll survive."

"Who knows?" He followed suit, kneeling beside her. His arms were strong and hard around her, and quickly she pressed her torso down on top of his, bracing herself for the impact.

"Geronimo!" Lonesome Fred shouted from the cockpit, and a second later they hit the water.

The force of their impact was tremendous, knocking Maggie back, ripping her arms away from Mack. She felt his body fall away from hers, and then everything blacked out, for minutes . . . for seconds. . . .

And then reality, unpleasant as it was, cropped up again. Mack was fumbling at her seat belt with desperate haste. Blood was pouring from a cut on his forehead, and cold water was lapping around her ankles. "Come on, Maggie," he muttered under his breath. "We haven't got much time."

She slapped his hands away, unfastening the seat belt with only slightly more efficiency. "Where are the life preservers?"

"Gone." He jerked his head toward the opposite side of the plane. The wing had broken off when they landed, and parts of the plane were floating rapidly away as the water poured in the side. "And this damn thing is going to sink momentarily. Let's go." He yanked her hand toward the raw opening in the body of the plane.

"But Lonesome Fred . . ."

"Dead. His neck broke when we hit," Mack said shortly. "Let's get the hell out of here."

She didn't even hesitate. She gave Mack a shove out of the plane, grabbed their knapsack, and dived after him into the greeny blue Gulf waters, which were damned cold for a Caribbean summer.

They both sighted the piece of wing floating in the choppy current at the same time. Maggie struck out for it, still holding the knapsack, but Mack reached it first.

The cold water had slowed the bleeding to a mere trickle, and Mack held out a hand to her, pulling her the last few feet to the wing and taking the knapsack from her, looping it around his wrist. "Are you okay?"

Maggie shook her wet hair out of her face. "All in one piece. What about you? Anything besides that cut on your forehead?"

"I don't think so." He squinted his eyes against the bright sunlight toward the slowly sinking plane. "I guess Lonesome Fred died the way he wanted to. Fitting coffin too."

"Pulaski, at this moment I really don't give a damn about Lonesome Fred," Maggie said in a dangerous voice. "Do you have any idea how far from land we are?"

"Nope. But I think we stand a good chance. There are lots of birds around, not just gulls, and I don't think they'd be too far out at sea. There's a strong current, and with any luck it will pull us in to shore."

"I wouldn't trust our luck," said Maggie. "The current could just as easily carry us out to sea. Do you suppose there are any great white sharks around?" She looked over her shoulder nervously.

"Afraid of sharks too?"

"No. Afraid of Hollywood movies," she snapped back. "Do you think we should kick?"

"I doubt it. We're being pulled along at a good rate. We'll either end up safe or dead, and at this point I think it's out of our hands."

"As long as nothing comes along and nibbles my toes, I can survive for a while. What about you?"

"Well, personally I'd like to be the one to nibble your toes," he said, "but I can wait till we reach shore."

"Pulaski, now is not the time for sexual banter."

"Maggie, I can't think of a better time," he shot back. "The sun is shining, the sky is blue, and it's a beautiful day. Why don't we enjoy it?"

She stared at him for a long moment. "You are absolutely demented," she breathed. "You are certifiably insane and—"

"I'm a survivor, Maggie. And so are you. We've got a rough time ahead of us, and we may as well do what we can to make it more bearable. Why don't you tell me what it was like growing up in Hollywood?" He reached out and put his cold, wet, strong hand on top of hers as she clung to the wing. The human warmth sank through her chilled skin, and Maggie relaxed.

He was right. The sun was shining overhead, the sky was blue, and the ocean, now that she was used to it, wasn't as numbing as she'd been afraid it would be. And if she and Mack were going to die, she at least didn't want it to be with a whine on her lips.

"Actually, it was pretty entertaining. Did you know that Deke Robinson was bisexual?"

"The heart throb of the fifties? Wasn't he married to your mother?"

"Her third husband," she said. "I was twelve when they got married. They had the strangest parties. . . ."

It kept them going for a long time. The sun moved through the skies as she kept him entertained with the most scurrilous gossip she could think of, most of it outdated but still fascinating. When she ran out of stories he told her of life on the road with a rock 'n' roll band in the sixties and seventies, of the psychedelic and sexual excesses that sounded amusing now that it was all over.

When she grew sleepy he tickled her, when she grew snappish he made her laugh. And when she thought she couldn't hold on any longer, when the sun was beginning to sink ahead of them, he gave her hope.

"I hope you've noticed which way the sun is moving," he said.

"The sun isn't moving, the earth is," she mumbled.

"Now isn't the time to be a pedant, Maggie. It's setting directly in front of us. Which is the west, unless life has changed dramatically in the last four hours. Which means we're moving in the right direction."

"But for how long?" She knew her voice sounded querulous, but she couldn't help it.

"Not too much longer now, I would think. Unless there are palm trees growing in the ocean."

"What?" she shrieked, and let go of the wing. The ocean was cold and black as it closed over her head, and she shot back up, sputtering and clawing for the wing.

Mack's hand caught her wrist and yanked her up. "No need to get so excited, Maggie. I told you we'd make it. There are palm trees over there."

Not only could they see palm trees through the twilight, they could see land, and a beach, and tangled underbrush. And before long the blessed, unbelievable feel of sand beneath their feet rushed up to meet them.

With a cry of gladness, Maggie abandoned the wing, staggering in to shore and collapsing on the beach. Mack was beside her, the knapsack looped around his wrist, and together they lay there on the beach, panting in exhaustion and relief.

It was an odd feeling, she thought, lying on her back and looking at the darkening sky, to come so close to death and then leap back. When they were hurtling toward the sea she'd had no time to panic, during the long hours clinging to that icy piece of flotsam she'd been too busy trying to convince both Mack and herself that she wasn't afraid to die. And the memory of Lonesome Fred, somewhere beneath the Caribbean Sea, feeding fishes, while they were safe and whole, came back to haunt her. She lay there in the gathering dusk and shivered, safe in the knowledge that Mack couldn't see her reaction.

When she finally accustomed herself to the feel of solid ground beneath her, she rolled over in the sand, coating her soaking jumpsuit in a layer of the gritty stuff, and stared at Mack. He was lying on his back, his breath coming easily enough, staring up at the twilight sky.

"How long do you think we were in the water?" she asked, and was relieved to discover her voice was calm and steady.

He stopped looking at the sky long enough to turn to her. "I don't know, Maggie. All I know is it's getting dark, and we're going to have to get moving before long if we want shelter for the night."

"Maybe there's a village nearby? Maybe even a town, with a Holiday Inn and a comfortable bed . . ."

"Dream on, Maggie. I think we're going to be spending the night on the beach. And if I don't do something about it right now, we'll be spending the night in the dark." He pulled himself upright, and Maggie could see the weariness in his big, strong body.

Reluctantly, she followed suit, staggering slightly as she tried to stand on the motionless sand. "I'll find some kindling."

"I don't suppose moonlight will do?" He asked it gently enough, but a chill ran across her.

"I'll take care of the fire. Why don't you see if there's something to eat? A banana tree or something."

"I bet we'll have to make do with salty chocolate bars and Jack Daniel's, if they're still in the knapsack. Don't worry, Maggie. We'll keep a light going." His concern was soft and gentle in his raspy voice, and Maggie wanted to tell him it didn't matter. A fire might draw unwanted attention—it would be a warm enough night and they'd be much better off without it. She opened her mouth to tell him so, then closed it again, hating her weakness.

Mack must have read her mind. He crossed the few feet of beach that separated them and brushed some of the sand off her pensive face. "Don't worry, Maggie May," he said again. "I don't like the dark much, either."

nine

Mack was right, of course. There wasn't even a run-down village or an abandoned shack anywhere near their beach, much less a Holiday Inn. Fortunately, before the darkness closed around them, Maggie had a decent fire going, keeping the night at bay.

Solemnly they divided and shared the soggy candy bars and the remnants of the bourbon, making the meager feast last. Maggie sat cross-legged on the sand, listening to the steady rush of the outgoing tide, trying vainly to dry out their dwindling supply of cash. She should have felt grateful. If the tide hadn't been coming in that afternoon, they would have been pulled out to sea, ending up as shark bait or something equally unpleasant.

But even so, given the solid ground beneath her, the warmth of the night, and the salt-laden candy bar that had at least taken the edge off her hunger, she was feeling disturbed and angry over God only knew what.

She was unable to make light conversation, and Mack didn't push her. He lay back in the sand, apparently at ease, his attention half on the fire in front of them, half on the night around them, and thankfully not at all on her. Or so she thought.

"What's on tap for tomorrow?" he inquired lazily, his voice cutting through her unhappy self-absorption.

"What?" She roused herself to stare at him across the firelight.

"I said what have you got planned for tomorrow," he said patiently. "How are you going to get us out of this mess?"

Slowly she pulled herself together, her battered pride and unhappiness pushed out of the way. "First I find us some transportation," she said, her voice firm in the night air. "And at the same time find out what country we're in."

"That might be a good idea," he said idly, leaning back in the sand.

"You . . . uh . . . don't have any idea where we are, do you?"

"Not a clue. I expect we're somewhere in Central America— Lonesome Fred was going to keep parallel to the coastline." He crossed his long legs, peering at the horizon. "Think you'll have any trouble finding where Van Zandt's holed up?"

"Maybe. But I'll find him sooner or later." She stared at his averted profile for a long, suspicious moment. She'd been sitting there, feeling useless and sorry for herself, and suddenly Mack had given her back her pride. Had he done it on purpose?

She had relied on him too much in the last twenty-four hours. First, to keep the night terrors from destroying her, then to keep her afloat during that interminable afternoon. It had been different when it came to stealing the car. She was perfectly comfortable having Mack rescue them. As long as she asked him to in the first place. She hated like hell having to accept his aid when it was presented unasked.

She had been prepared for him to try to take over the expedition, and in expectation she launched an attack. "That was a great pilot you picked," she said.

Mack shrugged, unmoved. "So I got a little overzealous," he drawled. "I didn't want to leave all the burden on you, Superwoman. I wouldn't want you to think I couldn't pull my weight."

Did he know what she'd been going through? Quite possibly. She had yet to meet a man who'd give up control so easily and yet still remain calm and strong. Apparently Mack was a man who could do it. Maybe. Maggie searched about in her own mind for the right words, gratitude without encouragement, comradeship without losing the upper hand. If she really had the upper hand at all.

"You pull your weight, Pulaski. I know I can count on you if need be," she said carefully. "I . . . I appreciate your help."

"Sure you do, princess," he said, much amused. "I'll keep my place next time."

She opened her mouth to protest, then shut it again. Her honesty was her major attribute, and she wasn't about to lie to him to assuage her own neuroses. They were in an extremely tenuous situation, and she needed to feel in control if she was going to get them safely out of it. And if Mack's feelings were hurt, that was too damned bad.

But he didn't look like a man suffering from wounded feelings. He lay there in the sand, entirely at ease, as if there was no place else he'd rather be. Maggie could only wish she felt the same way.

Her jumpsuit had long since dried, and she'd made an effort at brushing the sand from it. It was going to be a long, uncomfortable night, and having sand ride up her backbone wouldn't help matters. The sun had long ago withdrawn its warmth from the land, and Maggie shivered.

"Maggie." His ruined voice floated across the night breeze. "Come here."

She looked up at him suspiciously. "Why?"

"Because it's late, we both need sleep. It's getting chilly, and a little body warmth will come in handy, considering we don't have anything we can use for blankets."

"Pulaski . . ." she said warningly.

"For Christ's sake, Maggie, I'm not putting the make on you," he said, irritation finally breaking through his usual calm. "I'm tired and I'm cold and I want to go to sleep. And I'm not going to be able to sleep with you sitting there, miles away, brooding and shivering. Come here, or I'm damned well going to come over there."

She sat utterly still, glaring at him. It made perfect sense, of course. And she was pretty sure he wasn't about to rip off her jumpsuit and have his wicked way with her. Most of the time he barely seemed aware that she was female. Of course there were moments when an odd sort of sexual heat had flared between them, but those moments had been effectively wiped out by her cutting tongue. She'd done it before, she could do it again. And God, she was getting colder by the minute.

She pulled herself to her feet, moving around the small fire and kneeling beside him. "All right," she muttered wryly. "I'm trusting you to control your animal passions, though I know the temptation is great. Where do you want me?"

There was a light in his hazel eyes that told her he was considering a highly improper answer. She could come up with her own reply, and it was a very inviting position. But she remained kneeling, waiting for him.

Mack restrained himself nobly. "Between me and the fire, since you're clearly freezing to death," he said. "I may wake you up when I put more wood on it, but I figure them's the breaks."

"It's not that cold a night," she found herself saying. "You could let the fire die down."

"I was wrong about the moonlight, Maggie. If the fire died down, it would be dark." His voice was gentle.

She wished she could tell him not to bother. Just when she was trying to regain control, her old, irrational fears crept out again. "All right," she said, stretching out on the sand beside him, not touching him. "Wake me if you have to."

He grinned down at her. "What is this, a high school dance where the partners have to stay five inches apart? We aren't going to share much warmth this way, Maggie." And he pulled her across the sand into the shelter of his warm body.

She automatically stiffened, wondering if she'd read him wrong. But his hands were impersonal, holding her against him as if she were a child. Slowly she began to relax. What was she being such an idiot for, anyway? What would be wrong with sharing a little more than body warmth on a deserted beach?

What was wrong with making love to a man she found very attractive?

But she wasn't about to talk herself into it. Lying in the shelter of his big, strong body, she had to admit that she wanted him, and wanted him quite badly. Maybe more than she'd ever wanted anyone before. And despite Mack's nonthreatening, laid-back attitude, she suspected that he wanted her too.

But she didn't dare give in. They were safe enough on this beach, but if they made love now, they'd make love again. And again and again, every night they spent together, and then it wouldn't be as safe.

She'd had enough of failed relationships, of going into them blindly, openheartedly, only to have the men leave when they began to feel threatened or bored. It had been months since she and Peter had decided to go their separate ways, romantically, and she wasn't eager to trade her peace of mind for another round of passion and pain.

So Mack and his considerable physical attractions were going to have to be ignored. It was a good, sensible resolution, and she released her pent-up breath, relaxing against him.

"I don't think I like that decision," he murmured in her ear.

"Hmm?" she questioned sleepily.

"Never mind. I just got the impression I lost that round."

She didn't even bother to marvel at his uncanny ability to read her mind. He was doing it far too often—the longer they were together the better they knew each other's thoughts. It was one of the hazards of getting close to someone, but at least she'd avoid the other hazards. "You did," she murmured. "G'night, Pulaski."

"Good night, Maggie." His voice was deep, raspy, and amused. "Pleasant dreams."

They weren't. They were nightmares, memories from some of the worst times in her life. Suddenly she was sixteen again, alone in the darkness, with rough hands all over her, pawing at her, pulling away her clothes, cruel hands that she couldn't slap away, couldn't escape from, could only lie there and cry. . . .

"Maggie? Wake up, Maggie." The hands weren't on her breasts, pulling her clothes off her. They were strong, gentle hands on her shoulders, shaking her awake, out of the deep morass of dream and memory that had torn through her sleep and her defenses.

She opened her eyes. The flames of the newly stoked fire were flickering up into the inky black sky, and the man kneeling over her was in shadows. But she knew immediately that he was no threat, and she felt the panic and tension drain from her body. "I'm awake," she said. "I'm okay."

As her eyes grew accustomed to the darkness she could see his face, the tenderness and concern in his eyes as they stared down at her. Slowly he sank down beside her, gathering her body against his own. "You want to sleep, Maggie?" he whispered in her ear. "Or do you want to tell me about it?"

She shrugged against him, but her hands reached up of their own accord and clutched the rough khaki shirt in unconscious pleading. His body was warm and strong and curiously soothing beneath her fingers. Her voice was at variance with her hands, cool and composed. "There's not a whole lot to say. It happens to a lot of girls. The wrong man at the wrong time, in the wrong way." She waited for him to make some response to that, but he said nothing, just lay there, holding her, waiting.

"Except," she went on, unable to stop herself, "in my case it was my stepfather, when I was sixteen. And he wasn't completely to blame—I had a mad crush on him and I suppose he thought I was old enough to know what I wanted. It was a very dark night, and there was no light at all in the deserted pool house. And he was too stoned to realize when I said no, I meant it."

There was a long silence, and Mack's hold on her tightened imperceptibly, in wordless comfort. "What happened?"

"My mother divorced him, of course. She'd been planning to anyway, but when she heard what happened to me that night she kicked him out of the house. She'd already caught him in bed with another young actor, and she'd been willing to overlook that. But in my case her long-submerged maternal instincts came out and he was handed his walking papers."

"Another actor?"

"My stepfather was catholic in his sexual tastes. He took on all shapes, sizes, sexes, and relationships," she said bitterly. "I'm just glad he died of a drug overdose before he could get his hands on my stepsister."

"Who was your stepfather?"

Maggie laughed, a raw bitter sound that scraped her throat. "I had three. There was my father, Count Alexander Lagerfeldt, then Sidney Zimmerman, a banker, Deke Robinson, the heartthrob of the fifties, and finally Peter Malcolm, my mother's true love."

"How come you don't use your father's name?"

She shrugged again. "Sybil changed it to hers before I had much say in the matter. I was never close to my father—there never seemed much reason to go to the bother of changing it back."

"And it was Deke Robinson in the pool house."

"Deke Robinson in the pool house," she agreed. "Mother sent me to the best therapists. I survived the traumatic experience and I'm very healthy sexually. And I'd conquered my fear of the dark long ago."

"So what happened?"

She shook her head. "I don't know. It started again about a year ago. It built up slowly, and I haven't had time to deal with it. I know if I just have some time I can face it and it'll go away. I hate to be at the mercy of it," she said passionately.

"I'm sure you do. Are you still healthy sexually, or did that come back to haunt you too?" He said it in a light, bantering voice, and she responded in kind, grateful for the gentle teasing that was no threat at all.

"That's for me to know."

"And me to find out?" he replied.

"I didn't mean it that way."

"No," he said slowly. "I'm sure you didn't. Nevertheless, it's going to come to that, sooner or later. You know that, Maggie. Don't you?"

"Do I?" She was fencing, wary.

"You do. But now is neither the time nor the place. I'm perfectly willing to wait until the time and place are right. Are you going to run, Maggie?"

She took a deep breath. "No. You don't scare me."

He laughed, a silent expelling of sweet breath against her face. "That's good. Because there are times when you scare the hell out of me."

She smiled, a smug cat-that-got-the-canary smile that he couldn't see in the dark, and snuggled closer. "Keep it that way, Pulaski," she said. And willed herself back to sleep.

Maggie stamped with all her might on the clutch pedal, shoved the shrieking gear shift into third, and continued bouncing down the rutted road, a brilliant smile on her face, her tawny blond hair streaming out behind her. Her sense of well-being was completely out of proportion to her accomplishments, but she couldn't resist feeling absolutely wonderful and at peace with the world.

She'd woken up early, at first light, her bones and muscles cramped from sleeping on the hard sand. Mack slept on, and in the early morning light he looked as all men look when they sleep—young and vulnerable. Pulling herself into a sitting position, she'd stayed and watched him for long moments. He was a good man, Mack "Snake" Pulaski. Good and kind and generous. And sexy. Lying there with his shirt half open, his breathing deep and even, the stubble of beard rough on her hand as she reached out and touched him.

But she left him to sleep and headed off down what looked like it had once been a road.

It was forty-five minutes before she came to what passed for civilization. Four or five adobe buildings clustered together around the rough road, and the chickens and dogs outnumbered the curious inhabitants. Maggie had always had a facility for language, and it took her little time to be presented to the patriarch of the village and to ascertain that they were indeed in Honduras, though about as far from the border and the various camps of marauding rebels as they could be.

At first transportation was a complete impossibility. Once, however, the jefe accepted the fact that he had to deal with an inferior *norteamericana* woman, and once he caught sight of the always acceptable *norteamericano* money, impossibilities became easily accomplished.

And here she was, an hour and a half later, bouncing down the narrowing track, back to Mack, in a battered four-wheel-drive vehicle, a sack of food in the back, the sun beating down, the wind in her hair. God was in his heaven and all was right with the world. If she'd pinpointed their location and secured a running vehicle this easily, anything was possible.

She'd paid careful attention to the landmarks on her trek outward, and the distinctive triple palm tree signaled their campsite from the night before.

She pulled up as close to the beach as she could, put the balky vehicle in neutral, since she had dubious confidence in her ability to restart it, and leapt from the Jeep, racing out toward the ocean to show Mack her triumph.

But he was nowhere in sight. Last night's campfire was a circle of charred cinders, and she could see the indentation in the sand where the two of them had slept. She whirled around, but there was no sign of him anywhere on the deserted beach. She was alone—abandoned. He hadn't trusted her ability to get him out of this mess. Damn him, she thought, feeling oddly close to the tears she never shed. Tears of anger, she told herself, feeling bereft. Tears of rage.

ten

"That's a hell of a vehicle, Maggie." Mack's voice came from directly behind her. "Where did you conjure it up from?"

"Where were you?" She turned, her body radiating disapproval. "I thought you'd taken off." She kept her voice completely even, unmoved by the fact that he was standing there dripping seawater and stark naked.

He shrugged. "I thought the same about you, Maggie. Fortunately, I had enough trust to wait around and see if you were going to return."

She bit back the scathing reply. "I would have thought you'd had enough salt water yesterday," she said instead, running her eyes over his body with studied calm. If the turquoise Jockey shorts had been distracting, this was much worse. She was going to dream about his damned, beautiful body, she knew she was.

He shook back his long wet hair and smiled at her sweetly. "It's very refreshing." And he started pulling on the clothes he carried over his arm. "You ought to try it," he said.

"What I'd like to try is a long hot shower in a modern hotel," she replied, noticing that some of the tension left her as the clothes covered his body. She was becoming more and more vulnerable to him, and it was a vulnerability she couldn't afford. "We're in Honduras, but we're about as far from where we want to be as possible. If only Van Zandt had his damned camp in Costa Rica," she grumbled.

"Why?"

"Why?" she echoed, incensed. "Haven't you looked at the horizon?" She gestured extravagantly. "This country is nothing but mountains and ridges and steep little valleys. Its roads are nonexistent, its population sparse and suspicious. We are going to have a hell of a time making it to Tegucigalpa."

"Where?"

"Tegucigalpa. Capital of Honduras, center of rebel activities. That's where I find out exactly where Van Zandt is, and that's where the nearest Holiday Inn is. It's about a hundred and fifty miles as the crow flies, and I figure on these roads it'll take us three days."

Mack was fastening the buttons of his much-abused chambray shirt. "Then what are we waiting for?"

They traveled in almost complete silence for the first hour. Maggie was concentrating on her driving. Mack was concentrating first on the provisions she'd conned from the villagers and then on the shredded Texaco map he'd found in the glove compartment that was chock-full of empty shell cases from a weapon that was undoubtedly the size of an elephant gun.

"You still haven't told me how you managed to get this Jeep," Mack said finally. "And the food, for that matter."

"I found a village a little to the west of our beach."

"And how did you persuade them to part with such a prized possession? I thought your money reserves were running low, and somehow I wouldn't think a remote village on the east coast of Honduras would take Visa."

"Nope. They did, however, take our gun." She'd been trying to avoid her own doubts as to the wisdom of that unavoidable piece of barter, and Mack's reaction only reinforced her own.

"They did what?"

"I traded them one hundred dollars of American money and the gun. We were out of bullets. It wouldn't have done us much good."

"We could have bought ammunition, Maggie. Even without bullets we could have scared someone off with it. Or are you prepared to catch bullets in your teeth, Superwoman?"

"Don't call me that."

He was muttering to himself under his breath. "I just hope you know what you're doing."

"Trust me." Her voice sounded completely confident, hiding her very real doubts as the jungle around them seemed to thicken to her paranoid eyes.

"Oh, I trust you, Maggie. With my life." If the sound of his drawling voice wasn't completely reassuring, Maggie chose to ignore it. He flipped the crumpled map back, folding it over and laying it in his lap. "I think we ought to head back toward La Ceiba, catch the highway that goes through San Pedro Sula, and then on to Tegucigalpa. It's about as direct as we can get, it has the advantage of major cities and probably adequate hotels, and it would cut our trip in half."

Maggie bit back the odd little twinge of annoyance and relief. She hadn't had time to more than glance at the map—she hadn't even considered the possibility of heading back up the north coast to the bustling little resort area of La Ceiba. But paved roads and a bed for the night sounded almost too good to be true. "What do you suggest we use for money? I only have two hundred dollars left. And as you already mentioned, Visa isn't ready currency around here."

"It will be in the larger towns like San Pedro Sula," he replied. "Don't you think?"

"Don't throw me any crumbs, Pulaski," she snarled. "You're right, I'm wrong, and my ego isn't so fragile that I can't admit it. How do we get to La Ceiba?"

"I don't know how to tell you this, Maggie."

She bit her lips, glaring at the underbrush. "You may as well —you haven't held back so far."

"You've been driving toward La Ceiba for the last hour anyway. I should think we'll hit it by midafternoon."

"The hell I am!" she exploded. "I'm heading due west—"

"La Ceiba is due west, Maggie. Tegucigalpa is directly south of us," he interrupted calmly.

She would like to have driven the balky Jeep into a banana

tree before admitting he was right. She'd envisioned the geography in her mind, but turned it sideways. She'd been carefully heading west, thinking it was toward the Pacific Ocean and the Honduran capital halfway between, and instead she'd simply been moving farther away.

"Pulaski," she said in a deceptively gentle voice, "no one likes a smart ass."

"Maggie," he replied, his raw voice curiously sweet, "no one likes someone who's perfect."

"Then I guess I don't have to worry about whether you like me or not," she said with a brittle laugh. "I'm getting further and further from perfection every day."

"I like you, Maggie," he said. "I like you just fine."

"I don't suppose there's a Holiday Inn in La Ceiba?" she asked in a mournful voice, changing the subject.

"What is this fixation about Holiday Inns? I've seen enough in my younger days to last me a lifetime. Don't you want to immerse yourself in the experience anymore?"

"I want to immerse myself in a heated swimming pool, a hot tub, a sauna, and a king-size bed with clean sheets."

"Sorry, it looks too small to have a Holiday Inn. There might be some nice resorts by the beaches, but I would think you'd be happier if we took a small hotel in town."

"I wouldn't be happier, but I'd be smarter. All right, Pulaski, I know when I'm beaten. But tell me there's a Holiday Inn in Tegucigalpa."

"We can probably find a Fodor's Guide in La Ceiba that will tell us. That is, if Fodor even publishes one."

"I wouldn't think too many people are eager to travel in Central America nowadays," Maggie said. "Still, they must have some sort of guide. I've got a good memory for geography and history but I can't remember much about Honduras except that it's all mountains."

"Good memory for geography? Then why were we heading in the opposite direction?" Mack drawled.

"Shut up, Pulaski, or I'll hand you over to the rebels when

we reach Tegucigalpa. I'm sure they'd be more than happy to help you find Van Zandt. Or at least make sure that you wouldn't ever need to see him again."

"Empty threats, Maggie. Think of the long hot shower you'll get tonight. Probably a wonderful seafood dinner, maybe a local wine."

"Sadist. Hand me a tortilla and be quiet. I've got to concentrate on my driving."

"How are you going to concentrate on your driving when you're trying to eat—"

"Shut up, Pulaski," she said in a dangerous tone of voice.

"All right, Maggie. But I don't think—"

Whatever he didn't think was destined to remain lost as a bullet whizzed directly between Maggie and Mack, straight through the center of the cracked windshield.

"Hell and damnation," Maggie cursed. "Duck, Pulaski." She stamped on the gas, and the balky four-wheel-drive coughed, sputtered, and then jerked forward at a marginally faster speed. Another bullet whistled past her ear, followed by the ominous crack of a rifle, and Maggie hunched over the steering wheel, biting her lip and cursing in a low, steady voice.

"What the hell is this?" Mack demanded from his position on the floor of the front seat. "You sure you paid for this Jeep?"

"I don't have your talents for hot-wiring," she muttered as the Jeep careened wildly down the jungle track. Her vision was not the best, since she didn't dare do more than peer over the steering wheel, and she had more than one glancing encounter with the underbrush before righting the vehicle. "I can't imagine why someone would want to shoot at perfect strangers—" Another bullet slammed into the dashboard five inches from her hand, knocking out the speedometer, which didn't work anyway, and Maggie stamped on the accelerator once more.

"I can imagine. Didn't you take a good look at this Jeep, Maggie?" How Mack could manage to sound reasonable from his hunched-over position on the floor of the Jeep was beyond her comprehension, but his raspy voice was calm and collected.

"This was some sort of government vehicle, and I wouldn't be surprised if it once belonged to the local equivalent of the DEA. I imagine we've stumbled into a branch of the local import/export business that doesn't care for government visitors. Probably doesn't care for *turistas*, either. I think the sooner we get out of here, the better."

"I'm driving as fast as I can!" she snapped as they bounced and jarred their way through the underbrush. The only sound in the steamy noontime air was the sound of jungle birds and the laboring noise of the old engine. "Do you hear anything?"

Slowly Mack pulled himself back into the front seat as Maggie took some of the pressure off the gas pedal. "I guess we're out of range. For now."

"What do you mean 'for now'?"

"I mean I expect there are any number of drug operations in these jungles. And we'll have to count on luck to avoid them."

"Luck and my driving," Maggie shot back, daring him to say something.

Mack only raised his eyebrows and sunk down lower in the seat. "Sure thing, kid. Wake me when it's over."

They drove into La Ceiba just after three o'clock in the afternoon. Maggie's Rolex had survived its long submersion of the day before, but her nerves weren't holding up as well. The sight of the bustling port city, surrounded by white beaches and fertile valleys, and the sheer mass of people sent mixed emotions through Maggie.

"Civilization," Mack said.

"Yes. For what it's worth."

"For what it's worth, I think there's an airport here," he said. "I wouldn't be surprised if we could get a flight to Tegucigalpa."

"God, I'd give my right arm to get rid of this damned Jeep," Maggie said fervently.

Mack could have made the obvious comment, and she steeled herself for it. He'd never once offered to drive on the long, hot trip, even when she wrestled with the stubborn clutch, the stalling motor, or the windshield wipers, which had flown off their stalks when they'd hit a flash rainstorm. He hadn't given her a word of advice when she'd had to drive the damned thing almost straight down a cliff, hadn't done anything more than clench the door handle and his teeth when they'd skidded on the rubble and ended up sideways in a shallow streambed.

But nothing, absolutely nothing, would have made her give up in her battle to control the Jeep, and Mack must have known it. Even now he said nothing, simply waited for her to shove the damned gear shift into first and head down into the port city. She put her narrow, long-fingered hand on the gear shift, paused, and looked at him.

She had battled the jungle, the narrow track that was better suited to mules than motorized vehicles, battled and won. And never in her life had she known a man who could just sit back and let her fight her own way, in her own time. Who trusted her enough to know what she had to do. A sudden rush of gratitude, affection, and something more swept over her, and with it came the exhaustion she'd been holding at bay. He looked so solid sitting there, and suddenly she wanted to put her head on his shoulder, close her eyes, and forget her battles.

"Pulaski," she said. "Would you drive the rest of the way?"

She'd finally managed to surprise a reaction out of him. His warm hazel eyes were startled, his eyebrows rose in his newly tanned face, and his mouth quirked upward. "Tired of fighting, Maggie May?"

"I'm not fighting you."

"I know that. We both know who you're fighting." And of course he did, bless his heart. He knew her almost as well as she knew herself. In some ways even better. It was an unnerving thought, and one she didn't have the energy to dwell on right there and then.

"Yes, I'm tired of fighting. Drive till you come to the cleanest, quietest hotel you can find." She climbed out of the driver's seat, stumbled around behind the Jeep, and stood by the passenger's side.

Mack hadn't moved. He was sitting there, looking at her, warmth and compassion and something else in those wonderful eyes of his. Before she knew what he was doing, he slid his large, warm hand behind her neck, under the loose braid, and pulled her face down to his. His mouth caught hers in a gentle, open-mouthed kiss that was reassuring, restrained, and yet hinting at a passion that had been waiting to burst forth.

She was too surprised and too exhausted to react—to respond or to fight—and before she could make up her mind, he moved away, sliding over into the driver's seat.

She climbed in, the warmth of his body still clinging to the tattered seats. "You shouldn't have done that," she said. "We can't afford to complicate matters."

He said nothing, his face blank as he put the Jeep in gear and started down toward the city. "I'm simplifying matters," he said finally. And she was too weary to argue or even ask him what he meant.

Hotel La Ceiba was a small, quiet, unprepossessing little place on a side street in the surprisingly noisy town. Pulaski checked them in, prepaid the extravagant fee of eight dollars, and led her up to a small room on the third floor. The halls were narrow and well-swept, the room he took her to had two narrow beds, colorful rag rugs on the floor, and a crucifix on the whitewashed wall.

"Home sweet home," Mack announced, dropping the knapsack in the chair.

"It looks like paradise to me," Maggie said, shoving a filthy hand through her wispy hair and leaving a streak of dust on her sweating face. "I'm going to find the shower and scrape some of this dirt off me. What about you?"

He leaned against the door, and his eyes were distant, almost thoughtful, as they swept over her. "Why don't we meet in the lobby in a couple of hours? You look like you could use a nap, and I want to do a little exploring."

"Not without me," she said, struggling to sound professional in the thick afternoon heat. "It's too dangerous—"

"No one knows we're here, Maggie," he said patiently. "I want to check out the neighborhood, see if I can find a store that has a travel guide and cigarettes. I'll check into what kind of flights they have. At least we could probably rent better transportation in a town this size."

She wanted to argue, knew she should put up a fight, but she was too damned tired. "Suit yourself. But watch out. I didn't get this far to lose you."

"You aren't going to lose me, Maggie." Again there was that curious note in his voice, a thread of promise that was both frightening and reassuring. Before she could rouse herself enough to push him, he was gone, and she was left staring at the thin pine door with its flimsy lock.

The water was lukewarm, rusty, and not much more than a halfhearted dribble in the semiprivate bath, but Maggie didn't give a damn. The salty residue of their dunking made her skin itch, her scalp flake, and even if her change of clothes were still stiff with salt, they at least didn't smell of sweat and dirt.

She walked barefoot down the deserted hallway, her long blond hair hanging like a wet curtain down her back. She promised herself that once she got to L.A. she'd give in to her mother's blandishments for the first time and give her poor abused body over to the best hairdresser, masseur, and beautician Sybil Bennett could find.

The narrow bed was surprisingly comfortable. The room was shadowed with the late afternoon light, and the trade winds blew gently across her body as she stretched out for what she promised herself was only a short nap. She stayed awake long enough to wonder if Mack was going to stay in his own bed tonight, and then sleep claimed her.

She awoke exactly one hour later, her internal alarm clock efficient as always, and the room was dim and shadowed. Suddenly she was completely alert, knowing that she wasn't alone. She could see Pulaski sitting in the one chair the room boasted, his long legs stretched out in front of him, his expression brooding.

"I didn't hear you come in," she murmured sleepily, sinking back down on the bed. "Did you find anything useful?"

"I did," he said, still watching her with that odd intensity. And then he shook himself, an infinitesimal movement that Maggie nevertheless noticed. "I've got the latest edition of *Fodor's Guide: Central America,* published about five years ago, toothbrushes, toothpaste, and an airline schedule. There are flights to Tegucigalpa almost every hour from the airport just out of town."

"I don't know if I trust your abilities as a travel agent," Maggie said, stretching, her lazy smile taking the sting out of her words. "I think poor old Lonesome Fred left a little bit to be desired."

"That's why I didn't make the reservations. Someone stole the Jeep, by the way."

"What?"

"Don't worry, we can get a taxi out to the airport. I figure it was our gain, their loss. I agree with you, I'd rather not have to drive that monstrosity again. Come on, Maggie, stir your buns. Or aren't you hungry?" He rose, stretching, and in her sleepy state she allowed herself the luxury of staring at his lean, sexy body.

"Pulaski, I could eat a horse," she said, not thinking of food at all.

He grinned, and she wondered if he was reading her mind again. God, she hoped not! "Maggie May, I know a place where they make the best horse in Central America. Come on, kid. Let's do the town."

eleven

This night out was just what they needed, Maggie thought several hours later as she stared dreamily out into the harbor. The lobster stuffed with local Cuyamel fish, the odd, sweet-starchy vegetables, the salad, and the local *cerveza* left her replete and happy. The town was noisy, cheerful, and colorful, and the company could not have been improved upon. Mack was in an expansive mood, out to charm her out of any lingering paranoia, and she went gratefully, tired of looking over her shoulder, tired of worrying about the future.

Tomorrow would take care of tomorrow's problems, she told herself with a shrug. Tomorrow they would board a flight for Tegucigalpa and be linked up with Van Zandt in probably less than twenty-four hours. For now she could lean back in her chair on the terrace of the oceanfront cafe, sip her wickedly strong coffee, and enjoy herself.

"So tell me more about growing up as Sybil Bennett's daughter?" Mack questioned, his voice low and rumbly, his eyes warm and relaxed and flattering in the candlelight. "And don't tell me any more superficial Hollywood stories, tell me about you."

She grinned in silent acknowledgment of his perspicacity. She had a supply of stock answers about growing up in Hollywood. None of which would do for Mack Pulaski.

"Wonderful, exciting, exhausting, depressing. Sybil's always been a romantic—she never feels alive unless she's desperately in love. God only knows when it started—she was twenty when

I was born and I've always had the suspicion she'd been busy before me. She'd meet someone, fall in love, and of course have to marry him. That was the early fifties, and she'd seen what happened to Ingrid Bergman when she didn't follow Hollywood's idea of morality. So Mother would fall in love, get married, and immediately present the current husband with proof of her adoration in the form of an offspring. By the time said offspring was a year old, Mother would have lost interest, both in the husband and in the child, and gone on to new conquests."

"That mustn't have been pleasant."

"It was all right. Sybil is a very loving woman—it's just that children bored her once they got past the stage where they posed successfully. I think she thought of us as fashion accessories—pretty little girls to smile up at her adoringly, with or without cameras around. She didn't care much for grubby hands and blue jeans and sticky kisses."

"So who got the grubby hands and sticky kisses?"

"Granny Bennett, for as long as she lived. And Queenie, Sybil's housekeeper. And then me."

"You?"

"I brought up the other three. Kate and Holly and Jilly. I was a very maternal older sister, a little domineering, I suppose. By the time I was twelve, even my mother was coming to me with her problems." Maggie laughed, a wry, accepting sound in the warm night air. After a moment Maggie looked distracted and sad. "My ex-husband told me I was too much for any man to live up to. Peter Wallace said pretty much the same thing."

"Do you think that's true?" He was toying with his brandy glass, and his hazel eyes were warm and tender in the reflected lights from the street.

Maggie shrugged. "Close enough. I scare the hell out of men, and there's nothing I can do about it. I scare even you."

"Who says?"

"You did. Last night, on the beach."

Mack considered it for a moment, then nodded. "Yes, I suppose you do scare me. But I'm willing to bet it's not in the same way you scared the others."

"How do I scare you?"

He grinned. "As you said last night, that's for me to know and you to find out. Would you like more coffee or would you like to go for a walk along the water?"

"Neither," she said with a yawn. "It's after eleven already, and we need to get to Tegucigalpa as early as we can tomorrow. I want to go back to the hotel, take another shower, and go to bed."

"Another shower? You just took one."

"Yes, but you brought me lavender soap, shampoo, and conditioner. I've never appreciated the pleasures of civilization so much in my entire life, and I intend to take full advantage of them. Once we get to Tegucigalpa, God knows what will happen."

"Does this mean I get spared the Holiday Inn?"

"Nope. But it means we may not be in the Holiday Inn any longer than we were in the Travers Hotel. I want to take my creature comforts while I can."

"Sounds reasonable. Let's go." He rose, tossing a handful of paper money down on the table, and Maggie looked up at him for a long, pensive moment before following.

It wasn't until she'd stepped under the shower a few minutes later that Maggie realized what was bothering her. Mack had been warm, charming, and infuriatingly distant. Clearly he didn't feel the same strong sensual pull that she'd been fighting all night. It was probably the fault of the unaccustomed good food and alcohol, she told herself, rubbing the sweet-smelling shampoo through her tangled hair. She'd sat there, staring at his strong, lean body lounging comfortably in the chair across from her, trying to fight the insidious attraction that was threatening to overwhelm her. She was becoming weak in her old age, her strength and resolution wavering in the face of almost continual disasters. With Peter's death her life had undergone a change that she could no longer deny. Life and death were indelibly imprinted on her brain. Tomorrow Mack could be dead. Tomorrow she could be dead. It was useless to miss chances that might never come again.

Life needed to be lived to the fullest, Maggie told herself when she stepped from the shower, wrapping the threadbare towel around her tall body. And the next time Mack made one of his halfhearted passes at her, she was going to take him up on it. Because even if he was only marginally attracted to her, he was becoming an obsession with her.

She wasn't one for spending a great deal of time looking in mirrors, but tonight was different. She saw that she was attractive, with her wide-spaced aquamarine eyes, her Danish cornsilk hair, which was now hanging wet and shiny down her back, her good nose, high Nordic cheekbones, and generous mouth. And her body was strong and sleek and healthy, a good body for loving. But maybe Mack liked petite brunettes full of soft curves. After all, he'd said he'd always had the hots for Sybil Bennett. Maybe he'd settle for bedding someone with the same eyes.

"You're an idiot, Maggie," she said out loud, grimacing at her mirror. "You only get into trouble when you go after someone. Look at Deke. Look at Randall. Look at your marriage. Forget about sex and concentrate on a good night's sleep. Pulaski looks good to you only because there's no one else around."

Which was a fat lie and she knew it, but she stuck to it anyway, turning her back on the mirror and rubbing her body briskly with the towel before pulling her wet jumpsuit back on for the dash down the hallway. She'd washed all her clothes in the sink, with the hopeful thought that they'd dry by morning. Even in the heat of the Honduran summer the wet cotton chilled her flesh, and she shivered as she ran barefoot down the hall to her room.

There was a light burning by the narrow bed as she closed and locked the door behind her. A light that illuminated Mack lying on her bed wearing his jeans and nothing else. Waiting for her.

She held herself very still, pressing her shoulder blades against the thin wooden door behind her. "What're you doing there?" Her voice came out admirably controlled. "That's my bed."

Mack smiled up at her—a sweet, understanding smile. "I'm sleeping here."

"And where am I supposed to sleep?" Stupid question, she thought.

But Mack was still curiously gentle, almost reassuring. "Here," he said.

"Isn't the bed a little small?"

"We'll manage."

So why was she standing there, frozen like a panicky virgin? Hadn't she just stood staring at herself in the mirror, telling herself that the next time Mack made a halfhearted pass, she was going to take him up on it. So what was she doing cowering against the door and trying to find her way out?

"Uh, Pulaski . . ." she began nervously.

"I never thought I'd see you turn into a coward, Maggie."

"I'm not a coward. I'm just not sure if this is a good idea."

"It's an excellent idea. What're you frightened of, Maggie? That you'll scare me off like you scared all the others? Or that you won't?"

That moved her away from the door. "Go to hell, Pulaski. I don't need your two-bit psychoanalysis tonight."

"I know you don't. You need love."

That shut her up for a moment. When she'd gathered her wits back about her she laughed. "Isn't that a euphemism? Aren't you talking about sex?"

"No," he said flatly, his voice low and sexy in the still night air. "I'm talking about love, and you know it as well as I do. Come here, Maggie."

She could stand there, shivering in her wet jumpsuit, and keep arguing. She could order him from her room, and he'd go with that damnable, easygoing smile of his. Or she could reach up and begin to undo her top button.

The wet material made the button tricky to unfasten, and her hands were trembling. She managed the first one, her eyes looking into his shaded ones with a fearless gaze, then her fingers moved awkwardly to the next one. And then he was off the bed in one fluid movement, and unaccountably she remembered Snake's serpentine grace. He was standing in front of her, his hands brushing hers out of the way, and he was warm and strong and so very close.

"I can take care of it, Maggie May," he whispered, his fingers making quick work of the buttons that traveled down her chest, past her waist. When he pushed the jumpsuit off her shoulders and down to her waist, she just stood there naked, waiting.

"Oh, Maggie," he said, his voice a caress, a raw breath of emotion, and his eyes glazed as he watched her. "Maggie, Maggie, Maggie," he whispered, pulling her into his arms, her chilled flesh scorched by the heat of him. And suddenly she was shivering, trembling all over with heat and cold and light and darkness, with a wanting that she'd thought was gone forever from her life, and she slid her hands up his smooth chest to clutch at his shoulders, swaying against him with a quiet little moan of delight.

"This is a mistake," she whispered, her mouth pressing lightly, curiously against the warm, smooth skin of his shoulder.

"This is the smartest thing we've done so far," Mack murmured back. "You told me last night how sexually healthy you are. Why don't you show me?"

His hands slid down her back to her hips, pulling her up against him, and the wet jumpsuit slid to the floor around her feet. It was an odd erotic sensation to feel her naked hips pressed against the heavy denim of his jeans, to feel his strong, rough hands on her smooth skin, molding her to him. Suddenly she felt gloriously, wickedly, wonderfully alive, and she raised her face to his, laughter and delight and wanting filling her aquamarine eyes. Her hands boldly slid down the taut length of him to press against the heat that surged against the zipper of his jeans.

And Mack's hands left her hips to cup her face, holding it up to his as he stared down at her with wonder and longing and something distant and indefinable. "God, Maggie," he whispered. "Why didn't we do this days ago? Why didn't we stop long enough in the cabin in Moab and get this settled?"

"Pulaski," Maggie said. "Stop talking so damned much." And she reached up and pressed her mouth against his.

She'd never known kissing to be such an overwhelming erotic adventure. If there was an Olympic event in kissing, Mack would have walked away with the gold medal. He did things with his tongue and teeth and lips that Maggie would never have even thought of, till she was gasping and burning in his arms, and her hands were tearing at his jeans.

The narrow bed sagged beneath their combined weight, the dip in the center throwing them together. Mack had dumped his jeans on the floor beside her wet jumpsuit, and Maggie spared a moment to consider how uncomfortable they were going to be when they got dressed in the morning. And that was the last rational thought she had for hours.

The small pool of light from the bedside lamp threw shadows around Mack's face, making him appear dark and mysterious as he bent over her. But Maggie was beyond childish fears at that point. She arched her back as his mouth traveled down her smooth skin, tasting, teasing, arousing, and soothing. Her nipples were painfully tight with longing, and when his mouth caught one and then the other, she moaned with desperation as her fingers twined in his long hair and pulled him down against her.

His hands stroked down the smooth skin of her stomach, across her hips, his rough calluses another sensation of delight. She arched her hips against his hand in mute supplication, and he laughed, low in his throat.

"For someone who put up such a fight," he said, "you sure are in a hurry." And his hand slid between her legs.

She reached out and touched him, stroking the hot, surging length of him, her fingers gentle, knowing, inspired. She could feel his reaction, the sudden trembling that vibrated through his body, the tension in his muscles that matched her own and told her they had waited long enough.

With the silent understanding that usually comes only with long-term lovers, he knew that she was ready. He was above her, shadowed against the darkened room, kneeling between her legs. He hesitated for a moment, and with a sudden, matching clarity she knew what he was thinking. He was wondering whether she still needed to be in control.

And without a word she reached out her arms to him, pulling him toward her, against her, into her, taking him on his terms in a sudden rush of love and gratitude and sensuality that threatened to split her apart.

If she expected the filling of that aching, empty part of her to assuage her longing, she was wrong. It drove her past wanting into a kind of madness of desire that he matched, surging against her, his body shaking as he tried to control the steady, powerful thrusts into her.

And then suddenly she was talking, words tumbling out of her mouth—feverish, pleading, impassioned words, love words, sex words, begging him, praising him, moaning against him. Until his mouth silenced hers, his tongue driving deep into her mouth as his body drove into her warmth. And there was nothing she could do but cling to him as explosion after explosion wracked her body. She was distantly aware of him stiffening in her arms, the sudden exhalation of breath against her sweat-streaked face, and then he collapsed against her, cradling her head against him as he lay there, his pounding heartbeat a twin to hers, slowing in tandem, as they sank back to a semblance of reality.

His strong back was slippery with sweat. It felt good to her, strong and real and hot, and she moved her head to place her mouth against his slightly bony shoulder, opening it to taste the dampness their lovemaking had brought forth. Then his head moved down, catching her mouth, kissing her with a sweet passion that had only begun to be sated. And the slow coils of desire began to burn again, and she was wide awake once more.

There was no way she could deny it. Her body was already reacting to the renewed proof of his desire, tightening around him in reminiscent, anticipatory spasms of longing. "We're going to be sorry," she said, trailing hot, hungry little kisses down his chest.

"Maybe," Mack said. "Maybe not." And he flipped over, bringing her with him, and smiled up at her, a devilish, sexy grin that wrung her heart. "Okay, kid. Your turn to do all the work."

She looked down at him, considering for a long moment. "Pulaski," she said, shifting slightly and watching with pleasure as his eyes glazed, "you're going to be my downfall."

He looked up. "God, I hope so, Maggie May. I surely hope so."

twelve

It had been a strange, uncomfortable morning. Maggie woke up first, crawled from beneath the tangle of limbs, and made it to the shower before Mack could pull her back. She killed as much time as she could, then went directly down to the small, clean lobby to find out about flights to Tegucigalpa. By the time she came back to the room, Mack was up and dressed.

She didn't want to look at Mack and see that warm, tender look in his eyes that completely demoralized her. He seemed suddenly much larger, filling the small hotel room with his presence, and yet she knew it was an illusion. He wasn't much taller than her almost six feet. She felt nervous, unsure of herself and her reactions to the almost shocking events of the night before. The feelings he stirred in her left her disoriented, quiet, and in desperate need of time to think and reflect.

But right now time was their most precious commodity. So she entered the room, avoiding his gaze, moving straight to the window and looking out over the courtyard. The soft trade breezes blew her damp hair against her forehead, soothing her. "We're taking the first flight out of here—I've arranged for a taxi to take us to the airport. Was there anything you needed to buy before we go?" Her voice was cool, distant, friendly, and she allowed herself a brief look at him before her eyes skittered away.

Hurt and anger clouded his hazel eyes, but his rough, drawling voice sounded just as unmoved as hers. "I think I've got everything I need. Tegucigalpa's the biggest city in the country, according to Fodor's. I'm sure if we need anything else, we can find it there."

"Yes, I'm sure we can," she said, staring out at the leaves gently moving in the soft wind. She forced herself to turn, smiling brightly at him. "Let's go."

He waited. Watching her. He was going to say something, she just knew it. He was going to open that sexy mouth of his that had done such shocking things to her last night and say, "About last night . . ."

Without a word, he stuffed their damp clothes in the knapsack, fastened it, and hoisted it over his shoulder. "Let's go," was all he said.

They slept the short flight from La Ceiba to Tegucigalpa, careful not to touch each other. There'd been an uncomfortable moment when they'd taken their seats in the small commuter plane, and Maggie couldn't keep her eyes from meeting his as she fastened the seat belt.

"You're not the slightest bit nervous?" he asked her, his voice nothing more than politely curious. They might never have clung together on the shattered wing of a downed plane, might never have kept each other alive and alert during those endless hours.

"Not the slightest," she said, and it was only a little bit of a lie. "What about you?"

"Scared shitless," he said. "But then, I've never made any claim to being perfect. I have real emotions. I get angry, I get scared, I get hurt. What about you?" There was no mistaking the pulsing anger in his voice.

Maggie knew that sooner or later she was going to have to face what happened, sooner or later they were going to have to talk about it. But not right now, when she was trying to hide the fact that her palms were sweating, not right here when they were surrounded by tourists and businessmen and flight attendants.

"You should know by now that I do my absolute best not to

let things faze me," she said in her coolest voice. "Life is a great deal more comfortable that way."

"I'm sure it is," he snapped, and he didn't say another word the entire trip.

If his nagging, impertinent questions made her edgy, his silence was even worse. As they made their way through Tegucigalpa, Mack followed her with a leashed docility that she had little doubt would explode sooner or later. She found she was looking forward to it.

Tegucigalpa was a bustling, growing city, nestled in one of Honduras's many valleys, with new construction abounding on the outskirts and in the center of the capital. The pastel houses, the red-tiled roofs, the twisting little neighborhoods and charming, colonial ambience made Maggie think twice about settling for the anonymous comfort of the Holiday Inn Plaza. But not three times. That anonymity was just what they needed while she made contact with the head of the rebels.

The government of Honduras had cracked down recently, ordering the various bickering groups of rebels to maintain a lower profile in the country's capital. It might prove more difficult finding them than she supposed. She also had to figure out what she was going to do with Mack while she made contact. While it was unlikely that word of his involvement with the New York drug deal could have filtered all the way down here, Maggie didn't dare rule it out.

Mack waited in the spacious lobby of the new Holiday Inn Plaza while she checked in, followed her as she led the way to their room on the third floor overlooking the charming city and the mountains that ringed it.

Finally he spoke. "Where am I sleeping?"

There were two double beds in the spacious, American-style hotel. "Like a five-hundred-pound gorilla, Pulaski, you can sleep anywhere you damn please."

He didn't smile. "Which bed do you want?"

So it was going to be like that, was it, she thought dishearteningly. She had no one to blame but herself. She'd known it was a mistake from the start, she'd been deliberately cool all morning, and it was no wonder he was setting his own distances between them.

"The bed by the window," she said in an even voice. "I like to be near the light."

Mack nodded, dropping the knapsack on the other bed. And then he kicked off his shoes and sank down onto her bed, stretching out and placing his hands behind his head. "Good. I like this one better too." And his eyes were challenging.

Her eyes met his challenge for a long, unwavering moment. Then she sank down in one of the chairs. "I want you to stay here while I contact the RAO."

"The who?"

"The RAO. The . . . God, I can't remember what the letters stand for, and I don't really give a damn. It's the largest group of rebels. They're the ones working the most with the CIA—they should know where Van Zandt is."

"And you want me to stay here while you talk to them? Forget it, Maggie."

"Pulaski, we can't be sure they haven't been warned about you. Your voice is distinctive—all they'd have to do is hear that rasp and recognize you."

"Then I won't talk. I can be discreet, Maggie. But I'm not going to let you go into a lion's den alone."

"I don't need some goddamned man watching out for me!" The nervous tension that had been simmering within her all morning ignited, and fury lit through her like a forest fire. "Don't think that sleeping with me gave you some sort of rights over me. I can take care of myself, and I'm not about to start relying on some insecure male who's got something to prove and thinks he owns me. No one owns me, mister, and no one is responsible for my well-being but me."

He remained calm and unmoved during her tirade. "Got anything else to say, Superwoman?" he taunted gently.

Her anger evaporated as swiftly as it had come. "All right.

I'm sorry for flying off the handle. Why do you want to come with me?"

"Because it's my butt you're trying to save. I figure I have some responsibilities to myself, even if you won't let me have any toward you. It would be nice if you could look upon this as a cooperative effort—you save me when the need arrives, I return the favor when the time comes. But I know you have problems with that, and that's okay. I just don't want to sit in the Holiday Inn waiting to hear what's happened to you."

Maggie laughed, a forced laugh, but a laugh all the same. "Tell you what. Keep your mouth shut and your shades on. As far as anyone's concerned, you're my husband, Jack Portman."

"God, we're back to him again?"

"We're back to him again. I don't suppose I'll fool the RAO, but unless the informer at Third World Causes has been amazingly efficient, they shouldn't suspect you at all."

"You think there's an informer? Is that how people managed to find us time after time? Is that why Peter Wallace wound up dead?" They were reasonable enough questions, ones to which Maggie had no answers.

"I don't know. Maybe I'm being paranoid again. But you're not going to stay put and let me find out, are you?"

"You know me pretty well by now."

Maggie shrugged. She did know him pretty well by now, and she knew he was determined to stick to her like glue. "Well, then, we're just going to have to find out together. Let's go."

He'd already slid his feet back into his battered Nikes. "Yes, ma'am. I'm ready."

The headquarters of the RAO had been moved, at the Honduran Government's polite but inflexible request, from the high-rise office building in downtown Tegucigalpa to an unprepossessing location across the river in one of the less desirable neighborhoods. Everything looked prosaically normal, the neatly painted lettering on the plaque outside the soft pink building, the children playing in the streets. Even the armed soldiers standing guard outside the main entrance were relaxed and smiling. Until Maggie asked for Enrique Castanasta in her liquid Spanish.

"Who wants him?" the suddenly hostile soldier demanded in thickly accented Spanish. The expression in his dark, distrustful eyes suggested that no mere female could have anything of importance to discuss with such an illustrious person.

She hesitated. On the one hand, if she gave them her phony name it would give them some measure of protection. There was a good chance someone at Third World Causes was far too talkative and then she'd be in trouble. But Enrique Castanasta was not the sort to grant interviews to any American *turista* who happened to show up, even accompanied by a hulking, mute male. She was far more likely to get to see him and to find out where Van Zandt was if she told him a variant of the truth.

"Margrethe Bennett of Third World Causes, Ltd.," she said. Mack didn't make a sound, didn't move a muscle, but she could feel his sudden tension. "This is my companion, Jack Portman. We're good friends of Jeffrey Van Zandt, and we're hoping General Castanasta could help us find him."

The names meant something to him; she could tell by the flickering of his basilisk eyes. But which names—Van Zandt and Third World Causes? Or Margrethe Bennett and Mack's previously used alias? Or all of them? His reply wasn't illuminating. "Wait here."

Maggie stood there with the afternoon sun beating down on her bare head, wishing she'd managed to arm herself with a pair of mirrored sunglasses like Mack's. Her rumpled jumpsuit was already sticking to her in the heat, her feet hurt, and her nerves were strung as tightly as high wire.

"Why the hell did you give him your real name?" Mack muttered in her ear. "Weren't you taking a big chance?"

"It was either that or not get in to see Castanasta at all," she replied without turning. "Don't bug me, Portman. I know what I'm doing."

"I sure as hell hope so." He stepped back as the soldier reappeared in the doorway.

"He'll see you. Alone," he added, waving his machine gun as they both stepped forward.

Maggie shook her head. "We go together or not at all."

The soldier shrugged. "Suit yourself, gringa. I am certain it will make no difference to the general."

Maggie's shrug matched his, and her smile in the blazing afternoon sun was brilliant. "Perhaps," she replied. "But I wouldn't count on it if I were you. Many people would be distressed if the RAO didn't help us reach Van Zandt. People of influence and power, people who support your noble cause with their hearts and their money." She kept her voice neutral. Mack could probably hear the cynicism in her voice, if he even understood her Spanish, but the soldier in front of her took her words at face value.

"I will check." Once more he disappeared into the building, once more he reappeared, gesturing the two of them in with the barrel of his machine gun. It took all Maggie's willpower not to skirt the evil-looking weapon nervously.

"Senora Bennett, how may I help you?" General Enrique Castanasta was all shiny teeth and charm. His office was small and surprisingly luxurious, and everything was all affability. An affability Maggie instinctively distrusted.

"I'm trying to find Jeffrey Van Zandt. He's aided Third World Causes over the last three years, and we were counting on his help on a small matter. We have reason to believe he's working in a training camp somewhere north of the Nicaraguan border, and we hoped you might be able to help us."

"If only I could, senora," Castanasta said, the regret in his voice but not in his eyes. "We know of Third World Causes, though we are as yet unsure whether to count them as friends. And we know of Van Zandt and his training camp. Unfortunately the camp is not stationary, nor is it even always on this side of the border. For all I know, Senor Van Zandt might be in

Managua at this very moment. Or he might be back in Washington."

"Do you have any idea where there might be training camps?" she persisted.

Castanasta shrugged, smiling. "Who can say? I may be a general, senora, but I am merely a desk-bound bureaucrat. We exist here in Tegucigalpa to raise money and disperse it to where it is most needed. Two weeks ago we had two thousand troops on the eastern coast. Last week they were just north of El Paraíso. Who knows where they will be tomorrow?" He stood, and Maggie had no choice but to follow suit. She was aware of Mack behind her, silent, watching, waiting.

"I am sorry I can be of no further help, senora."

"Do you suppose the ACSO might know of his whereabouts?" She came up with one last try.

It was the wrong try. The RAO and the ACSO were competing rebel factions, competing for media attention and money, completely ignoring the fact that they were ostensibly on the same side. Castanasta's affable smile vanished, his small, rather cruel mouth snapped shut, and he moved to the door, the interview clearly at an end.

"Who can say with the ACSO?" he grumbled. "They are a pack of dogs, chasing their own tails. I would like to think the United States Government would be wiser than to waste the small amount of money they've allocated for us to fools like them. But that is probably a vain hope."

"Do they have offices in Tegucigalpa?"

"Senora, I do not know. I do not know if there are any members left alive. The last I heard they had all run to Costa Rica and were trading thousand-dollar weapons for a few miserable pesos. Rabid dogs, all of them." He hesitated. "They will be of no help to you and Senor Pulaski. If I do hear of anything, however, I will send word to the Holiday Inn Plaza."

"How did you know where we were staying?" Maggie was suddenly aware of a cold trickle of unease sliding down her narrow backbone.

Castanasta shrugged, his smile firmly back on his face. "Where else would *norteamericanos* be staying?" he inquired. "I will be in touch, senora."

They had no choice but to leave. All of Maggie's instincts were warning her of danger, but the faces of the RAO around them were bland, even helpful. But something was definitely wrong, and the center of her back prickled with the feel of a shotgun trained on it.

The two of them walked in silence down the dusty, deserted street. Their taxi had long since disappeared, and so had any other sign of life. They were at the corner when Mack finally spoke.

"I have a bad feeling about this," he muttered. "Did you trust them?"

"No. But then, why should I? Members of their group or the ACSO tried to run us off the road in Arizona." They turned the corner and headed uphill, back toward the center of the city. "I wish I could figure out what is bothering me about that meeting."

"Something's bothering me right now," Mack said. "When we got here there were children playing in the streets, old men gossiping, women doing laundry, dogs and goats roaming around. And now the whole damned place is a ghost town. I think we're in trouble, Maggie."

She wanted to deny it, wanted to reassure him, but she couldn't even open her mouth to do so. And then she realized what was wrong. "He knew your name."

"What?"

"He called you Pulaski," she said grimly. "I introduced you as Jack Portman, and he called you Senor Pulaski. We're in deep trouble."

The sudden silence of the hot afternoon was broken by an ominous sound. It was the unmistakable sound of a machine-gun clip being jammed into place.

"Maggie," Mack groaned. "I think we'd better get the hell out of here."

"Pulaski," she replied, "I think you're right."

thirteen

The empty, silent street suddenly turned into a blazing, white-hot nightmare. Maggie dived around the corner, Mack on her heels, as the roar of machine-gun fire shattered the stillness. And then they were running, racing down the rough cobbled streets with the certain, terrifying knowledge that their lives depended on it. Maggie didn't even turn back to make certain Mack was following; she could only run for her life and hope he was doing the same.

The maze of narrow, twisting streets heading back toward the center of town aided their escape. She could hear the pounding of booted feet, the martial shouts and orders from behind them, and she doubled her speed. Occasionally a face would peer from a window, someone would start out a door and then quickly retreat. And Maggie and Mack kept running.

A volley of shots rang out just as Maggie careened around another corner. She saw the plaster spurt off the side of a house as she turned to check for Mack. He was keeping pace with her, showing no signs of tiring, no signs of panic. She wondered if she appeared equally stoic. She doubted it.

The soldiers were gaining on them. Both she and Mack were in good shape, and they were fortunately unencumbered by heavy artillery. But the pounding footsteps and rapid-fire Spanish were getting closer and closer.

One more corner, and Maggie dashed around it. To be confronted by a tall stone wall.

Mack raced past her, leapt over the top of an abandoned car, and was on a shallow rooftop before she had time to do more than assimilate the situation. "Move your ass, Maggie," he shouted, his raspy voice raw with his heavy breathing.

The rebels were behind them, closing in. She had only a few seconds to spare, and it was a dangerous, possibly deadly, idea. But she was suddenly confronted with the chance that she might lose him, as she'd lost everyone else, through her stubbornness.

She ran to the wall, a wall she could scale in seconds, and held up her arms. "Help me, Mack."

He stared down at her in complete dumbfounded amazement, not moving. Seconds seemed to hang like hours in the hot afternoon, and the footsteps grew closer. May as well go all the way, Maggie thought. I may die for this stupid idea. "Help me," she said. "I can't make it."

She had a moment to admire the touching aspects of her plea. If she expected Mack to be similarly moved, she was in for a shock. A look of complete, absolute fury whitened his face, and without a word he leaned down, wrapping his hands around her wrists like steel manacles. He yanked her up, slamming her knees against the edge of the roof, just as the rebels rounded the corner. And then he jerked her after him, a second ahead of the next spray of bullets.

Finally they reached a different part of town. The streets, while still narrow and twisting, were free of litter, the charming pastel houses were newly painted and spotless. One or two older American cars could be seen parked along the side streets, and dogs and children, both clean and well-fed, roamed freely.

Mack dropped her wrist like it was leprous. "We're out of danger," he said flatly, and she could see the rage vibrating through his sweat-soaked body. A rage she couldn't even begin to understand. "I'll see if I can find us a taxi back to the hotel." And without another word, he walked away from her.

She stood there on the neat, quiet street and watched him go. She'd betrayed herself, and her highest principles, to bind him to her, to give him what she thought he wanted. She'd given him the power over life and death, and instead of bringing them closer, it had enraged him. And the tension and panic of the last minutes faded into a rage of her own.

He was back, moments later, with one of the local taxis. They rode together in silence back to the center of Tegucigalpa. She could feel Mack's anger, and her own fury matched his, until they both marched stiffly through the lobby, heading for their room with one infuriated accord.

"You realize that Castanasta knows where to find us?" Mack said angrily when they were alone in the elevator.

"Yes."

"What do you intend to do about it?"

"Not a goddamned thing. If he wants to blow you up, he can damned well do it, with my blessing," she said through gritted teeth.

Together they marched down the wide, luxurious hallway of the newly built hotel. She could feel him waiting, hovering on the brink of some sort of explosion as she fumbled with the key, and she found she was looking forward to it. They stepped inside the cool, dark room, and she closed the door, intending to turn around and confront him with his unreasonable behavior.

She didn't have a chance. He caught her shoulders in a painful, iron grip, turned her around, and slammed her with a great deal of unnecessary force against the wooden door. "Don't you ever do something like that again," he said, his voice shaking with fury.

"What the hell are you talking about?" she shot back. "And get your goddamned hands off of me."

His fingers only dug in deeper, and he slammed her back against the wall for emphasis. "That touching little scene in the alleyway. 'Help me, Mack,' " he mimicked savagely. " 'I can't make it.' " His voice was a simper. "The day you couldn't make it over that wall twice as fast as I could will be a cold day in hell, and I know it as well as you do! What the hell do you take me for?" He was absolutely roaring with rage.

"I was too tired—"

"Bullshit! You were playing games, Maggie. You decided I was some insecure male who needed my ego stroked, so you figured you'd let me save your life. In doing so you risked both our lives, and all for some stupid whim. Let me tell you, lady," he continued, thumping her against the wall for emphasis, "I don't need you or anybody else stroking my ego. I don't give a damn if you save my life time and time again. I don't have any overweening macho pride that will make me reject you in the long run, and you should know me well enough by now to realize it."

"If you'll stop throwing me against the wall," she managed through gritted teeth, "I'll explain to you—"

"I don't need any explanations. You may not know me, but I know you like the back of my hand. I know the way your mind works, and I know how you try to manipulate me so you can feel in control. Well, forget about control, lady. You've just blown it completely, and it's a whole new ball game. From now on you're going to have to be completely honest, with me and with yourself, and no more manufactured rescues, no more dewy-eyed little pleas for help. Got that?" He banged her against the wall one last time, and it was one time too many.

She lashed out with every ounce of her strength and knew immediately she was outclassed. He had been holding back when he'd jumped her in Utah, but now he was using every ounce of the power in his body to subdue her, and it was considerable.

But Maggie knew a few tricks of her own. She twisted, turned, slammed her foot down on his instep, then swiftly brought her knee up to his groin.

Thankfully, for both their sakes, he was faster than she was. He twisted out of range, still gripping her shoulders, and then they were on the heavily carpeted floor, rolling over and over as Maggie tried to punch and pound and hit him.

It was hopeless. He was much larger than she was, and his hands were everywhere. The silent afternoon was punctuated by the sound of their heavy breathing, the grunts and curses as she fought like a madwoman. All in vain. She ended up lying beneath him on the floor by the bed, her wrists held down by his arms, his body straddling hers, as she glared up at him, panting in exhaustion and fury.

She'd managed to connect more than once, she noticed with triumph. She'd split his lip by banging her head against him, there was a long scratch down one side of his face, and if she were really lucky, she might have given him a black eye. He just sat there, his weight holding her immobile, his face impassive.

And then suddenly the whole tension shifted and changed, from raw anger to a blazing sexuality that was free from rage. Slowly he leaned down and kissed her, full and hard on the mouth, and she could taste the blood she'd drawn. Without hesitation she opened her mouth to him, reaching out for him with a passion just as raw and overwhelming as her suddenly vanished anger.

He released her hands to rip at her jumpsuit, and she did the same, pulling his shirt off him, straining against him with a desperation that knew no bounds. And then they were naked on the rug, hot, straining flesh melting together. He entered her immediately, and within seconds she was arching around him, shivering and crying and moaning her release into his hungry mouth. And he joined her, his body rigid in her arms, and they sank together into that tiny death that was a triumph over the greater one they had just avoided.

It was a long time before either of them moved. Maggie thought she might have fallen asleep for a few moments, she couldn't be sure. She felt almost shell-shocked, comatose, unable to move even her eyelids.

Slowly Mack pulled away. She could feel him looking down at her, but she didn't want to open her eyes. Her muscles refused to obey her, which was just as well. If she could have moved, all she would have done was to hide her face.

"Open your eyes, Maggie," he said, and there was a strange note in his voice. One that sounded almost like laughter. It was so unlikely that she found she had to look, and sure enough he was smiling down at her, his clear hazel eyes torn between amusement and wonder.

"Do you have any idea how perverse that was?" Maggie inquired.

"Yup," he said. "Kinky as hell. Great, too. Does it bother you?"

Since he was still pinning her hips down, there was no way she could turn and bury her face in the rug. And in his current playful mood, that might have caused even more trouble. She just looked up at him, her face shadowed, and his smile softened. Leaning down, he kissed her again, very gently. "It does, doesn't it?" he whispered.

"Yes," she admitted on a broken sigh. "A little. And I think what bothers me the most is that it doesn't bother me half as much as it should."

He laughed then, a gentle, reassuring laugh as he pulled her unresisting body into his arms. "Don't worry, Maggie, I'm not suggesting we make a habit of beating each other up before sex," he drawled in her ear. "I think we had to let off some steam after this afternoon. But don't, and I mean this, Maggie, don't ever do that again. I don't need you playing games to pander to my machismo. I don't think I have any machismo."

"Oh, yes, you do," she murmured against his salt-sweaty chest. "In the best possible way."

"And you, my dear, are a total woman. In the best possible way," he added swiftly.

"A total woman who's got carpet burns on her butt."

"Why don't we move up to the bed for a short nap?"

"Sounds good to me," she said. "You move first."

"We can do it together." He hoisted her up, and she saw a sudden wince of pain cross his face in the darkened room.

"Are you all right?" she asked as he placed her gently on the bed, following her down and pulling her back into his arms. Back where she belonged, she thought absently.

"I may limp for a few days," he said on a note of laughter.

"You managed to connect once or twice when you were trying to kick me in the shins."

"Oh, no, Mack, I didn't mean—"

"Oh, yes, you did. Let's just be glad that you're more adept with your toes than your knee, or neither of us would be half as comfortable right now." He tucked her against him, and his mouth was soft and teasing on her shoulder. "Go to sleep, Superwoman. We can go another ten rounds tomorrow."

"Maybe," she murmured. "The question is, who won this round?"

His hand cupped her breast, and even in her sleepy, satisfied state, the nipple hardened against him. "I think we both did, Maggie May."

It was getting dark when Maggie awoke. Some inner sense warned her as the blackness was beginning to close around them, and she reached out and turned on the bedside lamp. Mack stirred sleepily, turning to bury his face in the pillow, and she smiled down at him, giving in to the impulse to run her hand through his shaggy blond hair. There was a surprising amount of gray mixed in with it, and, leaning over, she pressed her mouth against the nape of his neck in a light butterfly kiss before sliding off the bed and heading for the sybaritic bathroom.

Even the towels were huge and thick and wonderful. When she stepped back out into the lamplit room, Mack was sitting on the side of the bed. "I was going to join you in there," he said, replacing the telephone.

"I got cleaner this way," she said absently, rubbing her hair. "Who were you calling?"

Mack just looked at her. Her tone of voice had been anything but accusing, but they both could read the undercurrents. "Not the rebels, Maggie May. I called room service for some dinner, the cleaning service for our clothes, and I tried the U.S. Embassy, but it's after hours. They even have goddamned answering machines down here."

"Why did you call the embassy? They're not going to tell us where Van Zandt is. They're going to deny he even exists." She sat down beside him on the bed.

"I was thinking they might offer us some protection. Even if the CIA is pissed at me for interfering in their business. I still don't think the Feds want American citizens to be gunned down in Honduras."

"I'm not so sure. I think we're more than expendable. Don't call them again, Mack?" It was a request, gently stated, not an order.

"I don't want you dying, Maggie."

"I have no intention of dying. Or letting you get killed either. I've still got a few tricks up my sleeve. When the ACSO finds out the RAO tried to kill us, they'll bend over backward to be helpful."

"Unless the RAO gets to us first."

She shook her head. "They won't. All the rebels are here in Honduras on sufferance. Word will reach the government about the shoot-out this afternoon, and it won't go well for them. They wouldn't dare interfere with the tourist trade of an American hotel like a Holiday Inn. If this were Managua, we'd be in a different situation—they'd blow the whole place up without thinking twice. But I really don't think they'll dare mess around in Tegucigalpa."

"Does that mean we don't have to be careful?"

"That means we have to sleep with only one eye open instead of two," she said, dropping her towel on the bed and reaching for her one set of clean clothes. "When's dinner coming?"

"Half an hour."

"Then I'll go out and see if I can find us something else to wear. My jumpsuit has seen better days."

"I may have ripped all the buttons off it," he agreed smoothly.

"I think you ripped the whole damned thing apart," she said, pulling on her jeans. "Will you wait here for me?"

Again the request, not the order. "You don't have to be that polite, Maggie May," he drawled. "Yes, I'll stay put. Just don't come back with turquoise Jockey shorts this time."

"I promise. Maybe tiger-striped ones."

Mack was in the shower when she returned. Her excursion had been more than successful. There was no sign of any rebels in the area, and the desk clerk had been more than helpful. The plans were simple, straightforward, and already made. It would be interesting to see how Mack responded.

"We're all set," she announced when he came dripping into the room. "We're meeting with Lieutenant Mendoses of the ACSO tomorrow morning. He'll have maps, information, guns, and a Jeep."

Mack nodded. "And you trust him?"

"No. I've found out where there's another gun shop, and I thought we'd rent our own Jeep and switch when we get out of sight. But I think he'll tell us the truth about Van Zandt. He has nothing to lose and everything to gain by helping us. Van Zandt and his bosses aren't going to like the RAO's attempt."

"Why not? I'd think the CIA would like nothing better than for us to disappear."

"Disappear, yes. Gunned down on the streets of Tegucigalpa, no. We'll get to Van Zandt, sooner or later."

"We still have no guarantees he'll be able to help us."

"We have no guarantees of anything. If worse comes to worse, we can always fly to one of the Bay Islands and hole up for a while."

Mack smiled—a slow, sexy smile. "Why don't we skip Van Zandt and go directly to Option B? I'd much rather lie on a warm beach with you than chase around guerrilla-infested jungles."

"That's not all these jungles are infested with," she said dryly.

"What's that supposed to mean?"

"I'll tell you tomorrow. Dinner's here."

"How do you know it's dinner and not some unfriendly rebels?"

"Because I can smell the roast chicken," Maggie said. "Trust me, Mack. Right now we're safe." And she opened the door to General Enrique Castanasta.

fourteen

It would have been nice if she'd seen whether the gun shop was still open, she thought as she surveyed her nemesis with opaque eyes. She would have felt a hell of a lot more secure if she had a gun within reach. Castanasta was carrying enough artillery for half a dozen men, wearing handguns and knives like medals around his uniform. It took only one furtive glance to ascertain that he was alone, the hallway behind him deserted. And there was no gun in his hand.

"General Castanasta," Maggie said with ironic courtesy, "what a pleasure to see you again. I wasn't expecting you so soon."

"We can waste time fencing, Senora Bennett, or you can invite me in and we can come directly to the point." There was no answering polite smile on his face.

"Or we could come directly to the point without inviting you into our room," she said sweetly. "I think I like that option the best. That way if you decide to finish what you started this afternoon, there will be witnesses."

"Senora Bennett, you know as well as I do that if I had really wanted you and Senor Pulaski dead, nothing would have stopped me. A machine gun and armed soldiers against two civilians on foot is a very uneven match."

Maggie nodded, having come to the same conclusion. "So you just decided to scare the hell out of us, General? For what purpose?"

"If you would care to invite me in, I might tell you."

Maggie found herself in the midst of a paralyzing struggle. On the one hand, she wanted to turn and get Mack's opinion. On the other, she was still fighting like crazy having to rely on anyone else. So she stood there, motionless, fighting herself, until common sense finally reared its ugly head. It was Mack's life, after all. He deserved some say in the matter.

"One moment, please," she said to the general with exaggerated politeness, closing the door in his face. She turned to Mack, leaning against the door. "What do you think? Should we let him in?"

Mack stood there, staring at her for a long moment. And then he crossed the room, caught her face in his strong, warm hands, and kissed her full on the mouth. "Sometimes, Maggie," he whispered, "you absolutely amaze me."

She fought the treacherous warmth that swept over her. "That still doesn't answer my question, Mack," she said, keeping her voice stern.

"Sure, have him in. I don't think he'd come out in public if he was planning to murder us."

Maggie reopened the door, gesturing the general in with a flourish. The one bed was a wreck of tangled sheets and tossed pillows, and Mack was still casually buttoning his shirt, his feet bare, his eyes bland. There was clearly no question as to what the two of them had been doing all afternoon, and Maggie met the general's quizzical expression with a look almost of defiance.

"Senor Pulaski," he greeted him. "We were not properly introduced earlier today, but I of course know who you are."

"Of course," said Mack in his rasping voice.

"The question is, how are we to get you two safely to Chicaste?"

"Why would we wish to go to Chicaste?" Maggie perched on the wide dresser, her eyes never leaving Castanasta's hands in case they felt like straying to one of the guns strapped around his torso.

"Because that is where the CIA has set up military training

camps. And that is where Van Zandt has been serving as an adviser, off and on for the last three years."

That was also the name of the town that had escaped her memory, Maggie had to grant him that much. "You intend to help us?" She didn't bother to keep the skepticism out of her voice.

"I intend to help you, senora. If you were to meet with Mendoses and follow his instructions, I doubt you would make it as far as Danli."

"Lieutenant Mendoses didn't send armed men to chase us through Tegucigalpa," Mack said, sitting down on the bed and pulling on his shoes. Maggie took a moment to notice that he, too, kept his attention on Castanasta's weapons.

Castanasta hesitated for a moment. "I will, as you say, lay my cards on the table. You know that the RAO and the ACSO are bitter rivals. What you don't know is that the ACSO was behind the drug deal that Senor Pulaski so unfortunately stumbled into. They are riddled with informers, incompetents, and traitors, and we of the RAO want nothing to do with them. Unfortunately we have certain agreements. And one is that you were to be disposed of if you made an appearance. Your knowledge is very embarrassing to the ACSO."

"Sorry about that," Mack said.

"However, I have no desire to serve as executioner for those fools. We put up a good show, my men, eh? I think the ACSO was convinced we tried our best to eliminate you. We have no quarrel with you, senor, nor do we have any stake in keeping you alive. We do, however, have need of getting in touch with the training camp, and we are willing to assist you in return for you being the bearer of certain information."

"Why don't you send one of your own men?" Maggie questioned sharply.

Castanasta spread his hands. "Again I will be honest and tell you something that you probably already know. We are very short of men. We have no more than eight stationed in Tegucigalpa, and I can spare none of them."

"And how many do you have in Chicaste? Not two thousand, as you told me earlier."

"Not even two hundred, senora. We need money quite desperately, and we have been waiting for Van Zandt to bring it."

"Bring it from where?" Maggie demanded.

"Don't you mean from whom?" Mack interjected.

She considered glaring at him, then thought better of it. "You're right, I mean from whom. If it's coming from my country, I want to know who's sending it. The last military aid package was voted down, thank God, and . . ." Belatedly she realized that opinion wouldn't go over too well with the man in front of her, but he just shook his head.

"I already know that you don't approve of our revolution, senora. It is of no concern to me, as long as you do not interfere."

"Unlike Van Zandt and his ilk, I have no intention of interfering with the internal politics of countries other than my own," she said in a lofty tone of voice. "What you do is your concern."

"Gracias," Castanasta said ironically. "And you needn't worry—the money does not come from your government, it comes from private sources."

"Sure it does," Mack drawled.

"So what do you want from us? I trust you don't expect us to be couriers, bringing the money back to you."

"No, senora. In return for directions to Chicaste we only want you to pass a message along. They will send one of their men back to us."

"And we should trust you?" Maggie questioned, irony deep in her voice.

"You have very little choice, senora."

"I have Lieutenant Mendoses. I only have your word for it that he wants us dead."

"You trust Lieutenant Mendoses even less than you trust me, and rightly so," Castanasta said with a fair amount of acuity. "You know I'm right. We could have killed you this afternoon, and we didn't. What guarantee do you have that Mendoses will grant you the same?"

It was unanswerable. Maggie sat there, still and watchful, her expression giving none of her inner uncertainty away. It would be a shot in the dark, a blind choice that she could only hope was the right one. Common sense told her to trust neither group, but common sense also told her that they would never find Van Zandt without trusting someone. And her instincts, instincts that so far hadn't played her false, told her Castanasta was the lesser of two evils.

She turned to look at Mack, wishing there was some way she could communicate with him. His eyes met hers, and he gave her a short, understanding nod. "Better the devil you know," he said in the tone of one agreeing with her, and she had to wonder how he could read her mind so well after so short an acquaintance.

She turned back to Castanasta. "All right."

"It is settled, then. At what time were you to meet with Mendoses?"

"Eleven."

"We will meet at seven-thirty at Parque Central. Too early for the ACSO to be up and about," he said with a sneer. "I will provide a Jeep, guns, food, and maps. Better than what Mendoses could come up with, I promise you. You will be out of Tegucigalpa before they even realize you are gone."

"Sounds delightful," Maggie murmured. There was a sudden knocking at the door, and the speed with which Castanasta went for his gun was impressive enough that Maggie knew she could have stood little chance against him had he decided to move against the two of them.

A voice behind the door called out "room service" in Spanish, and this time Maggie really could smell the chicken.

"Relax, General," she said, sliding off the dresser and moving toward the door. "It's just dinner."

Reluctantly, he reholstered his pistol. "One can never be too careful in this part of the world, senora," he murmured. "I will leave the two of you to your meal. Until tomorrow." He passed the white-jacketed waiter without a second glance.

The two of them watched in silence as the dark-skinned, polite young man set a table for them, all neatness and flourishes and deferential silence. Maggie stood there, her appetite completely vanished, wanting nothing more than to have a chance to talk with Mack, and still the young man lingered.

"Gracias, gracias," she said finally, shooing him away when he was about to open the wine Mack had ordered. She stuffed a wad of pesos in his hand. "*Basta,* gracias."

The young man nodded, smiling his friendly open smile as she pushed him toward the door. She was just about to shove him through when his body suddenly turned stubborn, and he turned that smiling, innocent face on her. "Watch out for Castanasta," he said in perfect, unaccented English. "He is not much better than Mendoses." And then he was gone.

Maggie stared after him, momentarily numb with surprise. She contemplated racing after him, but he was gone before she could gather her wits around her.

She closed the door behind her, shaking her head. "Damn," she said. "I'm beginning to get very confused."

"Beginning?" Mack echoed. "Who the hell was that, anyway?"

"CIA, I presume," she said, pushing away from the door. "Did you order this much?" The table was filled with enough covered dishes to serve half a dozen people.

"I didn't think so. Maybe my Spanish isn't as good as I thought." He leaned forward, tipped the cover of one of the dishes, and smiled. "Now this is a meal I can enjoy."

Resting on a clean white napkin was a large handgun, army issue, neat, efficient, with no frills. Just a straightforward killing machine, Maggie thought as she picked it up. "What else did he bring?"

"Another gun, ammunition," Mack announced, uncovering the dishes one after the other. "Maps, papers, what looks like car keys. And chicken, thank God."

"So now we've got a third option," Maggie said, reaching for the neatly folded paper and opening it. "We can go with the ACSO, the RAO, or the CIA."

"More alphabet soup," Mack said, digging into the chicken. "I hope you don't mind if I start without you? I'm starving."

"Go right ahead," she said absently. "I think we go with the CIA. This is from Bud Willis."

"Who's Bud Willis?"

"Ex-CIA. A friend of Van Zandt's, stationed down here. Doing his bit to help out bloodshed wherever he can find it," she said bitterly. "He's in Chicaste, and says he can get us to Van Zandt."

"You believe him?"

"He'd have no reason to lie. He doesn't give a damn who does what as long as he gets paid. He'll get us to Van Zandt, all right, if I offer him enough money."

"Sounds good," Mack said, his strong white teeth making short work of the roasted chicken. And then suddenly he stopped eating. "You know, I just thought of something," he said, dropping the half-chewed bone back on his plate.

"What?" she inquired absently, holding the map in one hand and her own piece of chicken in the other.

"I must be building up quite a tab with Third World Causes, Ltd. I have a comfortable amount of money, but I don't know how far it's going to go."

Maggie grinned. "I never thought of that. Maybe I should have Beverly in the front office send you a bill before we go any farther. We can just stay put until you pay the first installment. I'd better warn you, I'm pretty expensive. I don't want you fainting when you get the bill."

"I think I'll manage. What if we get back and find I'm broke?" He retrieved his chicken leg.

"Then you'll have to work it off," Maggie said. "I think my mother needs her pool cleaned. That should take care of part of my consulting fees."

"Speaking of consulting—who do we trust, Maggie? I agree

with you, I think we should go with the CIA. That's what Van Zandt is, so it should give us a bit of a head start. Unless you want to reconsider the Bay Islands."

"Later. We've got to cross our fingers that our search will end in Chicaste. Then we can think about lying on a beach somewhere."

"Yes, boss. I hate to tell you, but I'll be thinking about it anyway."

"So will I, Mack," she said. "So will I."

It was a different white-coated waiter who retrieved the empty dishes, one who spoke no English and lacked their previous waiter's innocent smile. Maggie tipped him heavily in her relief.

Mendoses expected them at eleven, Castanasta at seven-thirty. The maps were skillful and well-marked, and they decided to leave in the dead of night. "In which case," Maggie said, "we should get some rest even if we can't sleep. The main part of our journey is on what passes for highways down here, so we'll be able to navigate with a flashlight."

Maggie continued, "We go first to Danli, which seems to be a good-sized city. Then to El Paraíso, and then through the jungle to Chicaste. We're supposed to be hunters, which will account for our guns and our going to out-of-the-way places."

"What are we supposed to be hunting with handguns?"

"Apparently there's lots of game in the area."

"Like what?" he demanded suspiciously. "Nice, harmless stuff like foxes and rabbits, I hope."

"And doves, though they're out of season."

"Doves? Who the hell would shoot doves?"

"It's a major sport down here."

"Okay, so they're out of season. Anything else lurking in the underbrush besides CIA and rebels?"

"They're the most lethal, I expect. We may run into a few wild boar."

"What?" Mack's raw voice managed a semblance of a shriek.

"Not to mention pumas, jaguars, and wild turkeys."

"Speaking of turkeys, Maggie May," he said in a dangerous voice, "you must be crazy if you think I'm going to go camping with pumas."

"Don't worry, Mack, I'll protect you," she said with a laugh. "Besides, Chicaste isn't that far. If we get a good start, we may reach the rebel camp sometime tomorrow afternoon."

"Somehow that prospect doesn't reassure me," he said dourly.

Maggie shrugged. It didn't reassure her either, but they had no choice. If they were going to get out of this mess alive, they would have to find Van Zandt. Staying in Tegucigalpa, caught between the ACSO and the RAO, they were nothing more than sitting ducks.

"How about L.A. in a week? I'll let you live out your fantasies with my mother."

"I've already lived out almost every fantasy I've ever had with you, Maggie May. Compared to you, your mother loses her appeal."

"For God's sake don't tell her that," she said on a note of laughter.

"I wouldn't think of it. You're the only one I want to talk to anyway. Everything set for tonight?"

Maggie looked at the knapsack, now full of clean, dry clothes, two guns, flashlight, the maps, and the papers. "I guess so."

"Then let's go to bed."

She turned to look at him. It was a prosaic enough request, it wasn't the first time she'd done it, so why did her pulse immediately begin to race, why did her stomach leap and her breasts tingle?

"I think that you're having a demoralizing effect on me," she said in a measured tone of voice.

"Well, I hope so. Take off your clothes and come over here, lady. Unless you're into another wrestling match." He started to get up, and she backed away swiftly.

"No, thank you. I'm still sore from the first one."

"I don't think it's the wrestling match that you're sore from. And at least I didn't give you a black eye. Come to bed, Maggie," he said in a softer voice, and there was no way she could put up any more arguments.

Mack's body was smooth and supple beneath her hands and mouth, and he was content to lie there letting her explore him with a curiosity and wonder that was outrageously sensual. When he could take no more he pushed her back onto the mattress and returned the favor, taking her to the point of almost painful delight, so that her hands were clutching fistfuls of sheet, and her toes were digging into the mattress, and her body was flushed and damp and trembling.

When he'd finished with her she was beyond rational thought. She lay beside him, curled up in his arms, as her heart slowed its breakneck speed and her breathing returned to normal. His hands were gentle on her, soothing her, calming her, and his lips teased her ear. He whispered something, and she couldn't hear him. Or couldn't believe him. He wouldn't, couldn't, have told her he loved her.

She made no response, just lay there in the circle of his arms.

An hour later they were stealing away in the dark moonless night. For some reason, Maggie wasn't afraid of the dark.

fifteen

"That reminds me," Mack said. "I take exception to something you told Castanasta." They were driving their brand-new Jeep Cherokee down Highway 4 toward Danli, and the newly paved, blessedly wide road might almost have convinced them they were back in civilization instead of heading into a jaguar- and puma-infested jungle.

"What?" She took another sip from her lukewarm coffee, coffee that Mack had saved from their dinner tray. They'd been driving for hours, night was giving way to sunrise, and Maggie still wasn't awake.

Mack, on the other hand, seemed completely alert and relaxed, slouched down behind the driver's seat of the Cherokee, one arm resting on the open window as his fingers tapped out a song on the steering wheel. "When you told Castanasta you had to see Van Zandt on a small matter. I rate my life just a bit higher than that."

"Don't give me grief, Mack," she said wearily. "Maybe I should have left you with the RAO. After all, Castanasta did say he wanted to help us."

"You certainly are grumpy for someone with little cause," he replied in a bright tone of voice.

"And you certainly are disgustingly cheerful for someone with little cause," she fired back.

"What do you mean, little cause? The road is paved, the sun is rising, no one's trying to shoot at us for the moment, we've got food, warm bottled Coke, guns to keep off ravaging wildlife, and I've been extremely well laid. What more could one ask?"

"Mack!" Her voice held a definite warning.

He laughed. "I knew that would get a rise out of you. Come on, Maggie May, lighten up. We've got a few hours of peace before the next battle—we may as well enjoy it."

"Maybe. I'm just having second thoughts on the wisdom of taking Bud Willis's help."

"Why?"

"Because this brand-new Jeep didn't come from a mercenary's pocket or from the rebels. They're in such rotten financial shape that the Jeep we lost in La Ceiba would look like a luxury vehicle."

"So where do you think it came from?"

"Directly out of the CIA budget. They must want something from us, and I'm not going to be too cheerful until I figure out what it is."

"I'd think it would be fairly obvious."

"To you, maybe." There was a long pause, but he didn't volunteer any suggestions, just kept his eyes on the broad highway in front of them. "Okay, I give up. What's fairly obvious? What does the CIA want from us?"

"Silence. They don't want us messing around in Houston, in Honduras, in Chicaste, in Moab, Utah, for that matter. They want us out of the way."

"You think they're going to kill us?"

"Maybe. Somehow I doubt it. My opinion of the CIA isn't very high, but I think they draw the line at murdering U.S. citizens in cold blood. However, I wouldn't put it past them to look the other way if someone else gets ambitious enough to do the job."

"Lovely thought," she said. "Bud Willis?"

"You know him, I don't. Is he capable of it?"

"Sure. Bud Willis is capable of anything. But the financial thing still holds true—he knows I can better any bounty placed on our heads." She sighed. "It's a scary thought, to think that our own government would be out to kill us."

"No one said they were. I think they just don't want any interference. Isn't that why we're looking for Van Zandt? To find out what they want from us, and to get the word to whoever that I'm not about to make waves. I just want to be left in peace."

"That's sounding more and more tempting," Maggie said. "It's also sounding more and more unlikely."

"Thanks a lot," Mack muttered. "Now you're getting me depressed."

"Sorry." She drained the rest of her coffee. "But it doesn't help to hide your head in the sand."

"Tell you what, Maggie May. Why don't you go back to sleep and let me see if I can recapture my good mood," he said dourly.

"Suit yourself. Wake me if you see any wild boars."

"No comment."

They had breakfast in Danli, then headed away from Mack's beloved highway onto rougher turf. Maggie was content to let him continue driving. Her nap had helped to soothe her temper, and even the enervating heat of the jungle didn't bother her. She had a curious sense of destiny. If the CIA was waiting for them with a firing squad, if the ACSO or the RAO had set them up, there was nothing they could do but deal with it when it happened. In the meantime they were doing the only possible thing they could in their search for Van Zandt. And with any luck, that search would come to an end in a few hours.

The road deteriorated rapidly. With Mack driving and Maggie as navigator, they made it through a series of small towns, down one mountain and up another, through flash rainstorms, dry, baking heat, and everything in between, all in the period of several hours. It was almost dark when they drove into the smallest, dirtiest-looking town so far, and Mack pulled the Jeep up in the deserted town square, turned it off, and leaned back, stretching with the first sign of weariness he'd shown that day.

"Where the hell are we, Maggie?" he demanded, rubbing his forehead.

"Somewhere between Danli and Chicaste."

"I already knew that, darlin'," he said. "Do you have the faintest idea how far we are from the rebel camp?"

"We have to be close. But how close I can't really tell. Going up and down these damned mountains adds miles to the trip. Chicaste might be the next town down the road or it may have been three towns back."

"Don't say that."

"I'm sure we haven't passed it yet. It can't be more than a few more miles down the road."

"You want to see if we can find something to eat? We've finished everything in the backseat. We don't really know what our welcome will be like when we find Willis and Van Zandt. They may kill the fatted calf or they may—"

"Don't even say it." She climbed out of the Jeep, stretching wearily, her long arms reaching toward the darkening sky. "I wonder where everybody is?"

"Probably home eating their dinner and watching *Family Feud* reruns," Mack said. "Which is where we should be."

"Why don't you stay with the car while I go see if there's someplace we can buy dinner?"

"I've got a better idea. Why don't you stay with the car?" Mack countered.

"How about we both go?" Maggie capitulated with a sigh.

"What if someone decides to steal the Jeep? I didn't mind seeing the other one go, but I've gotten sort of fond of this one."

"I don't really give a damn if Scotty beams it up to the Enterprise," she said. "Even a brand-new Jeep doesn't have the world's greatest springs, and I'm not really looking forward to climbing back in it tonight."

"Maybe you won't have to, Maggie." It was a new voice—fresh, American—with the faint trace of a Midwestern accent.

"Willis," Maggie said. "Where the hell did you spring from?"

"This is my town, Maggie. No one comes within ten miles of

it without my knowing it," the man said. He was hidden in the shadows of the alleyway just off the main plaza, and all Maggie could see were his combat boots and the barrel of his gun. But it was Willis, all right. She'd know that cool, passionless voice anywhere.

"This is Chicaste?"

"This is Chicaste. Now, you wanna tell me what the fuck you've been doing messing around all over Tegucigalpa? I got word from my own man down there, I got word from Castanasta, and I got word from the ACSO. You're one foolhardy lady, you know that? I would have thought you'd learned your lesson by now. Last time I saw you, you weren't in any mood to go putting that nose of yours where it doesn't belong."

"I still don't put it where it doesn't belong, Willis," she said in a cool voice. "I have business down here."

"With me?"

"With Van Zandt. You want to tell me where he is?"

"Maybe. Maybe not. Who's your friend?" The gun barrel gestured at Mack's silent form.

"None of your damned business, Willis."

"Sure it is, Maggie. If you want to see Van Zandt, you're going to have to play the game my way. I told you, this town is mine. You come anywhere near it and I own your ass."

"Don't threaten me, Willis."

"Don't fuck with me, Maggie." He stepped into the light. He was a wiry man, with a Marine hair cut, skeletal cheekbones, and the emptiest eyes Maggie had ever seen. It had been four years since their paths had crossed, and she'd almost forgotten how deathlike he looked. He grinned at her, that travesty of good fellowship that fooled no one. "Is that Pulaski?"

"If you knew, why did you have to ask?"

"Just wanted to see whether you'd lie to me."

"I have no intention of lying to you, Willis," she said calmly. "I need your help, and I know you aren't going to give it to me unless I'm straight with you."

"Maybe I'm not going to give it to you anyway."

"Maybe. But I don't think you would have brought me down here if you weren't going to help me."

"You got it wrong, lady. I didn't bring you down here."

Mack spoke for the first time, his raw voice soft and oddly menacing in the warm night air. "Then who did?"

Willis cackled. "Mancini did a good job on your throat, didn't he, friend? You should have learned your lesson back then."

"I guess I'm a slow learner," Mack said with deceptive gentleness. "You didn't answer my question, friend."

Willis smiled his death's-head grin. "Van Zandt brought you guys to the elegant resort of Chicaste."

"Why?" Maggie broke in.

"Well, now, Van Zandt didn't confide in me. You know Van Zandt, Maggie. He tells you just what he wants you to know, and then expects you to kiss his ass for it. All's I know is that he wanted you two out of Tegucigalpa and down here. So I sent word to my man there, he passed the stuff along, and here you are."

"And where's Van Zandt?" Mack asked.

"Beats the hell out of me," Willis said cheerfully. "He's been the mystery man the last few months. Maybe he'll show up tonight, maybe he won't. He's gonna have to find us soon, 'cause we're out of here in the next twenty-four hours."

"Where are you going?" Maggie asked.

"None of your damned business. I know where your sympathies would lie, Ms. Bleeding Heart Liberal," he sneered. "And they don't lie the same place as my paycheck."

"You're going over the border into Nicaragua," she guessed.

"Hey, that's the name of the game, lady," Willis said. "We train here, and then we go in and zap the shit out of them. Makes no nevermind to me—a greaser is a greaser, I always say."

"Christ," Mack muttered under his breath.

"Shit, another bleeding heart," Willis said. "Well, if you two can swallow your principles, I've got my woman cooking a meal for us. I figured you'd get here by dinner, and Consuela's a damned good cook. Good in bed too."

"How fortunate for you," Maggie said acidly.

Willis grinned. "What can I say? I'm a man who likes the finer things in life." He headed up the street, not even bothering to see if they were following. "Better lock your car," he called back over his shoulder. "These greasers'll pick it clean before you can pick your nose."

"Helluva charming guy, Maggie," Mack observed. "Where did you two happen to meet?"

"Shut up, Mack," she muttered under her breath, starting after their host. "I never said I liked the bastard. But you've got to admit, we're closer to Van Zandt than we've ever been."

"Maybe," he said. "Maybe not. We only have his word for it that Van Zandt's going to show up, and I don't think his word is worth pigshit. You going to tell me how you happen to know a piece of garbage like Willis?"

She considered it for a moment. Willis was way ahead of them, but she knew him well enough to know that he could hear every word. His senses were fine-tuned after years in jungles around the world, ducking from snipers and doing some sniping of his own. But she had nothing to lose by telling him the truth. "I used to work for the CIA," she admitted.

"You what?"

She really had horrified him this time, she thought with grim amusement. "I said I used to work for the CIA, back when Willis still ostensibly worked for our government. Don't worry, I didn't get past the first training mission. I didn't have the right temperament for it. My killer instincts weren't finely honed enough for them."

"Thank God for that." There was a long pause. "You want to talk about it?"

"What's to talk about? A change in careers?"

"There's more to it than that, Maggie May. I keep telling you I know you very well, and you never believe me. You can't hide anything from me."

"I'm not hiding anything," she said, and realized how defensive she sounded.

"Okay, Maggie. I get the message."

Willis had disappeared into one of the larger adobe buildings at the head of the small square, and they followed him into the warmth and light of a sparsely furnished house.

Who knew whether or not Willis's Consuela was good in bed, but there was no question that she was a great cook. All through the spicy meal of beans and sausage, tortillas, chicken and raisins in bitter chocolate, Maggie kept looking toward the door, listening for telltale noise upstairs, waiting, waiting. She could feel Mack's matching tension as if it were her own, and even the delicious food began to pall as they sat there in the barren little room watching Consuela move like a timid rabbit around the kitchen, her wary eyes always on Willis.

Finally Willis shoved his empty plate away, belched loudly, and announced, "Fucking Mex food. I can't wait for . . ." He let the sentence trail off.

"For what, Willis? What nasty little war are you going to next?" Maggie questioned sweetly.

Willis laughed. "Almost caught me that time, Maggie. You're good, kid. I gotta admit it. It's a crying shame you didn't have the balls to make it in the Company. You could have been one of the best."

"Thanks," she said. "But I found better things to do."

"I'll bet you did. How long you been shacking up with Mr. Laryngitis over there?"

Mack leaned back, all deceptive ease, and smiled at Willis. "What makes you think we're shacking up?"

"You forget, friend, that I've known her longer than you. I've seen that look on her face before. You finally get over Randall, Maggie?"

She could feel her face flush, damn it. "Yes, Willis, I finally got over Randall."

"We had bets going," Willis said affably, leaning back in an unconscious imitation of Mack. "How long did it take you? You were pretty far gone."

Mack hadn't even turned to look at her. "I think we're a little more interested in Van Zandt's whereabouts than Maggie's ancient history, friend." He gave the last the same mocking emphasis.

"Tomorrow morning."

"He'll be here tomorrow morning?" Maggie demanded, hope rising.

"I'll tell you where he is tomorrow morning," Willis corrected her. "Shit, Maggie, don't be so goddamn antsy. If lover boy over there isn't enough for you, you can always join me and Consuela. I've got a pair of handcuffs that would be just your size—"

"Go to hell, Willis," Maggie said.

He shrugged, turning to Mack. "What can I say? The woman doesn't like me, God knows why. I try to be charming." He turned and said something in rapid-fire Spanish to the cowering Consuela, and then turned back with a grin. "You'll be staying in the room behind the kitchen. It's not the Waldorf, but then nothing in this fucking country is. Why the hell can't they have revolutions in civilized places, like France?"

"I wasn't aware they were having a revolution in Honduras," said Maggie.

"Hell, you know what I mean. Besides, with these crazy countries, it'll probably be the next one to go. Remind me not to sign up."

"I trust, hope, and pray that I won't ever have to be within a hundred miles of you again," Maggie said fervently, no longer hiding her disgust.

"Ah, Maggie, I love it when you're angry," Willis said, reaching out to pinch her breast.

His hand never connected. One moment he was leaning over her, grinning, the next he was flat on his back, spread-eagled, with a very large, very angry Mack pinning him to the rough stone floor. He held a knife to his throat, one he'd managed to pull off of Willis himself, and the mercenary lay there, motionless, numb with shock and fury.

"Listen, friend," Mack said in his husky growl, "it's time you learned a few things. One, you keep your goddamn hands off my woman. Two, you make the supreme effort and behave like a polite human being the rest of the time we're here, and three, you tell me, right now, where the hell Van Zandt is."

Maggie didn't move, didn't say a word. Willis was one of the fastest, best in the business. There were very few people who could floor him, and she was still not quite comprehending that Mack had done just that.

Apparently Willis was suffering the same shock. "What the hell . . . ?"

Mack pressed the knife a little harder against his throat, and a tiny spot of bright red blood stained the knife. "Right now, friend," he growled.

"Go fuck yourself," Willis said.

"Listen, asshole, I'll cut off your ears, your nose, and your balls if you don't tell me, and tell me fast," Mack told him in a genial tone of voice, and Maggie started to choke. "I haven't had a very pleasant time these last few weeks, and I'm not about to put up with it any longer than I have to. And, quite simply, I don't have to wait till tomorrow morning. You're going to tell me now, Willis. Aren't you?" His voice was gentle—dangerously so.

Willis hadn't gotten to the top of his ill-chosen profession without learning how to read his enemy. "Hey, all right, man," he said, grinning. "So you're a little impatient. All you had to do was ask nice."

Mack matched his smile. "I'm asking nice, Willis. Where's Van Zandt?"

Willis grinned up at him. "Switzerland."

sixteen

"Switzerland?" Maggie echoed in stunned disbelief. "What in God's name is he doing in Switzerland?"

"Waiting for you."

"What?"

"If you could get your friend off me," Willis grunted, "I might tell you."

"I'll get off you," Mack said, "but there's no 'might' about it. You'll tell us."

"Okay, okay," Willis muttered. Mack pulled away with a lithe, fast motion that kept him deftly out of reach. He ended up sitting back on the floor, a gun trained directly on Willis's groin as the mercenary's hand was halfway to his own gun.

"I wouldn't try it if I were you," Mack said affably. "I told you, I'm getting impatient, and I certainly wouldn't mind shooting you. So move your hand away from that gun and tell us what the hell is going on."

"Maybe he should toss the gun in the middle of the room," Maggie suggested.

"No, I don't think there's any need for that," Mack drawled. "Willis may be pissed as hell at me, but I don't think he really wants to kill us. That's right, isn't it, friend?"

Willis was still looking ripe for murder, but he gave himself a little shake and came up with that snarling grin of his. "No, I'm not going to kill you. I won't say the thought hasn't crossed my mind, but there's no money in it. And there's a fuck of a lot of money in keeping you alive."

"Explain," said Maggie.

Willis shrugged. "You know Van Zandt as well as I do, Maggie. He said if you made it this far you were to meet him in Zurich on the twenty-third."

"He's out of his mind," said Maggie.

"Maybe. You'll have a helluva time getting from the mountains of Honduras to the mountains of Switzerland, I know that much. I don't think Van Zandt took that into account. He just said meet him there, and he'll have the answers."

"Forget it," Mack said. "We've been on enough of a wild-goose chase as it is. We're not going halfway around the world chasing after someone who may or may not be able to help us."

"Oh, Van Zandt will be able to help you," Willis said. "Make no mistake about that. He's got the Mafia in his back pocket, he can get the Feds off your back, and these greasers'll believe anything he tells 'em. One word from him and you'll be a free man."

"Then why hasn't he given that one word?" Maggie cried. "Peter Wallace would still be alive if Van Zandt weren't so damned mysterious. If he'd only—"

"I don't think Wallace would still be alive, Maggie," Mack said suddenly.

"What do you mean?"

"Ask Willis. He knows what I'm talking about, don't you, friend?"

Willis grinned. "Not as sharp as usual, Maggie. Van Zandt killed Wallace."

"What?" she shrieked.

"I thought he might have," Mack said. "But since you didn't mention the possibility I decided to keep it to myself. Wallace said Van Zandt's name as he was dying. At first I thought he was mixing us up. You thought he was sending us to find him. Later it came to me that Wallace was naming his murderer."

"For God's sake, why?" she demanded, completely confused.

Willis shrugged. "Van Zandt's like me—he likes to tie up loose ends. He's into something more than you think, and it's my guess that Wallace found out about it. So Van Zandt had to take him out."

Maggie shivered in the hot night air. "And what makes you think he won't do the same to us once we get to Switzerland?"

"He might," Willis allowed. "But he could have paid me to do it easily enough and saved a lot of trouble. Hell, I might have done it on the cuff, as a gesture of goodwill. He knows I owe him one. But he told me I was to do what I could to keep you alive. So he must have a reason, a use for you."

"We could go to the government. . . ."

"They won't believe you, Maggie. Van Zandt's got them so confused they'll believe anything he tells them. He's got everybody running around in circles, you included, and your only chance is to play the game and hope you can win."

"No more games," Mack said in a flat voice. "We're not going to Switzerland, we're not going to meet with Van Zandt. It's over."

"The hell it is," Maggie said.

Willis appeared greatly amused. "Sounds like you two are going to have a restful night of it. I'm betting on you, Maggie." He rose, wiped away the trickle of blood from his neck, and gestured to the cowering Consuela, who'd sat in the kitchen during the last hour staring down at her lap. "We're out of here tomorrow morning. If I were you, I'd make my plans before then."

"If we were going to get to Switzerland, Willis, how would we go?" Maggie inquired.

"La Ceiba's the only international airport. You could get a shorter flight from Danli, then fly back to a major city in the U.S. That is if your friend dares show his face. Van Zandt's got a lot of people stirred up, looking for you, and I don't know if their orders are to let you be or shut you up." He turned and spoke to Consuela, and she jumped up nervously, wringing her long, beautiful hands. *"Buenas noches,"* he said. "I may see you tomorrow, I may not. If I don't, give Van Zandt a kick in the ass for me."

"I'll be sure to."

"You won't get the chance," Mack said when Willis and Consuela disappeared up the narrow stairs to the upper floor. "We're not going to Switzerland."

"What are our alternatives? Go back to the U.S. and wait for someone to gun you down?"

"What about the Bay Islands?"

"I'm not about to spend the rest of my life hiding out, and neither are you. And I'm not about to let that bastard Van Zandt get away with it. I never trusted him, I should have followed my instincts. But Peter was so damned sure, and look where it got him."

"I don't want you to wind up in the same place, Maggie."

"I won't. I'm smart and cynical and tough, and I'm not about to turn my back on him. You can wait it out on the islands and I'll come back and get you when it's over. But I've got to see this through to the end."

He sat there, staring at her, frustration and something else warring in his hazel eyes. He sighed in capitulation. "I guess we go to Switzerland."

"No, Mack. I'd do better alone."

"Stuff it, Superwoman. We go together or not at all," he demanded.

"Don't call me that," she said automatically. "Which reminds me. Why the hell did you jump Willis? Didn't you realize how dangerous he is?"

Mack just looked at her. "I really can take care of myself, Maggie," he said. It was a gentle reproof, but Maggie still didn't like it. "Besides, I had the sudden, overwhelming need to kick some ass."

"Great. Pick someone a little more innocuous next time, will you? Or at least do it when I'm not around."

Mack smiled. "I'm afraid your presence had a lot to do with it. My long-dormant machismo reasserting itself, I guess. Sorry about that, boss. It won't happen again."

"Christ, I let you drive," she said, flustered.

"So you did. In return I'll let you be on top tonight."

"Mack." Her voice carried a very definite warning.

"Maggie," he mimicked her, rising with one fluid gesture and reaching out a hand to pull her up. "Let's go check out our sleeping quarters."

She looked up at his hand. She didn't need his help, she could stand on her own, and she opened her mouth to tell him just that. He knew what she was thinking, she could tell by the half-amused look on his face. But he still held out his hand, waiting.

"You think you've got me psyched out, don't you?" she muttered.

"Do I?" Mack asked.

She sat there for another long, stubborn moment. And then she reached up and placed her hand in his. "You do, damn you," she said as he pulled her up and into his arms.

It was a relief to be there, to feel the strong, steady thud of his heartbeat against her breasts, to revel in the warmth of his arms around her. She wanted to lean her head against his shoulder and close her eyes to the latest impossible development, and it took all her pride and energy to give a gentle push.

He released her readily enough, and she knew with a sudden flash of understanding that he always would. He'd never tie her down, force her to do things his way, keep her a prisoner when she needed to be free. The only thing that would keep her chained to him would be her own needs. It was a frightening thought.

"You're right, we ought to check out where we're sleeping, and make sure Willis didn't stuff the mattress with tarantulas," she said, her voice just slightly shaken.

The back room contained a narrow, stained mattress on the stone floor, a threadbare blanket, and a window that wouldn't close, letting in all sorts of bugs. There was no moon that night, and the kerosene lamp Willis had left them made little dent in the darkness. Maggie controlled the shiver that crept across her backbone.

Mack put out a gentle hand, brushing her tangled hair away

from her flushed face. "I think this is a night for sleeping with our clothes on. What do you think?"

She went back into his arms of her own accord this time, holding him tight, resting her face against his muscled shoulder. "I think you're right. At least they won't have mosquitoes in Switzerland."

"Small comfort," he said, sinking down on the hard mattress with his arms still around her. "The beds will be better too."

"Maybe," she said sleepily, burrowing against him. "Mack?"

"Yup?"

"Turn out the light."

His arms tightened for a moment. And then he plunged the room into darkness.

She lay there in the circle of his arms, willing herself to relax in the blackness. Tonight she didn't have the advantage of soporific sex, tonight she had only a hard mattress and a scratchy blanket. And Mack. She sighed, letting the tension drain out of her. It was enough.

She was instantly awake. The blackness was like a thick velvet curtain around them, smothering, and she fought back the panic that threatened to strangle her. And then she heard it again, the noise that had penetrated her sleep and pulled her out of it with wrenching force.

She sat up, yanking at Mack's still-sleeping figure. "Wake up, Mack," she whispered in his ear. "We've got to get out of here."

"What? Why?" he mumbled sleepily. "What's happening?"

"Shhh." She shoved her hand across his mouth. "Something's going down, and we'd better get the hell out of here."

"What?" he said again, finally alert.

"I don't know. And I don't want to wait around long enough to find out. We're in the midst of a war here, and I don't feel like being a civilian casualty." She was sliding her running shoes on, and Mack quickly followed suit.

"Shouldn't we warn Willis?"

"Willis can take care of himself. Come on. I think we'd better go out the window. They may be watching the front door."

They were watching the windows too. No sooner had Maggie followed Mack out the window to land on the packed dirt than she found herself facing a gun barrel. And above it the dark, angry eyes of a man in uniform. From what side she couldn't even begin to guess.

Mack had already raised his arms, and Maggie quickly followed suit. It was a very nasty-looking gun. The sounds in the village square were louder now, and there was no doubt that a great many troops were amassed in Chicaste. Their captor, however, was alone.

"Listen, you don't have to hold that gun on us," Maggie said earnestly in her idiomatic Spanish. "We're friends of Willis's. Of the rebels," she said, lying.

The man grinned, showing very white teeth. "Unfortunate for you, senorita. Because we're enemies of Senor Willis, and the rebels. I'm Captain Esteban of the Liberation Army, and we're here to clean out this nest of vipers. And their American advisers."

Damn, Maggie thought. Blew it again. She gave Captain Esteban a brilliant smile. "Do I look like an adviser? We're tourists."

"You do not look like an adviser, senorita," the captain agreed. "Your man, however, is another matter. He is like a caged lion, and a very dangerous hombre, I suspect."

Mack said nothing, and Maggie spared him a fleeting glance. Mack did look grim, and dangerous, and she was no longer surprised he'd managed to flatten Willis.

"But, Captain," she said sweetly, edging closer and ignoring the gun still pointed at the two of them, "I promise you that I would never—"

She didn't have to finish the sentence. He wasn't as fast as Mack, and her foot connected with his groin before he even saw her move. Seconds later he was on the ground, moaning. And then he was silenced by Mack's very efficient right cross to the jaw.

"Let's get the hell out of here," Mack said as he grabbed the captain's gun.

"My sentiments exactly," Maggie said breathlessly. "Are we going to try for our Jeep?"

"I don't know how else we'll get back to Danli. I'm game if you are."

"Let's do it."

Together they crept into the surrounding underbrush. Any noise they made was covered by the sound of gunfire, the rapid staccato of machine guns, and the steady crak-crak of semiautomatics. Maggie touched the handgun in her belt for luck, and her hand was cold and sweaty. The adrenaline was pumping through her system, her heart was racing, and she was terrified. She looked at Mack in the midnight darkness, wondering if he felt the same.

They circled the village, managing to steer clear of the rampaging groups of soldiers. In the dark there was no way to tell who were the good guys and who were the bad. As a matter of fact, Maggie was no longer so certain if the light would have made any difference. She was heartily sick of revolutionaries and counterrevolutionaries, and the fabled spotless conformity of Switzerland began to appeal to her greatly.

The Jeep was still there, in a more deserted part of the square. Maggie could see what looked ominously like a firing squad up ahead, and a cold sickness filled her. Consuela was one of the people lined up against the wall, still wringing her long hands. There was no sign of Willis.

Maggie started forward, but Mack's arm shot out and dragged her back. "Get in the Jeep, Maggie."

"But Consuela . . ."

"We can't help her. Come on, Maggie, we don't have much time." His voice was low, urgent. "Get in the car, or I'll knock you over the head and cram you in there."

"The hell you will. I'm not going to let them kill—" She

didn't get a chance to finish the sentence. Mack's devastating fist shot out, and she had only enough time to register a faint surprise. Then everything went mercifully blank, just as she heard the volley of gunfire in the distance.

It started with a slow, throbbing pain in her head. Not just the top of her head but the whole damned thing, starting with her jaw, radiating up through her cheekbones, throbbing through her ears, stabbing her eyes. Even her hair hurt. She lay in a tumble, trying not to move, all her energy concentrated on the hope that if she could just hold still it wouldn't hurt so much.

It was a vain hope. It took her a few moments to realize she was being jounced along in the darkness at a rapid pace, another minute to recognize the backseat of the Jeep Cherokee. Even from her semicomatose state she could see the lightening sky through the windows. She must have been unconscious for a long time for it to be dawn already.

Then other things began to intrude—gunfire, screams, and the unmistakable smell of fire. And Maggie realized it wasn't dawn lighting the sky behind them. It was the burning village of Chicaste.

The Jeep bounced over something, careened to the left, and then pulled straight ahead. She didn't dare move her head or even try to lift it, when the slightest effort might make it fall off her neck and roll on the floor. She lay there, panting slightly as she tried to control the pain, and then she remembered.

It was Mack driving the Jeep at such a murderous pace through the jungle. It was Mack who'd slugged her in the jaw, knocking her unconscious and possibly loosening every tooth in her head. It was Mack who'd stopped her from trying to save poor Consuela. The memory of that volley of bullets came back to haunt her, and she could feel her fists clench.

The bastard, she thought, not moving as the Jeep racketed along. The heartless, despicable bastard. How dare he interfere, how dare he hit her, how dare he take over, ignoring her, forcing his will on her, treating her like an idiot?

The answer was simple and unavoidable. Because she had been an idiot. There was no way she could have helped Consuela—she could only have brought the further wrath of the Liberation Army down on their heads. But she'd been too furious to realize it, and Mack's cooler head had prevailed, stopping her from killing both of them. She owed him her life.

It wasn't an easy thing to live with. He'd helped her more than once, but it had never been as clear as it was now. She had no choice but to face the fact that her own stupidity had almost screwed them completely. And she'd needed to be rescued from herself.

Damn it, damn it, damn it. If only they could go back a few hours, maybe . . . But no, she knew she'd do the same thing again. She couldn't calmly climb in the Jeep as they shot an innocent victim like Consuela. She'd always have to fight, even if it killed her. But she had to wonder how Mack could live with the memory of Consuela's lost eyes as she faced her executioners.

"Am I about to have a gun placed to the back of my head?" His rough voice broke through her absorption. "If so, you'd better give me some warning."

Instinctively, she felt for the gun. It was still tucked in the waist of her jeans. "Why should I put the gun to the back of your head?" God, it hurt to talk! Her jaw felt as if it was made of cement, and even her eyelashes ached.

"Because I forcibly overruled you. There wasn't time for a democratic discussion of the issue."

Slowly, gritting her teeth, she pulled herself into a sitting position. There was no way it wasn't going to hurt, and the only thing she could do was ignore the pain. She took a deep, shaky breath. "So might makes right?"

"In this case."

"Did they kill her?" Her voice was flat, emotionless.

"Would you believe me if I told you I didn't know?"

She considered it. "You don't lie. At least, you haven't lied to me. I heard the gunfire before you slugged me. Are you telling me you didn't see whether she fell?"

"They weren't shooting at the people lined up in the square. They were shooting at your friend Willis," he said grimly. "He must have thought he could sneak past them when they were busy with their prisoners. He was mistaken."

"Did they kill him?" She was no more than distantly interested.

"I expect so. He fell. I didn't stop to watch. I just drove the hell out of there before they could stop us." He quickly glanced back at her. "Do you mind?"

"About Willis? No. He was bound to come to a bad end sooner or later."

"What about me?" Mack persisted, and she could hear the diffidence, the peculiar uncertainty in his voice.

"What about you?" she countered.

"Are you planning to use that gun on me for interfering?"

"Do I have to say it?"

"Yes."

"All right," she said wearily. "You were right, I was wrong. You did what you had to do, and I'm grateful. I'd like to break your neck, but I'm grateful. Will that do?"

"It's a start."

"What the hell do you want from me? Do you want me to grovel at your feet?"

"No. I'd like it not to be so hard for you to be wrong once in a while. That's all. Nobody's perfect, Maggie May. Not even Superwoman." His voice was surprisingly gentle, and she felt her anger slip away.

She wanted to reach out and touch him. She wanted to reach

over and turn off the car and climb into his arms and hide there. She wanted to cry against the warmth of his chest. No man had seen her cry in twelve years, and she'd promised herself no man ever would again. But now she wanted to cry to Mack.

But the flames still lit the sky behind them, and the sound of gunfire carried through the dense underbrush, and they couldn't afford to wait. "I'll try and remember that," she said, deliberately making her voice light and wry. "You got any idea where we're headed?"

"Back to Danli. We'll take a commuter plane out to La Ceiba, and then see what sort of connections we can make for Zurich. Unless you've changed your mind?"

"I haven't changed my mind. Van Zandt's been stringing us along, and the only way we're going to put a stop to it is to find him. I told you, you can stay—"

"Don't bother telling me again, Maggie. Whither thou goest . . ." he said. "We've got a long night ahead of us. You want to tell me about him?"

"Who? Van Zandt?" She was stalling.

"You know damned well who. Raymond, Ralph, whatever his name was."

"Randall," she said, facing the inevitable. "You want to tell me about your love life, Mack? If it's going to be such a long night, I'm sure you've got a hell of a lot more to tell."

"Somehow I get the impression it wouldn't be half as interesting as you and Randall."

"How about we save it for some other long night?" Maggie suggested a little desperately.

"That bad, is it? You can't even talk about it. I guess Willis was right when he said they didn't think you'd get over it. Apparently you haven't. Who are 'they,' by the way?"

"Can't you take no for an answer?"

"Not tonight. I've been pushed to the edge, Maggie, and I need some distraction. Tell me about Randall. And 'they.'"

Maggie sat as still as she could in the bouncing backseat. And then with a sigh she capitulated, climbing over into the front seat and almost kicking Mack in the face. " 'They,' I imagine, were Willis and the other people I worked with at the CIA. And Randall, most likely."

"Randall was CIA too?"

"No. Randall was a private citizen with a low threshold for boredom. He was head of a huge import/export conglomerate, and he was more than happy to help out the government on any little matter, as long as it was dangerous."

"How'd you meet him?"

"Randall was good at getting people out of tight situations. An agent was trapped in Eastern Europe, and Randall went to help him. I was assigned to the case." Her words were clipped and emotionless.

"And what happened?"

"I got involved with Randall. Not realizing that he wasn't involved with me. When the situation exploded Randall disappeared, I quit the company, and we all lived happily ever after." She turned to stare at Mack's averted profile. "It was no big deal. Everyone gets a broken heart somewhere along the way— Randall was mine. It happened a long time ago, and I got over it."

"Did you?"

"Yes." Her answer was flat, unequivocal, and completely certain.

"When?"

"You can't let anything alone, can you?" she shot back. "Don't you believe me?"

"Yes, I believe you. I just want to know how long it took."

"Why? You want to figure out how long it'll take me to get over you?" It was bluntly, boldly stated, and she didn't give a damn. There in the car, with the darkness and the fire and blood all around them, it no longer seemed worth the effort of hiding her feelings.

"Maggie," he said, "you aren't ever going to get over me. And that's a promise. Now answer my question. When did you get over Randall?"

"Last week, damn it."

He must have been expecting it. He laughed, and the sound was light and soothing and sexy in the still air, bringing life back into a night of death and despair. "When?"

"When you stepped out of the shadows in Moab, Utah. Now shut up and let me ache in peace," she snapped. "You fractured my jaw, I probably have a concussion, and my whole body hurts from this damned Jeep. Leave me alone, for God's sake."

"Yes, ma'am," he said cheerfully. She held on to both sides of her seat, trying to keep from bouncing, and watched the jungle road ahead. "Just one more thing," he added.

"What?"

"I'm not going to get over you either. Okay?"

She considered it for a moment, then leaned over to place a sweet kiss on his cheek. "Okay," she said softly.

They reached a small airfield just outside of Danli as dawn broke, the sky gold and gray and greeny orange, which reminded her of the fire they'd left behind.

"I hope you're going to do better than Lonesome Fred this time," she said.

Mack smiled at her, and in the early daylight she could see the shadows of exhaustion and something else darken his face. But his eyes were still warm and gentle on her, promising something she didn't dare ask for.

"Don't be so smug, Maggie May. It's your turn to get the pilot."

Pride and determination reared their twin heads, and she found herself stiffening her back and smiling at him. "You're a hard taskmaster," she said, climbing out of the Jeep and landing on the packed earth with a thud.

"No, I'm not, Maggie. Your only taskmaster is yourself." He leaned back in the driver's seat and propped his arms behind his head, closing his eyes. "Wake me when it's time."

She stared at him for a long moment. Before she even turned away she heard the gentle sound of a snore in the early morning air, and when she headed across the airstrip she found she was smiling.

It took her longer than it would have taken Mack. First she had to find the tin shack that served as an office for the small airfield, then she had to wait around till someone showed up. She used the time to good advantage, checking out the two twin-engine planes left baking in the early morning sunlight. She liked what she saw. They were in excellent condition, old but beautifully maintained. Either one of them could get them to La Ceiba, without any detours via the Atlantic Ocean.

Maggie squatted down in the dust, leaning against the tin building and squinting into the sunlight. For some unaccountable reason, she felt good. Damned good. Her whole head ached, and she wouldn't be surprised if she had a hell of a bruise. She would have killed for a cup of coffee and a candy bar. And she had only the faintest idea where she was heading. So why wasn't she sitting there crying?

Possibly because the sun was shining, the sky was a deep, cerulean blue, and she and Mack were alive and well, lucky to have escaped the slaughter in Chicaste. Once they found Van Zandt they'd find out what the hell was going on. For now she was content to sit in the lazy sunshine waiting for a pilot.

She had to admit that Mack had something to do with her odd peace of mind. He'd certainly done his share to contribute to her sense of physical well-being. She'd been celibate for six months, ever since her relationship with Peter had dissolved, and she'd forgotten just how good sex was. There was even the remote possibility that she'd never known.

Luis Camerera appeared at the tin building at just past nine, according to Maggie's battered Rolex. He was clean, sober, young, and intelligent, and had spent three years in the tiny Honduran Air Force. Maggie gave him twice what he asked for the flight to La Ceiba and went to fetch Mack.

It took her a while to find the Jeep. He'd moved it, for heaven only knew what reason, she thought as she spied it in some tangled underbrush. Maybe to get it out of the sun, but he could have told her. . . .

There was no one in the driver's seat. Suddenly she was very wary. He could have stretched out in the backseat or he could be stretched out across the two front seats, but somehow she doubted it. Her instincts were screaming at her, and she crossed the last few yards to the Jeep at a dead run.

It was empty. No sign of Mack, no sign of the knapsack that held all their worldly goods. The only thing in the brand-new Jeep Cherokee was blood, all over the front seat.

Maggie moaned and sank to her knees beside the Jeep, clinging with numb hands to the door handle. Whoever had gotten Mack probably hadn't gone far. Whoever it was would most likely return and finish her too. But she didn't care. She'd failed him, and now she was more alone than she'd ever been in her entire life.

"What the hell are you doing, Maggie May?" Mack's voice was heavy with irritation and exhaustion. "That's very artistic, kneeling there, but not too useful. You want to help me cover the body?"

She didn't move for a long moment, as relief washed over her with such force that she shook. She grinned down at the dust beneath her, releasing her grip on the door handle, but when she rose and turned back to Mack her expression was bland.

"Whose body?" she inquired.

Mack wasn't fooled. He jerked his head toward the underbrush. "God knows. The rebels, the Liberation Army, maybe even CIA. I didn't have any say in the matter—when I opened my eyes his knife was heading for my throat."

"Is he dead?"

"Bodies usually are," he replied. "Did you find us a pilot?"

"I found us a pilot. Clean-cut, sober, intelligent. Let's just hope he didn't send a friend out to investigate the Jeep."

"I guess we have no choice but to find out, do we?" Mack said, hoisting the knapsack over his shoulder. "Come on, Maggie May. Let's go."

"Don't we need to cover . . . ?"

"I just said that to get your attention. He's taken care of, kid. You look like you could use a little taking care of yourself. I didn't know you were so squeamish about death."

Only when I thought it was yours, she thought. "It's not something one should get used to."

"You're right. It's also not something one should dwell on when there's no choice in the matter," he said, and she had to agree. "Come on, sweetheart. Let's get the hell out of here."

"Sweetheart?" she echoed, stunned. The endearment came from out of the blue, suggesting all sorts of unexpected things like commitment and happy-ever-after.

Mack managed a white, shaken grin. "Sorry about that. It won't happen again."

"Good," she said, lying. "See that it doesn't." And they headed toward the plane.

eighteen

Luis lived up to Maggie's initial impression. He'd just finished his check of the engine when the two of them arrived back at the tin shack, and they took off immediately. The flight was peaceful, smooth, and completely uneventful. Maggie couldn't resist giving Mack a look of smug satisfaction, but it was lost on him. He slept the short flight to La Ceiba, woke up long enough to be uncharacteristically surly while she made arrangements for a flight to take them to New York, and then proceeded to sleep during that flight too.

She sat beside him on the 727 sipping at her Bloody Mary and trying to concentrate on the clouds outside the window. But her glance kept straying to Mack.

He hadn't shaved, and his chin was stubbled. His eyes, now as they lay closed in sleep, were still ringed with shadows that showed purple against his tan. He'd managed to wash his hands and face in the men's room, but there was still no denying the fact that the two of them were incredibly grubby, covered with dirt and sweat and dust. And, God help them, dried blood.

The thought of her huge old apartment awaiting them at the end of their flight made her almost dizzy with anticipation. Not that it was necessarily awaiting both of them, she reminded herself. Mack was proving stubborn and withdrawn today—she wouldn't put it past him to refuse to accompany her into Manhattan for the respite they both so desperately needed.

She leaned back against her own seat and crunched on the celery stalk from her drink. If only they hadn't had to toss their guns, she thought wearily. She'd feel a lot better if she still had that heavy, nasty piece of machinery tucked in the waistband of her jeans. But they really had no choice in the matter—no airline in the world would let them on carrying that kind of hardware.

If they could just make it to her apartment, they'd be all right. She had two handguns there, with licenses, ammunition, the works. Though of course the problem would surface again —Swissair was unlikely to encourage armed passengers in this day of skyjacking.

Well, they'd cross that bridge when they came to it. Right now all she wanted to do was get home and stand in the shower until she used every drop of hot water in her huge, prewar building. Maybe she'd leave enough for Mack, maybe not. Her own trip to the La Ceiba Airport ladies' room had disclosed an impressive bruise on her strong chin. She almost regretted washing away some of the grime when it made the purple and blue stain so spectacular. She owed Mack one. And sometime, somehow, she was going to collect on that debt. He hadn't had to hit her quite that hard.

She leaned back in the seat, wishing she could close her eyes and sleep as Mack slept. But her nerves were strung too tightly, too much was hanging in the balance. Mentally she went over the things she'd have to procure. New clothes again, tickets to Switzerland, more money and/or credit, the name of a contact in Switzerland who could get them guns. And somehow or other she was going to have to get in touch with Third World Causes, Ltd. and see how they were faring in the wake of Peter's death. And she had to do that without running afoul of the informant. If there even was one, she thought wearily. It seemed as if it had been half a century ago when she'd walked in and found Mack leaning over his body, but in fact it had been only five days ago.

Van Zandt, the evil genius behind all this, was safe in Switzerland, awaiting them, but that didn't mean all the other forces he'd sicced on them wouldn't be lying in wait. They'd be doing well if they just made it safely in and out of the city without Mancini and his hoods or the CIA and the FBI closing in on them.

Mack stirred in his sleep, and she abandoned her worries to watch him. It was an indulgence, and one that she deserved, she thought, tilting the seat back and staring at him out of gritty eyes. Every now and then she could see a trace of Snake in the sexy curl of his mouth. It must be strange for him to have another identity hidden in his past, cropping up at unexpected times.

She'd been like most adolescent girls and experienced her share of pubescent passion for Snake. But when it came right down to it she preferred the man next to her, with his surprising gentleness, his quirky humor, his warmth and tolerance. Not to mention his quick mind, his bravery that was simply an accepted fact, not something he had to prove. She liked the way he teased her, the way he let her be when she needed it, and the way he helped when she needed it. She liked the way his mouth felt on hers, the way his body fitted to hers, and she liked the slow, deliberate way he made love. And the fast, savage way he made love, she thought, remembering those moments on the floor of the Holiday Inn and feeling her pulse race. What would it be like to make love to him in her own bed, a bed she'd never taken any man to?

She was looking forward to it. Hell, that was putting it mildly. The very thought of it made her heart race and her palms sweat. Right now Maggie felt that if Mack just touched her, she'd ignite.

Down, girl, she told herself. It's a logical reaction. You're finally, temporarily, out of danger, and your body's just reasserting its natural prerogatives. With a sigh she turned away, looking across the aisle to the other sleeping passengers, to the clouds beyond. In a matter of hours they'd be back in her apartment. And then, whether he liked it or not, she would have her wicked way with him until they were both in a state of passionate exhaustion.

She shut her eyes, trying to ignore the gritty feel of the dust and too many disturbed nights. A few more hours, and then peace, God willing. She could hold out that long.

If she'd hoped Mack would wake up in a more cheerful mood, she was doomed to disappointment. It was a dark, gloomy day when they landed in New York, and the runways were wet with soaking rain. Mack awoke when the plane touched down, and his expression was abstracted, distant, and shadowed.

They sat there as the people around them rushed for the exits, neither of them saying a word. It had been almost a month since Mack had been in New York, longer than that for Maggie, if she didn't count the short time at the airport when Peter had sent her off on her current quest. It was home to both of them, Maggie thought. So why didn't they feel any relief?

"We're going to my place," Maggie said in a low voice.

"No."

She ignored that. "Just long enough for me to make plans. We need more money, we need clothes, we need plane reservations."

"Forget it, Maggie. I know what I have to do."

"Don't be a turkey, Mack. We've already agreed. We're going to Switzerland and face Van Zandt."

"I've changed my mind."

"Mack . . ." Her voice held a warning.

"I'm going alone."

"The hell you are."

"You don't have any say in the matter, Maggie," he said wearily. "Too many people have died because of me. I'm not going to let you walk into danger again. This is between Van Zandt and me, and I intend to take care of it. Without your help."

"Too bad, Mack. You've got my help, whether you want it or not," she shot back. "I hate to remind you, but I'm in charge of this expedition and I—"

"Not anymore."

"Listen, you macho pig, just because I'm not made of steel doesn't mean that you're suddenly the boss of the world," she snapped. "I have as much right—"

"Maggie," he said gently, "you're fired."

She stopped mid-tirade, too startled to do more than stare. "What?"

"I said you're fired," he repeated. "I hired the services of Third World Causes, Ltd., and I can fire them. You're out of a job, Maggie. Go back to your office and help them out of the mess Peter's death will have thrown them into. I can take care of the rest of this on my own."

"You can't do that."

"Of course I can. I just did." He unbuckled his seat belt. "The plane's empty. Shall we go?"

"Not until we get this settled," she began, but he rose and moved past her, starting down the narrow aisle, and she had no choice but to chase after him, feeling uncomfortably like a terrier snapping at his heels.

The winding tunnel was empty of passengers as she followed him off the plane and into the terminal. The flight attendants had even dispensed with their mechanical smiles, watching them go with undisguised relief. Mack kept marching, ignoring her as she hurried to keep pace with him, and for a moment she contemplated tripping him as she headed toward customs.

"Listen, you jerk," she yelled at him, "if you don't slow down and listen to me, you won't have to worry about Van Zandt— I'll kill you first. Damn it, Pulaski, will you stop for a moment?" She grabbed his arm, but she might have been a flea for all the difference it made. He just kept going, dragging her along with him with supreme disregard.

"Where do you think we're going?" she demanded finally, when even using all her strength did little more than slow his pace a trifle.

"You're going into the city. I'm putting you in a taxi and then I'm finding the next flight out for Switzerland," Mack deigned to reply. "And I'm not about to argue with you, Maggie. This is nonnegotiable—you're staying, I'm going." They reached customs, joining the shortest line, with Maggie desperately wracking her brains for ways to defeat his sudden stubbornness. It wouldn't take them long to get through customs, considering they had only the battered knapsack and not an ounce of contraband on them. And then Maggie had little doubt he'd do just as he said, bundle her into a taxi and send her off. She would, of course, order the taxi to turn around and drop her back off, but the maze of terminals at JFK wouldn't help matters. And there were any number of airlines flying to Switzerland—she'd have to try each one before she found the one Mack was taking.

"Mack, listen to reason," she said. "I have contacts, and I know Van Zandt a hell of a lot better than you do. You don't stand a snowball's chance in hell if you go alone. For God's sake, Mack," she said, suddenly desperate, "I don't want to lose you."

That got his attention. He looked at her, their eyes almost level, and the stubbornness faded into the warmth she had become used to, and that sexy mouth of his curved in a smile that would have done Snake proud. "Maggie," he said in his gravelly voice, and his hand reached up to gently touch her chin. She winced, and he leaned over and kissed her, first on the lips, then on her bruised chin. "You almost convince me, sweetheart. But I can't risk it, I can't risk you. And there's nothing you can say or do to make me."

"Do you have anything to declare?" the bored customs man demanded, and Mack moved ahead.

It took them only a few moments to pass customs, and then they were moving on down the wide corridors, heading for the gate that kept passengers from the rest of the world. Police and security guards were all around them, paying them not the slightest bit of attention, and Maggie's hopes rose. At least they weren't on the lookout for them yet. Maybe Van Zandt's machinations had failed, maybe no one connected them with Peter's death.

Suddenly Mack's footsteps slowed. They were nearing the security gate, and hurrying passengers pushed around them as he came to a dead stop. Maggie almost barrelled into him, and she had opened her mouth to complain when she saw the expression on his face.

"What is it?" she demanded.

"Mancini." His voice was flat, unemotional, and her gaze followed his.

He looked more like a stockbroker than a criminal, Maggie thought. Mancini was a beautifully groomed, beautifully dressed man in his mid-forties. He looked like any other rising executive, until you looked into his eyes. Even from that distance Maggie could see their cold, empty depths, so very like Willis's, and she shivered.

There were at least half a dozen men crowded around him. Similarly well-dressed, similarly well-groomed, an army of yuppie gangsters. And they were all staring straight at Mack and his companion.

"What the hell are we going to do?" Mack said, more to himself than to her, and she could hear the ragged edge of desperation in his raw voice. It had been one complication too many, but it gave Maggie just the chance she needed.

"They're not going to shoot us in broad daylight," she said. "They certainly won't want to make a fuss."

"No. But with that many reinforcements he'll have no trouble getting us out of here without anyone looking twice," he said wearily. "And I don't think customs is going to take us back."

"No, I doubt it," Maggie agreed. "So there's only one thing we can do."

Mack just looked at her as the crowds threaded their way around them. "And what's that?"

She grinned. "Take off your clothes."

"Maggie, in another time or place that would be a terrific idea, but I don't think it's going to help matters right now."

"Sure it is," she said cheerfully. "Do as I say. I'm about to save your butt." And she began to unbutton her shabby, sweat-stained shirt and talk very loudly in Danish.

It took Mack only another moment to catch on. And then he began to undo his own shirt, never looking toward their reception committee by the security gate.

"This may or may not get us out of this," Maggie said in the fluent Danish she used with her father, "but we stand a good chance of being arrested before Mancini can get his hands on us. And if we're arrested, we may end up being stuck in jail on suspicion of murder, but at least you won't be heading to Switzerland on your own, my friend." She dropped her shirt on the floor, then reached for her bra. Thank heavens for her Scandinavian blood, which didn't allow for false modesty, she thought, then said it aloud in Danish.

Mack, not understanding a word of this, nodded sagely and said *"Jawohl."* His shirt ended on the floor, and he reached for his belt. A moment later he dropped his trousers, to stand there in his glorious turquoise Calvin Klein briefs.

"Jeg ilsker dig," Maggie said, laughter and tenderness suddenly overwhelming her. *"Jeg ilsker dig,* Mack." I love you, damn it all. How did that happen? It must have been when I wasn't looking, she thought, and continued to babble on.

The briefs were about to follow Mack's jeans, and Maggie's own pants were unzipped when the airport police arrived.

"Here, now, you can't do that," a very Irish-looking airport cop protested, scooping up the clothes from the floor and trying to drape them around Maggie's nude torso.

She smiled brightly at him, babbling in Danish. "I happen to love that man over there in the Jockey shorts," she said, looking innocent. "And if you don't arrest us, there isn't going to be much left of him to love."

"Jawohl," Mack said solemnly, tugging at the waistband of his briefs as another policeman was trying to pull them up.

The Irish-looking cop, Officer Ryan, his nameplate proclaimed, was sweating at this point. "Come on, lady, don't you speak English?"

"It's a slow death to be trampled to death by geese," Maggie said in Danish, remembering her Scandinavian grandmother's favorite saying. "Arrest us, for Christ's sake." Mancini was still watching, waiting.

Officer Ryan was still sweating. "Come on, lady, gimme a break."

There was no help for it. Maggie threw off the shirt he'd been trying to drape around her and stepped out of her jeans, taking her underwear with it. Ryan gulped, threw the shirt back around her, and started cursing.

"Okay, lady, you and your friend asked for it. You have the right to remain silent . . ."

Maggie stopped her babbling, pulled her pants back up, and caught Mack's eyes. The stubbornness had vanished; they were warm with laughter. *"Jeg ilsker dig,"* she said one last time, reveling in the chance to say it, delighting that he couldn't possibly know that the mighty had fallen.

"Ich liebe dich," he said in his inappropriate German. And it didn't take someone with Maggie's gift for languages to know what he was saying to her. I love you, whether in German or in Danish, was only too easy to understand. And she could only hope it was a coincidence that made Mack say that to her. Perhaps it was the only German he knew, apart from *jawohl*. But somehow she doubted it.

Officer Ryan had managed to get a shirt back around her. It was Mack's shirt, but that was a minor problem. The turquoise briefs were covered, and Ryan's partner had brought out the handcuffs. Maggie stood there tranquilly enough as they handcuffed the two of them together, and she allowed herself a small glance at Mancini. All she saw was his narrow, beautifully tailored back as he left the airport, surrounded by his army.

She looked back at the handcuffs binding her to Mack, then up into his eyes. "Get out of this one, Mack," she muttered under her breath. "I dare you."

nineteen

Officer Ryan leaned against the door and glared at the unrepentant two. He'd brought them to a small, windowless room on the lower floor of the Honduro Airways building, dispatched his partner to phone in, and now he stood there glowering, his forehead still shiny with sweat.

Maggie casually began to button Mack's shirt with her unhandcuffed hand. He'd taken their wallets, credit cards, identification and all, and his pink complexion had turned bright red when he realized his prisoners weren't crazy foreigners at all. But he hadn't asked a question or said a word apart from ordering them to sit quietly at the conference table in the air-conditioned little room.

And so they sat, their arms stretched across the table, wrists bound together. Mack looked comparatively peaceful, Maggie decided. The decision had been taken out of his hands, and for the moment he seemed to accept it.

The door opened, Ryan's partner stuck his head in long enough to murmur something to the policeman, and then disappeared again after receiving his orders. And then Ryan did turn to them.

"Well, I hit the jackpot this time, didn't I?" he said, more to himself than them. "Wanted for murder, the both of you, down in Texas. Not to mention arson and car theft. You're a likely pair, the two of you."

"Both of us?" Maggie shrieked, having innocently assumed Pulaski was the only suspect.

"Arson?" Mack said, sparing Maggie an amused glance.

"The two of you bombed a motel in Texas, stole a car, murdered a man named Peter Wallace, and then fled the country," Ryan announced. "You care to make a statement?"

"You have the right to remain silent, Mack," Maggie warned.

"Yes, but what the hell are we going to do about a lawyer?"

"I don't know, kid," she drawled. "You just fired me."

"I don't think you're going to have much luck assembling our defense from a prison cell."

"I don't think we're going to be in a prison cell," she said.

"Why not? As far as I can tell, that might be the safest place," he countered.

"Such innocence. Mancini could get to you faster there than anyplace else. Fortunately, I'm a damned good lawyer, and I can get us out of this before that happens." She gestured toward the listening Ryan. "Better watch it. Little pitchers have big ears."

"Don't mind me, folks," Ryan said affably. "This is all very interesting."

"I'll bet it is," said Maggie, the lawyer in her reemerging. "What are we waiting for, Officer? The paddy wagon?"

"We're waiting for word from my superiors. Then it'll be off to Center Street with you, I expect. That is, if you don't mind," he added with exaggerated courtesy.

"I thought you said we weren't going to jail, Maggie May," Mack said, flexing his wrist in its metal casing.

"You aren't." A new voice entered the conversation, coming from the open door, and Maggie let out a cry of relief.

"Jackson!" she cried. "My savior. At least, I hope so."

Mike Jackson, head of the Washington branch of Third World Causes, Ltd., ducked inside the door, followed by another man. "Not me, Maggie. Hamilton here is doing the honors."

Maggie took one look at the man, at his nondescript three-piece suit, his forgettable face, medium coloring and middle age, and recognized him for what he was. "And why is the CIA saving us?" she questioned coolly.

Hamilton's nod of approval recognized her perception. "Orders, Miss Bennett," he said in a voice that matched his bland exterior as he flashed his identification at Ryan. "Thank you, Officer," he said. "You've done an excellent job today, and I'm sure we can count on your discretion in this matter?"

Ryan looked torn. On the one hand, having made such a glamorous collar was more excitement than he usually had in months. On the other hand, his shift was almost over, and the paperwork involved in an arrest like this one was monumental. Not to mention the hassle of going up against the U.S. Government. He shrugged, accepting his dismissal. "Sure thing," he muttered. "But tell 'em to keep their clothes on in public next time." He glowered at everyone in general. "You still want 'em cuffed?"

"That won't be necessary, Officer Ryan," Hamilton said. "They won't be going anywhere until we're ready."

Ryan slammed the door shut behind him. Hamilton took a seat at the table, Jackson followed suit, and Mack just watched them. Maggie felt oddly distant and removed. Things were out of her hands, finally, and for once in her life she was ready to give up control. Let the CIA figure it out this time; let Jackson, Peter Wallace's heir apparent, deal with it.

"We need your help," Hamilton said without preamble.

"Fancy that," Maggie said lightly, sparing a glance at Mack's stony profile. "Mine or Pulaski's?" She knew the answer. She just wanted to make certain Mack heard it from the source.

"Both, I'm afraid. Van Zandt won't have it any other way."

"God knows, we have to please Van Zandt," Mack said. "What do you want us to do, and what are you willing to give us in return?"

"I wouldn't say that now is the time for bargaining," Hamilton said sternly. "You're in enough trouble as it is. Your only chance of clearing things up is doing as we say."

"Mr. Hamilton"—Mack had leaned across the table, and

Maggie could see the barely leashed temper ticking away in his eyes—"I have not done one thing wrong, and I'll be damned if I'll let some shady branch of the government blackmail me so that I can get my basic civil rights."

"Basic civil rights in this country aren't worth a pig's ass," Hamilton said. "If we wash our hands of the situation, you'll be tied up in courts and trials for so long you'll be senile by the time you're free. And then Mancini and his friends will be waiting."

He grinned, a savage semblance of a smile. "Maggie assures me Mancini won't have to wait that long."

"Probably not. The CIA doesn't owe you anything, Pulaski. You've caused us a great deal of trouble, but we're willing to overlook that and help you if you're willing to help us."

Mack managed an obscene snarl, and Maggie decided it was time to intervene. "Exactly what do you want us to do, Mr. Hamilton?"

"We want you to meet with Jeffrey Van Zandt and find out what he wants from you. And then we'd like you to kill him."

Dead silence reigned in the climate-controlled room. Maggie looked at Jackson, but he showed no surprise. Hamilton still had that bland, nondescript expression on his face, and Mack merely looked cynical.

"Why?"

"He's a traitor," Hamilton said promptly. "God only knows what disasters he's been responsible for during the last few years. He's been arranging drug sales between the rebels and the mafia and then raking off most of the profits. But he hasn't been doing it alone, he's been answering to somebody. We want to find out who that somebody is, and we suspect that whatever Van Zandt wants you for has something to do with it."

"I hate to bring reality into this Le Carré fantasy you're living," Maggie drawled, "but I must point out that your organization is equipped to handle this sort of thing. Why don't your people track him down, find out what's going on, and then take him out? All in a day's work for you guys. We're sort of new at this stuff."

"Don't you think we would have if we could?" Hamilton said, irritation breaking through his determined blandness. "Jeffrey Van Zandt is one of the best. No one's going to get near him unless he wants them to. We've been working on this for months and we've had no luck whatsoever. For some reason he wants the two of you in Switzerland, and you're our only chance." He leaned back, a faint smile playing around his thin lips. "And I might add, we're your only chance."

"And if we don't choose to take it?" Maggie said.

"Well, then I'm sure Mr. Jackson will do his best for you. But when the government doesn't care to be helpful, things can take a very long time."

Maggie looked at Jackson. He was a beefy, balding man in his early fifties, with soulful eyes and the instincts of a barracuda, coupled with an intellect Wallace had once termed frightening. When he shook his head Maggie knew they had no choice whatsoever.

Mack had clearly come to the same decision. "I go alone or not at all," he said suddenly.

Before Maggie could protest, Hamilton shook his head. "That won't do. He wants you both there. If you show up alone, he won't come near you."

Mack's fist clenched, and his eyes met hers across the table. She smiled, a rueful, faintly triumphant smile. "You're stuck with me, Mack," she murmured. "Listen, you never know when a Mata Hari might be useful."

"She's very good with a gun," Jackson offered. "And she thinks on her feet. You couldn't do much better—"

"Thanks," Mack broke in. "But I've been traveling with her for more than a week now. I know how good she is. I also know that I don't want any more deaths on my conscience. I'll take jail."

Maggie controlled her temper with a great effort. "Then I'll just have to go alone," she said sweetly. "He may or may not refuse to see me. He may decide to have me killed if he doesn't get what he wants, but that's all right, you'll be safe in jail. Until Mancini gets you."

"You wouldn't!"

"I would. And you know it, Pulaski."

Hazel eyes glared into the famous Bennett aquamarine eyes, and the two men sat by, watching. Finally Mack sighed, leaning back. "You would, wouldn't you?" he snarled. "Okay, Hamilton. I guess we go to Switzerland. When?"

"Seven-thirty tonight. You'll arrive in Zurich tomorrow morning around eight. We've made reservations, gotten your passports, clothes, luggage—"

"My passport blew up in my apartment three weeks ago," Mack interrupted.

Hamilton held up a restraining hand. "Please, Mr. Pulaski. We've taken care of that. You have three hours before departure, and I've made arrangements at one of the airport hotels where you can bathe and change and have something to eat. But I suggest we hurry. If you miss tonight's flight, it'll be another twenty-four hours."

"Why don't you just send us over on Air Force One?" Mack snapped.

"It's in use," Hamilton replied, unfazed.

"What about guns?" Maggie broke in. "Can you arrange to have us carry our own through customs or at least find us some once we arrive?"

"The latter. Your contact will arrange all that. When you arrive in Zurich you'll check in to the new Zurich Holiday Inn—"

"God, no!" Mack groaned.

"Perfect," said Maggie.

"The Zurich Holiday Inn," Hamilton continued with a prissy little glare. "Our man will make contact there."

"How will we know him?" Mack demanded. "Will he wear a red rose in his lapel?"

Hamilton ignored his sarcasm. "You'll know him. He'll bring

you any weapons you might need. Any questions you have at that point you can ask him. He'll be briefed on the entire affair."

"Let's hope so," Maggie said. "No further questions, your honor. Just one small point. We won't kill him for you. We'll find out what he wants, find out who he's working for, and we'll do our damnedest to hand him over to you. But we're not going to be your executioners, no matter how much he deserves it."

Hamilton smiled faintly. "Suit yourself, Miss Bennett. I suspect you won't have any choice in the matter when it comes right down to it. With Van Zandt it's going to be a case of kill or be killed. I trust that it will be the former."

"We'll see," Maggie said, hiding the gloomy conviction that he was right.

Mack's glare took in the three of them. She could see the hesitation still lingering, but then he shrugged, accepting his fate. "I guess it's our funeral," he said succinctly. "Let's go."

She should be feeling better, Maggie thought, leafing through *Vogue* in her luxurious first-class seat on the 747 currently soaring over the Atlantic. She was clean, well-dressed, well-fed, even reasonably well-rested. Mack was beside her, immersed in the CIA file on Van Zandt and looking quite glorious in a cream linen Armani suit. Her own St. Laurent jumpsuit was a perfect fit—no mean feat when the wearer came close to six feet tall. They were as far away from Mancini and his men as they could be, and the charges from Texas were being dropped. All they had to worry about was Jeffrey Van Zandt.

That was more than enough to worry about. All her instincts about Jeffrey Van Zandt had proven true, and God only knew what they would face when they reached Zurich. And what he would want from them.

It was three in the morning, Zurich time. Maggie had already adjusted her watch, the scratched and dusty Rolex, her one constant through this entire adventure. The watch, and Mack.

She still couldn't quite believe what had escaped from her

when she'd been babbling in Danish. Once the words were out in the open, she couldn't call them back.

It was a strange notion, to be in love with Mack. Whenever she thought of love she thought of that twisted fascination she'd had for Randall. Or she thought of some idealized, pleasant cloud of emotion where all was gentleness and smiling peace. With Mack it was neither. It was vast irritation, ridiculous humor, tenderness, warmth, and passion that turned her blood to fire. There was no pleasant cloud of forgetfulness with Mack— it was real and solid and overwhelming. But would it hurt as much as it had with Randall? She had the nasty feeling that if Mack were to betray her as Randall had, she wouldn't recover. A part of her would wither and die.

Well, she didn't have any spare parts, she thought briskly. And Mack had offered her nothing, promised nothing. Granted, they couldn't really talk about the future when they were running for their lives. But the man had been married twice already. Not a good omen.

Who was she kidding? She and Mack had shared a bed and some blissful passion. But when the danger was finally over, when they went back to a semblance of their normal lives, then their relationship would doubtless be over too. It would be better for both of them, better than eventual disillusionment.

But in the meantime she was going to keep him alive. Between the two of them they'd track Van Zandt down and hand him over to the CIA contact in Zurich. And then they could worry about the future.

"What's that expression mean?" Mack's rasping voice broke through her abstraction. "You look like you just realized what we've gotten ourselves into."

She turned to look at him. His eyes were still slightly bloodshot, and she could see the traces of the black eye she'd given him centuries ago in the hotel room in Tegucigalpa. "I know what we've gotten ourselves into," she said quietly. *Jeg ilsker dig,* a little voice echoed in the back of her brain, and she squashed it down.

"I'm glad you knew what you were doing," he said wearily. "You want to tell me why?"

"Why?" she echoed.

"Why you wouldn't let me rot in jail? It wouldn't have been that long—Jackson could have gotten me out."

"Maybe. But Mancini would have gotten you. You should know that as well as I do. That's a major reason you were hiding out in Moab, Mack. And if the mob wants to get you, there's no real way to stop them."

"Are our chances any better in Zurich against someone like Van Zandt?"

"I think so. He wants something from us. Mancini only wants us dead," Maggie said.

"What's this 'us'? Mancini wants me."

Maggie shook her head. "Not anymore, I suspect. He saw the two of us together, he'll know we've been traveling together for the last week. I'm sure he'll decide to have me taken care of as well as you."

"No," he said, and there was anguish in his raw voice.

"Maybe not. Do you want to take a chance on it?" He didn't say anything, and she leaned back in the seat, stretching her long legs out in front of her. "I didn't think so. Take a nap, Mack. We're going to make it."

But it was she who slept the rest of the night, waking only when they landed in Zurich. It was a warm, sunny day, and Mack's despised Holiday Inn looked massive, comfortable, and very Swiss. They were settled into their large, spotless suite by eleven, with nothing to do but pace and wait.

Maggie ordered a huge breakfast for both of them, and neither of them could eat more than a few bites of fruit. Of course Mack turned on the television, only to turn it off when he discovered they got only two channels, and both of them were in German.

"German soap operas are almost better than this," Maggie said, dropping down on the huge bed.

"Better than what?" he said, pacing.

"Better than waiting. Better than staring out the window at Zurich, better than wearing a path in the carpet. How long are we supposed to wait here?"

"Until Van Zandt shows up, I suppose," he said, moving back to the window.

"And what if he shows up before our contact does?"

"Then we'll have no weapons," he said, turning back from the window, "and we'll be sitting ducks."

"Cheerful thought," Maggie said, watching as Mack headed back to the window again. That suit was definitely an asset to a body she had come to accept as impossibly sexy anyway. She patted the too hard mattress. "Wanna take a nap?"

He stopped his pacing, turning to stare at her, and slowly his brooding eyes lightened, and his grim mouth curved in a smile. "Now there's an idea. But I don't know if I'm sleepy."

She matched his grin. "Maybe we could get a little exercise? Just enough to tire us out a bit." She reached up and began unfastening the buttons of her jumpsuit.

His smile broadened to a lascivious grin. "Maybe I'm glad you came after all," he said, shrugging out of his jacket. "If we're going to die, we may as well die happy." He was advancing to the bed when a loud knocking reverberated through their soundproof door.

"Damn," Mack said, jumping a mile. His eyes met Maggie's suddenly alert ones. "Do you think it's Van Zandt?"

Maggie was already off the bed, her nerves strung as tightly as piano wire. "There's only one way to find out," she said, advancing on the door just as the pounding began again.

"Who is it?" she called out in German.

"Room service." The reply was in flat, Midwestern American, and the two of them exchanged glances. It didn't sound like Van Zandt, but then the voice was muffled through the door.

"We didn't order anything from room service," she said in English.

There was a pause. "Let's just say I'm a friend of Hamilton's, and no, I'm not wearing a rose in my lapel," the voice replied.

Mack shrugged at Maggie's inquiring glance. "Let him in. What have we got to lose?"

"Our lives," she muttered. She unfastened one lock, then the second, and pulled open the door. And then almost slammed it shut again. "Oh, God, no!" she groaned.

Bud Willis sauntered into the room, his skeletal grin firmly in place. "Your friendly CIA contact, making house calls," he announced himself. "Howya doing?"

twenty

"I guess it's only the good who die young," Maggie said, shutting the door behind him.

"You got it," Willis said. "Surprised the hell out of me when I heard you guys made it out of Chicaste in one piece. I thought for sure those greasers would have gotten you."

Mack's smile resembled a snarl. "We made it. Last time I saw you, you were running from a hail of bullets."

Willis shrugged. "What can I say? I run fast."

"Or they didn't want to hit you," Maggie added. "What did you do, Willis, sell them out too? And how come you're working for the CIA? I thought you were kicked out years ago."

"Maggie, Maggie, you should know that things are never as they seem with the Company," Willis chided her. "And not that it's any of your fucking business, but I don't sell people out. I follow orders."

"With the CIA that's the same thing," she said. "So what did you bring us?"

Willis dropped his briefcase on the king-size bed. "Guns, Maggie. What else?" In his three-piece suit and Italian shoes, Willis looked like a completely different animal than the jungle savage. Until you looked into his empty eyes, she thought, suppressing a shudder. He snapped the locks, opening the case, and Maggie looked down with combined satisfaction and distaste.

"They'll do," she allowed. "Anything else?"

"Why, Maggie, one would almost think you didn't like my company."

"She doesn't," Mack said.

Willis gave him his mocking grin. "Too fucking bad, friend. I'm your contact here in Switzerland, and the only chance of help you two have."

"If you're our only chance of help, then we're better off alone," he said. "Get out."

The smile on Willis's face tightened for a moment, and his face grew even more skeletal. And then he was once more all mocking charm. "Sure thing, guys. You'd need me if you were going to hand Van Zandt over to us. But we all know it's not going to come down to that, don't we, sugar lips?" He'd turned his attention back to Maggie, pinching her cheek, and out of the corner of her eye she could see Mack move with that sudden, lightning stealth that still managed to shock her.

But she could move fast, too, and she didn't want their hotel room turned into a battleground. She shoved Willis away, putting her body between his and Mack's. "Good-bye, Willis. Tell them to send someone less sleazy next time. Like Jack the Ripper."

Willis smiled, but he moved to the door. "Our paths are going to cross again, Maggie. We both know it."

He was halfway out the door before her voice stopped him. "Willis, answer me one thing."

"Sure thing, sweet cakes."

"Did Consuela survive?" The memory of those dark, haunted eyes and her slender, wringing hands had haunted Maggie for the last twenty-four hours, and she simply had to know.

Willis dismissed the question with a shrug. "I doubt it. I didn't wait around to see. What's it to you?"

She almost moved out of the way to let Mack at him. Only her fear that the two might be evenly matched stopped her. In the end she had no choice. Mack's hands came down on her shoulders, the fingers strong and kneading the tight muscles.

"Get the hell out of here, Willis," he said.

Willis grinned. "I'm history, friend. For now." And he shut the door very quietly behind him.

Maggie turned and threaded her arms around Mack, hiding her face against his shoulder. "The man," she whispered, "is swamp scum."

"That's being generous," Mack whispered back. "Now what were we doing when we were so rudely interrupted?"

The waiting, Maggie decided, was the hardest part of this entire adventure. Twenty-four hours later there was no word from Van Zandt, Willis had vanished into the sewers where he belonged, and the four walls of the hotel room were beginning to close in on them. When *Dynasty* dubbed in German began to look good, Maggie knew she was in trouble. It was another matter for a tube addict like Mack. He could watch anything and be reasonably entertained. But Maggie was made of sterner stuff.

"I'm just glad I didn't have to hide out in Moab," she said. "I think I would have gone completely mad."

"You are completely mad, darling," Mack said evenly, pulling his attention away from the German Carringtons. "Why don't we get out of this place? Go for a walk, go shopping? It's a beautiful day, and if Van Zandt arrives and we're not here, he can damn well come back later."

"I don't know. As long as we're in this room, I feel safe. Once we leave it, all bets are off."

"It doesn't do us much good to be safe if we're both crazy," he said reasonably. "And since you've decided sex isn't an option, I find I'm in need of some exercise to work off my frustrations. You can come with me or you can hide out here."

"Mack, I explained to you last night—"

"You had a dozen excuses, Maggie May," he said dispassionately. "All very logical, rational excuses that don't amount to a hill of beans. When it comes right down to it you're scared to death—"

"I am not," she shot back, pushing away from the window. "I can face Van Zandt and anything he wants to dish out without batting an eye, and you damn well know it."

"Sure, I know it. I'm the one you can't face, Maggie. You're scared to death of me—no, scratch that—you're scared to death of your feelings for me."

"And just what do you think my feelings for you are?"

He'd snapped off the television and he stood there looking at her, his eyes dark and disappointed. "Maggie, I toured Scandinavia in the early seventies. I know as well as anyone what *jeg ilsker dig* means."

"Listen, Mack, my Danish isn't that good. I just said whatever came into my mind, and you shouldn't take it seriously. I—"

"I'm not interested in excuses, Maggie," he cut her off. "You knew what you were saying. And you know you're lying right now. But I'm tired of it, Maggie. I'm tired of fighting your fragile ego and your need for control, and I'm tired of watching you fight yourself and your needs. I'm tired of being jerked around, and Maggie"—he had moved very close to her, and she could see the anger in his eyes, feel the warmth of his breath on her face—"right now I am damned tired of you."

He turned around without touching her and started for the door. She watched him go without moving. One word and he'd turn back. She knew that full well, but her mouth wouldn't open. A hand clamped down on her heart, squeezing it, wrenching it, so that she longed to cry out for him. But she couldn't.

He didn't look back. The door closed behind him, and the quiet, well-oiled click reverberated through her tense body. She stood there trying to summon up righteous indignation, anger, and outrage at his harsh words. But those emotions wouldn't come at her bidding. The one thing she prided herself on was her scrupulous honesty. And she couldn't hide from the fact that he had every reason to be angry.

Her excuses last night had sounded weak even to her own ears. Mack had just looked at her. Listened to her drone on and on with excuses, and said not a word. Just given her his sweet, slightly mocking smile and turned over and gone to sleep, leaving her to lie awake beside him for half the night, her body acutely aware of him, her mind obsessed with him, her heart crying for him. She knew she loved him and she panicked, and tried to push him away.

"Bastard," she said now, moving to drop down on the bed. "Having a temper tantrum because I wouldn't put out. It's time to grow up, Pulaski," she said severely into the pillow.

The words echoed around the empty room. "Yes," she said wearily, "it's time to grow up. For you, Maggie Bennett. You know perfectly well he wasn't angry about the sex. He was angry about the excuses, about the lies. And he had every right to be angry." The bright sunlight from the Zurich summer was streaming in the window, but Maggie shut her eyes, not even noticing. "Every right," she murmured miserably. "Christ, Maggie, why are you so goddamned stupid?"

When she woke up the bright sunlight had turned dark and gloomy. She squinted at her watch, shook her head, and stared again. It was midafternoon—Mack had been gone for hours.

Where the hell could he have gone for so long? It took her less than two minutes to grab her shoes, her sweater, and the purse with the small, efficient gun inside it. And then she was racing down the empty corridors, her heart slamming against her ribs.

The clean wide *strasse* outside the new Holiday Inn Zurich was crowded with neat, prosperous-looking people. Tourists and native Swiss alike, all moved with quiet deliberation, heading toward their destinations. And nowhere in that crowd of people did she see Mack's slouching, rangy figure.

She stood there for minutes, hours, at the edge of the sedate traffic, her eyes sweeping over the multitudes as she fought the panic that clawed at her insides. And then she saw him, moving down the sidewalk with that sexy walk of his, the Armani suit hanging on his wonderful body with negligent charm, and suddenly Maggie realized just how crazy she'd become. How could she have turned that down when, on top of everything else, she loved him? It was ridiculous to fight it anymore. She was going to go after him and tell him, and if all the straitlaced Swiss wanted to stare at her, let them.

The traffic lights were in her favor. She started across the wide street toward him, trusting in the obedient Swiss drivers, not quite believing when she heard the sudden squeal of tires, the horrified screams as the huge black Mercedes sedan bore down on her.

Everyone around her scattered, but Maggie was mesmerized, unable to move as the car headed directly for her. The windows were smoked, and she was unable to see the driver. Not that it matters, she thought abstractedly. Even if she knew who it was, she wouldn't be in any state to tell anyone. Unless, of course, she were able to move. But her feet were still paralyzed, and all she could do was stand there and watch as the car headed straight for her.

There was a sudden, sickening crunch as flesh and bone and muscle thudded into her, flinging her to the edge of the road. The Mercedes bumper nicked her leg, but Maggie was beyond noticing. Mack had seen her standing there like a frightened rabbit; Mack had pushed the polite Swiss out of the way and tackled her, dragging both of them out of the way of the murderous Mercedes.

And suddenly the paralysis that had afflicted everyone but Mack broke, and they were surrounded by several dozen chattering, concerned bystanders. Maggie could hear the voices, hear the mishmash of languages, all expressing concern, but she couldn't move. Her face was pressed up against Mack's chest, and she could do nothing but shiver.

"Are you all right?" His raw voice was rough in her ear. She nodded against him, making an effort to stand up. She didn't get very far, as her muscles trembled and her knees refused to support her.

Mack scooped her up in his arms, rising with an impressive amount of grace, considering his burden. "She's fine," he said in German and English to the chattering magpies around them. "Just shaken up a bit. I'll get her back to her room."

Half a dozen languages urged them to see a doctor, another half dozen suggested the police. Mack made no response, crossing the wide, deadly *strasse* and moving back into the Holiday Inn without a backward glance.

She hid in the shelter of his arms, using every ounce of her energy to calm the trembling in her limbs. She felt close to tears, and desperately she tried to push them back. She'd regain her self-control, and she and Mack could calmly figure out who had tried to kill her and why.

He managed the door to their room with surprising ease, kicking it shut behind them. With a great effort, Maggie lifted her head, willing her eyes to be calm. "I'm all right now," she said evenly as he carried her over to the bed.

He looked down at her, his eyes stormy with emotion. "Are you?" he said dubiously. "Okay." And he dropped her on the bed and turned away.

The shock of the fall left her momentarily speechless, her hard-won calm disappearing for a moment as she watched him stalk to the window. She could feel the tears edge up on her again, and she swallowed hard, pushing them back. She needed him more than she had ever needed anyone in her entire life. And she could do nothing but sit there and try to fight back the weak, sniveling tears that she hated and wait for self-control to return.

She waited, but it didn't come back. Instead, the tears kept creeping back up, stinging the back of her eyes, so that her fingers clenched the thick bedspread in a vain effort of control. Her heart was pounding, her breath was strangled, and she was losing the battle. She was going to cry in front of him, she was going to break down completely, and her last defenses would be gone. And at that terrifying thought the last wall broke, and a loud, gulping sob broke the tense silence between the two of them.

Mack whirled around, startled, watching her as her face crumpled and the tears burst forth.

"Go away," she said, weeping. "Get out of here. I don't want you to see me like this." God, it hurt. The sobs were ripping her apart, and she wrapped her arms around her body and curled up in a little ball. She'd stored up a lot of tears over the years, and they all chose that moment to stream forth. She lay there howling in pain and misery and aching loneliness, crying for every hurt that she'd hidden from over the years.

When Mack's hands first touched her she tried to slap him away, but he was stronger than she was, and a moment later she was cradled in his arms, sobbing against his neck. He held her carefully, his warm, strong hands stroking her, his voice low and soothing. Slowly he rocked her, back and forth, as she wept against him. Her nose was running, and without a word he handed her his handkerchief. She started hiccuping and coughing and he pounded her back for her. And still she wept.

It was dark in the room when the storm of tears finally abated, dying away with a strangled sigh. The last ounce of tension left her body, and she realized she was lying in the cradle of Mack's arms, stretched out on the wide bed, feeling limp and peaceful.

"You still with me?" he murmured in her ear. "Or did I lose you along the way?"

Maggie sighed, a loose, watery sigh, and snuggled against him. "God, Mack," she whispered. "I feel completely wasted. This is almost better than sex."

He laughed, a silent, gentle little laugh. "Nothing's better than sex, Maggie. How long has it been since you cried?"

"A lifetime," she answered. "I've destroyed your suit."

"It's supposed to look rumpled."

"I've been an idiot."

"Yes," he agreed.

She lay there in silence for a long while, letting her body rest against his. Never had she felt so peaceful, so trusting. She could tell him anything, and it would be all right. She closed her eyes, letting her hands catch his. "I don't want to be in love with you," she said.

"I know that." His voice held no emotion but acceptance.

She paused. "But it doesn't seem to matter whether I want to or not, does it?"

"You tell me."

"I love you, Mack. I can't fight it anymore. I love you, I'm in love with you, and I'm in deep trouble," she said gloomily. "I feel like a witch who's lost her powers."

"Maggie, how many times do I have to tell you—you don't have to be strong all the time? You're allowed to feel things like everybody else."

"I don't want to hurt like everybody else." There was no disguising the fear in her words.

He laughed, a gentle, warm sound that almost reassured her. "Trust me, Maggie. Just trust me."

twenty-one

Damn Mack, she thought sleepily, burrowing deeper into the pillow. He's put the television on again. How did he expect her to sleep with all that noise in the background? Two heated male voices, arguing away . . .

In English. Maggie's eyes flew open. She was lying on the bed with the bedspread pulled over her, her brain still fuzzy with her exhausted sleep and the aftermath of her brush with death. The shadows on the wall were dark and ominous, the voices low and angry. Slowly Maggie sat up, peering through the dimly lit room.

"You're awake," Jeffrey Van Zandt said flatly, moving into the light. "Your bodyguard here wouldn't let me wake you up, and we've been standing here for half an hour making the most unbelievable small talk. How are you, darling?"

The whole thing had taken on the quality of a nightmare, Maggie decided. There was Van Zandt, his preppy-perfect looks making him resemble a young William F. Buckley; that charming smile on his even, patrician features; his Ralph Lauren shirt faded to just the right shade; his linen trousers perfectly wrinkled; the sleeves of his well-tailored jacket shoved up his arms. It took an experienced eye to notice the bulge of a well-made shoulder holster under that jacket, and Maggie had experienced eyes.

She tossed the bedspread to one side and swung her feet to the floor. A wave of dizziness washed over her, reminding her that she hadn't eaten for almost twenty-four hours, but not a trace of it showed in her face. "I'm just fine, Jeffrey," she said politely. "A bit tired, but then we've been running halfway around the world recently. You've certainly led us on a merry chase."

Van Zandt smiled, flashing all his orthodontically perfect teeth. "You've outdone yourself, Maggie. I never thought you'd get this far. I'm glad to see you've enjoyed yourself along the way." His glance trailed down Maggie's front, and her eyes followed his, noting that Mack had left her shirt unbuttoned.

Mack moved past Van Zandt and sat down on the bed beside her, perfectly at ease. "We've had our moments," he drawled in his raspy voice. "But don't think you're going to get much gratitude from either of us." His eyes met hers for a brief moment, and one hand reached out and did up her buttons. The casual sexiness of it took her breath away, momentarily distracting her attention from Van Zandt. But then his hand left her, and the moment might never have existed. Except for the lingering warmth on her skin.

Van Zandt shrugged, taking one of the chairs without asking and switching on the light. The bright glare only illuminated his bland good looks, and the nightmare deepened. "You win some, you lose some. Personally, I think Maggie looks a hell of a lot better than she has for a long time. You've been good for her, Mack. Much better for her than Peter Wallace."

"Why did you kill him, Jeffrey?" Maggie went straight to the point. "And what in God's name do you want from us?"

"I'm sorry about Peter, I really am. But he gave me no choice. I hadn't realized Third World Causes was quite so efficient. He was able to trace the drug deal directly back to me. He made the mistake of confronting me with it, and I had no choice but to . . . uh, silence him," he said delicately. "I had expected it would be very neat—the police would arrest Mack and Mancini would see that he came to a quick end in some Houston jail. I hadn't counted on you, Maggie, I'm afraid."

Mack sent her a warm look that took some of the nightmare quality away. "That was a mistake on your part, Van Zandt.

One should never underestimate Maggie." And he reached out and caught her hand.

Van Zandt's lip curled, and some of the preppy charm faded. "True love is so inspiring." He yawned. "And you just may get your chance to live happily ever after."

"That would be nice," Mack said gravely. "You want to tell us how? What is it you want from us, Van Zandt?"

"First of all, you can forget about Hamilton and the Company's plans to trip me up. You'll find that I have protection in high places, very high places indeed. If you handed me over to either one of those two gentlemen, I'd be out so fast your heads would spin. So don't waste our time, okay, dearies?"

"Jeffrey, all we want is for you to leave us alone," Maggie said. "Call off all your nasty little friends, and Mack will keep his mouth shut. He doesn't give a damn if the rebels and Mancini control all the drug traffic in the western hemisphere. Just call them off, and we'll all be happy."

"They don't control the drug traffic in the western hemisphere, Maggie," Van Zandt said in a gentle voice. "A Belgian gentleman named Hercule Mersot is the head of a syndicate that runs seventy-five percent of the world's drug traffic. Mancini answers to him, believe it or not. If the rebels want to deal drugs, they answer to him. And I, I must confess, answer to him."

"Now why am I not surprised?" said Maggie.

"Because you're a bright woman, my dear."

"And what does Hercule Mersot have to do with us?"

"I'm afraid I've been greedy. You can play both ends against the middle for just so long, and then people begin to get suspicious. The Company is distressed with me, but I certainly won't have any trouble placating them. The rebels are so deeply in trouble and in debt that they're not worth worrying about, and Mancini will always listen to reason. No, my only problem is M. Mersot. I'm afraid he's begun to suspect that I've been a little generous in helping myself to my share in certain deals. And he's not a man who likes to be trifled with. So I need you two to take care of him." He leaned back and smiled with the air of a man who's explained a very simple problem to everyone's satisfaction.

"Are you out of your mind?" Mack broke in. "We aren't hired killers. Why don't you hire someone with natural ability? Someone like your good buddy Willis?"

"Unfortunately, Willis is somewhere in Honduras," Van Zandt replied, and Maggie breathed a small sigh of relief. She had no idea whether that misinformation would help her, but anything was possible. "And despite Willis's many talents, he's exactly the sort of man who could get nowhere near Mersot. Not to mention the fact that I wouldn't trust him. No, I need two relative newcomers. People who would go about things with a fresh approach—therein lies the only hope of success. And that's where you come in."

"Why should we kill him? Why don't you do it yourself? Don't you think they'll suspect you're behind it?" Maggie demanded.

"I can talk my way out of anything," he said with his usual overwhelming confidence, and Maggie almost believed he could. "You and Mack will be long gone—"

"I'm sure we will," Mack interrupted.

"Living happily ever after," Jeffrey continued reprovingly. "Mersot's partners will have no idea that two innocent tourists could have gotten to the great Mersot, and they'll be too busy fighting over control of his empire to dwell on it. It should all work out very well."

"And this Mersot lives in Switzerland?" Mack asked.

"You got it. Halfway up the Jungfrau. You'll have to take three cog railways and then hike across mountain meadows to get to his chalet, but you're both strong and healthy."

"How does he get there?"

"Helicopter. I think that might look a little suspicious on your part. There are a few roads that are passable this time of year, but the helicopter is so much more efficient. All you have to do, my dears, is go in there and kill him. He won't give you any trouble—he's a charming old man devoted to his gerbils. I'll get rid of his armed guards for you."

"Decent of you," Maggie said. "And what makes you think we'll do this?"

"Several reasons," Van Zandt replied. "First, it's your only chance to get me to call off my business associates. You might be able to avoid one set of them, but all of them together is rather more than even Maggie could fight off. And if Mersot has me killed, I won't be able to help you." He yawned delicately, like a cat. "And more important, you really wouldn't have to make it back to the States before you met your long-postponed fate. That little encounter with my Mercedes was in the nature of incentive."

Maggie just sat there, looking at him, her hand still in Mack's. He'd boxed them in quite neatly, and they had no choice in the matter. One couldn't reason with the Van Zandts of the world. It was merely a question of kill or be killed. And Maggie had no intention of being killed. She looked at Mack, a question in her eyes, consulting him. He knew everything she'd been thinking, knew and agreed. He nodded, once.

"How?" she said to Van Zandt. "When?"

Van Zandt smiled his smug little smile. "Tomorrow."

"Tomorrow?" she echoed, shocked out of her acceptance.

"Why put it off? Wouldn't you like this all to be over with?"

Maggie ignored the pleasantry. "How and where?"

"I've written it all down. I even have train schedules, maps. Everything you might need. Mersot will be alone up there, the alarm system will be turned off. All you have to do is waltz in there and kill him."

"Sounds too easy to be true. How do we know you're not sending us into a trap, with Mersot's men waiting to pick us off the moment we come within range?"

"Not a bad idea, but I could have taken care of you anywhere along the way. It wouldn't make sense for me to import you to Switzerland just to kill you. Untidy, not to mention a little too spectacular. There are enough tourists around the Jungfrau to notice if someone opens fire."

"Why aren't we reassured?" Mack grumbled.

"Maybe because you're sadly paranoid," Van Zandt purred. "Take it or leave it, my friends."

"And if we leave it?" Maggie said.

Van Zandt showed all his perfect teeth. "Then you're dead. By my hand or perhaps by one of Mersot's employees if someone happens to let him know you came to Switzerland to kill him. Or you may survive for a while until Mancini tracks you down. Whichever way, your days would be numbered. Far better to take a chance my way."

"And if we do this," Maggie said, "what happens to you? Do you get away with all this?"

"For a while. Unless the two of you decide to come after me. People are so unforgiving," he said with a sigh.

Mack smiled grimly. "They do have a habit of holding grudges," he agreed.

"I'm sure you won't fall prey to such base emotions," Van Zandt replied.

"Trust me," Mack murmured, and Maggie felt his hand tighten on hers. She squeezed back, in complete agreement.

"We do have some sense, Jeffrey," she lied with a charming smile.

Van Zandt's eyes were bright with cheerful malice. "You do," he agreed. "But you're tiresomely idealistic, darling, you know you are. I'll have to hope Mack will curb your martyr tendencies." He rose, slender, graceful, infinitely charming. "I'll be in touch."

"You want to make sure we do it?" Mack questioned in a caustic voice.

"Oh, I'll know when you do it. The reverberations will be felt all around the world." He smiled. "Good luck, my friends."

"Will we need it?"

"Oh, I expect so, Maggie. I do expect so. Things are never

easy." And he drifted out the door with a gentle wave of his hand.

Maggie stared at the closed door. "Should we go after him?" she inquired in a calm voice.

"It wouldn't do us any good," Mack said. "He was right, wasn't he? We don't have any choice in the matter. Even if we could protect ourselves from some of the people after us, there's no one who can protect us from everyone."

"No."

He let go of her hand, rising to pick up the packet of material Van Zandt had left them. "Do you think this is a setup?"

"Undoubtedly. I'm sure he wants us to kill Mersot. I'm also certain he's not planning for us to leave the chalet once we do so. In the CIA they learn to be as thorough as the Mafia. No loose ends."

"No loose ends," Mack echoed, dropping the papers back on the table. "I guess we play this game to the end. You want to go out for dinner?"

"No."

"Room service?"

"No."

He turned to look at her, something in her tone of voice catching his attention. "What do you want then?"

"You," she said simply, and waited. He had every right to turn away, to turn her earlier refusal against her, to reject her. But unlike herself, Maggie thought, Mack hadn't a self-destructive bone in his body.

One moment he was across the room, abstracted, the next he was pushing her down on the bed, his mouth capturing hers in a kiss of surprising sweetness. "You know that I love you, don't you?" he whispered against her mouth.

She laughed, an oddly carefree laugh, given their life-or-death predicament. "I know, Mack," she said, sliding her arms around his neck and pulling him against her. "I know."

There was an odd, *Twilight Zone* kind of sense to their trip the next day. They followed Van Zandt's directions dutifully, trying to blend in with the cheerful, smiling tourists, trying to come up with light conversation when both of them wanted to sit huddled with their own dark thoughts. They left their rental car at the train station in Interlaken for the first leg of their journey of death via Lauterbrunnen to the tiny, perfect little Alpine town of Wengen. And then on up, another seven miles to Kleine Scheidegg, to face the terminus of the cog railway and the advent of the worst part of their journey.

Van Zandt's maps were clear. Maggie and Mack had dressed wisely, with sturdy walking shoes, layers of clothing, and loaded guns. When they finally left the chattering merrymakers they sank into a silence that neither of them wanted to break. Somewhere deep inside, Maggie thought, she had to find the courage to face what lay ahead. It might be the murder of an evil old man, it might be Mack's death and her own. She'd faced death before, without flinching. But somehow with Mack it was much harder. She didn't want to die, and she didn't want to lose him. More than ever she wanted to live, to love, to experience everything clean and joyous. But first she had to climb this beautiful, sunny Alpine meadow and head into a valley of death.

Mersot's chalet was a deceptively innocuous building, miles away from the center of the tourist activity, almost hidden by the overhanging cliffs of the Jungfrau. They followed sheep tracks, narrow, beaten little paths that provided dubious footing, and Maggie was almost relieved when they finally caught sight of the sprawling, Austrian-style building hidden against the cliffs.

"That must be it," Mack said unnecessarily.

"Yes." She rubbed her ankle absently. "Do you see anyone around?"

"No. But they wouldn't have to be out and about. I heard a helicopter earlier—maybe it was the guards leaving."

"Maybe. I wish I could trust Van Zandt to get rid of them."

Mack grunted. The brisk mountain wind was blowing his hair against his high, lined forehead, and his eyes were narrowed against the bright glare of sunshine. Somewhere along the way he'd lost his mirrored sunglasses and never bothered to replace them, and his eyes and his expression could no longer be hidden from her. She almost wished she could have sought the security of not knowing Mack's doubts equaled her own. "The one thing I trust about Van Zandt is that he really wants Mersot dead. And we're not going to be able to kill him if he's surrounded by guards. He'll have gotten rid of them. It's up to us to make sure they don't come back before we're out of there."

"Are we really going to kill a stranger, Mack? He's never done us any harm. . . ."

"I don't know," he said grimly. "Maybe we can reason with him. But if worse comes to worst, we're going to have to remember he's behind an obscene amount of the drug deals in the Western world. You might be lucky enough never to have seen someone strung out on heroin. You might have even missed what coke can do to people. I've seen far too much of it. Any man who gets obscenely rich trafficking in other people's pain and despair and death deserves what he gets."

"At your hands?" She couldn't keep from asking.

The look he gave her was one of exasperation. "No, damn it. Not if I think about it. The whole trick to this, Maggie, is not to think about it. Not to meditate on what we're supposed to do—just go in and do it. If it's my life or his, the choice will be easy. I'm just hoping it'll be that clear."

It was a deceptively long distance, down across the remote Alpine meadow to the chalet, which seemed to grow larger and larger as they got closer. The barriers were more numerous—barbed wire, no trespassing signs in six languages, locked gates and electrified fences. They ignored them all, keeping at a slow, steady pace.

They skirted the long, winding drive that led into an underground garage, keeping well out of sight of the windows. The security devices were as sophisticated as any Maggie had ever seen: heat and light sensors, microscopic trip wires, probably guards on the lookout from the charming gabled windows. But no one appeared from the depths of the chalet. Everything remained still and silent and deserted.

They reached the north face of the chalet without incidence. According to Van Zandt's instruction, it was the easiest side to penetrate. French doors led onto a terrace that no one used because of the sharp winds. It wouldn't be locked. Once inside, they were on their own.

Maggie stared at the door, the empty panes of glass winking in the sunlight. She was about to reach for the handle when Mack pulled her hand back.

"I think it's wired," he whispered, his raw voice only a breath of sound in the wind. "Don't touch it. We'll look for another way in."

She nodded, moving back toward the edge of the terrace, when the sound of the dogs stopped her for a moment. She had a healthy respect for attack dogs, and the gun wouldn't hold off a truly determined pack.

"They're chained up, Maggie," Mack said, reading her hesitation almost before she felt it. "Let's keep on."

She looked at him. They were almost the same height, his warm hazel eyes on a level with hers. A thousand things ran through her mind, a thousand things she wanted to tell him before it was too late.

But time was already up. They stood there, motionless, as the French door opened into the blinding sunlight. A small, grandfatherly man stood there, with carefully combed strands of white hair plastered to a pink skull, luxurious waxed mustaches adorning his face, dark, cheerful eyes, and a beaming smile greeting them.

"How delightful to have such visitors," he said affably, his accent only faint. "I was expecting Van Zandt. But you're equally welcome. Won't you come in, Mlle. Bennett and M. Pulaski?" And he waved them toward the door with the machine gun that sat far too comfortably in his patrician hands.

twenty-two

"You can drop your guns on the table to your right," Mersot continued as he followed them into the cool, dim interior of the chalet. "And I would suggest you do it carefully. I'm an old man, and unused to modern weapons such as the one I'm holding. I would hate to make a mistake."

Maggie placed the small, efficient gun Willis had brought her on the little table by the door, moving away as Mack followed suit. Her mind was working feverishly, her eyes darting around the shadowed hallway, looking for something, anything, that might help them.

"I'm quite alone, Mlle. Bennett," Mersot said. "But I'm afraid that's going to work to your disadvantage. Since I feel unable to watch you both while I wait for my men to return, I'm going to have to . . . er . . . incapacitate you for the duration."

"Like hell . . ." Mack grated, and the machine gun swept around to aim directly at his groin.

"Don't be a hero, M. Pulaski. My friend Van Zandt has been surprisingly efficient in disposing of my men. I have no choice but to be as efficient while I wait for them to bring him back."

"Van Zandt?" Maggie queried innocently.

"Don't waste your energy, mademoiselle. The man is very brilliant in his own way, but he underestimated me quite badly. I've had reports on your sojourn during the last two weeks. I knew the moment you reached Switzerland. I know more about you than your own mother, and I know you were innocent enough to think you had a chance of killing me. I hope you're beginning to realize how foolish that notion was."

"Foolish indeed," Mack murmured. "So what are you going to do with us?"

"That remains to be seen. If you can come up with any reason why I might spare your lives, any way you might be useful to me, then I'll let you live. I'm not a bloodthirsty man, my friends. Just tidy. But if, as I suspect, your continued existence on this planet is only a liability to me, then I'm afraid my men will have to dispose of you. We have marvelous glaciers up here, and crevasses where a body could be frozen till the millennium. In the meantime, if you would be so kind as to follow me?"

"Where are we going?" Maggie asked with matching courtesy.

"I'm going to lock you in my wine cellar, Mlle. Bennett. It's windowless, and very dark indeed. I don't imagine I'll even need to bother tying you up, given your little problem with the dark."

"Damn you," she said, fighting back the sense of horror that his words had brought forth.

Mersot nodded his head in acknowledgment. "As for you, M. Pulaski, I'm simply going to lock you in the utility room. I don't happen to know your particular weakness."

"Sure you do, Mersot," he drawled in reply. "It's Maggie. You know I'll do anything you tell me to rather than risk her being hurt."

Mersot smiled faintly. "I must say I guessed as much. She won't like being locked in the dark, but I'm afraid it's necessary. I need you too frightened even to think, Mlle. Bennett. Come along, children. With luck this will all be over by nightfall."

Since the ending to this particular venture would probably involve their deaths, Maggie didn't find the notion terribly encouraging. She used every last ounce of her energy to keep her face bland and unconcerned. It would be bad enough, locked in the darkness without Mack to hold her. It would be even worse if he knew how terrified she was.

The chalet was even larger than it had appeared from the outside. Mack and Maggie moved down the hallways, through salons and offices and game rooms, always mindful of the gun behind them and the sweet, smiling old man holding it. They went down two flights of stairs and halted in front of a steel door with an electronic lock. Mersot punched a few buttons and the door opened with a quiet hiss. With a courtly politeness, Mersot gestured her inside.

She stalled for a moment. The room was pitch black; only the dim light from the hallway illuminated the first rows of wine racks. The floor was cement, and it smelled dry and cool and musty. She opened her mouth—to reason, to argue, to beg and plead—but her eyes met Pulaski's, and she shut it again. He looked even more desperate than she felt. For her, she realized, and the knowledge started a small fire burning inside her, warming her chilled flesh, lighting her darkness.

She shrugged. "See you in a while, Mack," she said airily, and stepped in the room.

"Very brave, mademoiselle," Mersot approved. "Do not bother trying to pick the locks. They're all electronically controlled, and you would end up with a very nasty shock indeed. *Au revoir.*" And the steel door swung shut silently behind her.

Only for a moment did the panic sweep over her. Only for a brief, terrified second did she lose control and feel herself begin to shatter. And then Mack's look came back to her, the feel of his arms around her, and she knew that the darkness wouldn't win this time. She would. She'd wait out her time in the pitch-black hole and figure out a way to stop Mersot. And if it involved killing him . . . She lost the last of her qualms with the quiet sound of the steel door closing in upon her.

She sank to the floor, pulling her knees up to her chest. The coolness of the wine cellar wasn't much worse than the Alpine heights in a strong wind, and the light sweater would be enough protection. She was almost tempted to try to break into one of

Mersot's bottles—he would have only premium vintages. She could also trash the place, smashing bottle after bottle of probably priceless wines. But Mersot would have no qualms at all about incapacitating her further, and despite his disclaimer, he was more than adept with that machine gun. No, she'd be a good, obedient girl, sit quietly on the stone floor, and figure how the hell they were going to get out of this mess in one piece.

It was amazing how time could lose its meaning in the darkness. It could have been hours, it could have been minutes, it could even have been days, she realized with sudden horror. The darkness was closing around her, smothering her, and she was losing her ability to keep it at bay. Summoning Mack's image worked only for so long, and then it turned to mockery, and Deke Robinson's hands were all over her, and he was laughing at her tears. And then Randall replaced him, cold and remote and hateful. And then Peter Wallace, as she'd last seen him, a bullet hole the size of a crater in his chest, his eyes open and reproachful, his mouth open but no words coming forth. Just blood.

"No," she thought she screamed, but the sound came out in a tiny whisper that echoed eerily in the darkness. Think of something else, she ordered herself. Think how Mack is faring, locked away in some utility room. Some nice, light utility room. Was he thinking of her? Or was he trying to figure some way out of this mess, the way she should be? And once more the memory of Mack worked its calming magic, bringing her panic back under control.

She heard the tiny ping of the electric lock moments before the doorknob turned. She raised her head, prepared to use the last ounce of energy she possessed to direct a defiant glare at the man opening the door. It was wasted on Mack.

He just stood there, staring at her. "Are you still with us, Superwoman?" His voice was not much more than a raw whisper, but she could see the worry and tension vibrating through his body.

"Don't call me Superwoman, Mack," she replied automatically. It took an embarrassing amount of effort to pull herself to her feet, but he didn't help, knowing that she didn't want any. "What's happening?"

"Mersot made the mistake of putting me in the room with the electrical circuits. He didn't realize that any rock 'n' roll musician, even a lead singer, knows his way around power boards. I rewired the place."

"What do you mean, you rewired the place?" She was dizzy, but not about to tell him that. She leaned against a wine rack, just for a moment.

"Rewired the alarm system. Anyone who touches the alarm switches or the turnoffs will get a hell of a jolt. Not enough to kill them . . ."

"Pansy," Maggie murmured, and Mack grinned.

"What can I say? I lack the killer instinct."

"Speaking of killer instinct, where's Mersot?"

"Up with his gerbils."

"His what?" she echoed.

"His gerbils. He has a passion for them. He had to show them off before he locked me in my little prison. He has this huge rodent farm with maybe a hundred gerbils crawling around."

"Yuck."

Mack shrugged. "I can think of worse hobbies. I think, Maggie, that we ought to get out of here."

"I think you're right. What time is it?"

"Sometime after four. We've been here a couple of hours—"

"Is that all?" she inquired faintly, pushing away from the wine rack and stepping into the light.

He just looked at her. "Was it awful?"

She shook her head. "No, Mack. I just closed my eyes and thought of you."

"Did you?" He moved then, into the shadow of the doorway, and kissed her full on the mouth, a brief, thorough kiss that put the last of her faltering courage back into her. "Come on, Maggie May. Let's get out of here before his henchmen return."

The corridors were still deserted as they made their way stealthily up the flights of stairs. They made it as far as the top level, a few short yards from freedom, when their one chance of escape was ripped from their hands.

"Leaving so soon?" Jeffrey Van Zandt inquired sweetly. "I hadn't realized you'd finished your mission."

Maggie just stared at him. She could feel Mack's tension, knew that any moment he might lunge for Van Zandt, and she knew she had to forestall that move. "What the hell are you doing here?"

"Taking care of loose ends," he said. "I'm a thorough man. Most of us are, in this business. Is Mersot dead?"

"No."

Van Zandt shrugged. "No matter. He will be within the hour. This place is set to blow at five o'clock, and it would take more demolition experts than Switzerland has ever seen to stop it."

"I'm hurt," Maggie mocked. "Didn't you trust us to be able to kill him?"

"Actually, I rather thought you'd manage it," he admitted. "The bomb was to take care of any extraneous details."

"Such as?"

Van Zandt smiled. "Such as proof of my involvement in Mersot's empire. Such as any leftover guards who might have reason to suspect me. Such as the two of you. You've been more than helpful, you realize. Everyone's been so busy looking for the two of you, trying to figure out how you were involved in the drug deal, that no one had any time to think about me. I've created the most wonderful paper trail, which is going to survive this, and with any luck I'll come out smelling like a rose. I'll think of you both, often," he added with genuine regret.

"I'm touched," she said.

"I knew you would be. Let's go and find Mersot, shall we?" he said. His own gun was smaller than Mersot's machine gun, but quite impressive nonetheless. And theirs were somewhere back by the French doors, hopelessly out of reach.

"Do we have a choice?" Mack's calm matched Van Zandt's.

"You know you don't. Where's Mersot? Not with his little rats, I hope?" Van Zandt inquired with a shudder of distaste, and Maggie felt her first glimmering of hope.

" 'Fraid so," Mack said. "Not to mention a machine gun."

Van Zandt dismissed the weapon with an airy wave of his own. "It doesn't work."

"Says who?" she demanded hotly.

Van Zandt smiled. "I say. How many times must I tell you, Maggie? I'm a thorough man. I saw to his little pet weapon the last time I was out here."

Her rage and frustration threatened to choke her, and if she'd been alone with Van Zandt, she would have gone for him, ignoring the weapon that rested so casually between them.

"If you'd bothered to tell us, Van Zandt, we might have been more successful in taking him out," Mack said, his voice holding nothing more noticeable than faint disapproval.

"Didn't I happen to mention it?" Van Zandt murmured. "How careless of me. Lead the way, Pulaski. That way you can have the pleasure of seeing the shock on Mersot's face."

Her first glance of the room at the top floor of the chalet made her appreciate Van Zandt's distaste. Mersot had his back to the door, and he was bent over a huge expanse of something that resembled an elaborate miniature train set. Until one looked more closely, and saw all the rodents scurrying back and forth in their little glassed-in village.

The late afternoon shadows were lengthening outside the expanse of windows that looked out over the valley. They must have made a noise, for Mersot looked up, into the wall of windows, and saw their reflection.

She couldn't help but flinch when the machine gun instantly met their eyes. The only sound in the room, above the scurry of a thousand rodent feet, was the useless click of the firing mechanism.

Mersot looked down at his weapon, shrugged, and dropped it, turning to face them with his charming smile still intact. "We keep underestimating each other, Jeffrey," he said. "It is a great

215

shame that we could not trust each other, work together. There would have been no stopping us."

"Alas, Hercule, I am a greedy man," Van Zandt murmured. "No matter how large my share is, I always seem to need more."

"That is too bad." Maggie watched with an odd detachment as Mersot's stubby fingers moved along the mahogany trim of the gerbil platform. "But I have had to weather other disappointments in my life. I can weather this one." And before she could move, his fingers found a white button and he pressed.

The results were not what she had expected, and indeed not what Mersot had intended either. There was a blue-white flash, the crackle of electricity, and Mersot's small, portly body was flung across the miniature city, crushing the glass with the force of the blow.

Mack moved before anyone else could, taking the old man's pulse. "He's dead."

"Quite a neat trick, Pulaski. I presume you're responsible? A nice jolt of electricity does wonders for an old man with a heart condition." Van Zandt edged closer, peering at his fallen nemesis.

Maggie moved forward, averting her eyes from the old man's body, trying to ignore the smell of scorched flesh, as she tried to pull the scattered remnants of her self-possession back around her. "Listen, Jeffrey," she said in an urgent tone of voice. "This is your chance. If Mack just fixes the electricity, we can all get out of here. It'll look like he died of natural causes, and no one will ever suspect that you had anything to do with it. You'd be home free. . . ."

"Not as long as the two of you survive," Van Zandt corrected her patiently. "No, I'm sorry, but the chalet has got to go, and the two of you with it. It's unfortunate, but I don't really have an alternative. I've been too softhearted as it is."

He'd turned his back to the table, ignoring Mersot's lifeless body, unaware of the horde of gerbils rushing through the smashed glass, swarming over their master's corpse, scurrying on little claws down his trouser legs to swarm across the floor. Maggie controlled her own shudder of revulsion, keeping her face calm and earnest, as the army of gerbils advanced on Van Zandt's pants leg.

"Jeffrey, think how much we've meant to each other. . . ." She was grasping at straws, and Van Zandt's soft giggle mocked her.

"Not a thing, Maggie. I never was your type, and I have to admit, you're not mine. I wish this could end differently, but I know that you wouldn't let Peter's death go unavenged. And I've got to come up with at least one scapegoat when I go back and confront the Company and Mancini. I still may be able to salvage . . ." His voice trailed off in a strangled scream as the first wave of gerbils gained his leg. And then they were swarming over him, a sea of rodents, clawing their furry way up his body, and all the time Van Zandt kept screaming, a terrified, high-pitched scream.

Maggie just stood there, watching in fascinated horror, until Mack dived across the room and tackled her, bringing her to the floor. Just in time, as Van Zandt began shooting at the gerbils scurrying over the floor, riddling the floor, the miniature village, and the fallen body of Mersot with bullets before he ran out of ammunition.

Maggie could barely see, crushed as she was beneath Mack's strong body. Van Zandt threw the gun at the gerbils, still screaming, and began beating at his body. And then he ran, racing around the room, beating at the clinging rodents, until he tripped over a fresh wave of them. He went stumbling, staggering, screaming toward the wall of windows. The next moment he was gone, with a crashing of heavy glass, over the balcony and down, down, down. . . .

Maggie lay there on the floor, Mack's body pressing down on her. The gerbils were at eye level, scurrying around, half mad with fear and panic, and as grateful as she was to them for their rescue, she didn't want to be their next host. "Let me up, for Christ's sake," she said in a strangled voice.

A second later Mack pulled her to her feet. "Had enough, Maggie May?" His voice was hollow. "This place is set to blow at five, unless Van Zandt was lying. I think we ought to get as far away as we can."

She swallowed a sudden, shuddering breath. "Yes," she said. "Let's get out of here."

"That's probably a good idea," Bud Willis drawled from the doorway. "Christ, you guys are a two-man demolition team." He kicked at the gerbils, stepping into the room and surveying it with his cold empty eyes.

"What is this, a convention?" Maggie demanded, his sudden appearance putting the final straw on her rapidly eroding courage. "What the hell are you doing here?"

"I've been on Van Zandt's tail for the past three days. I didn't figure I could count on the two of you to take care of him. I guess I was wrong. That Mersot?" He gestured toward the old man's body, which in the ensuing melee had tumbled to the floor. Gerbils were still crawling over him, and Maggie turned away with a shudder.

"That's Mersot. This place is going to blow up, Willis. Not that I really feel you deserve a warning, but I'm a nice guy," Mack drawled. "We're out of here, unless you have any objections."

"No objections," he said absently, looking around him.

"Do you want to come with us?"

He grinned, that death's-head grin. "And interfere with the happy couple? No way. We'll meet up again, sooner or later. In the meantime, Pulaski, watch your back."

Mack's hazel eyes were narrowed with dislike. "I'll do that," he said. He looked at Maggie, and she waited dismally for an order. An order that never came. "What's your pleasure, Maggie?"

Relief and love swept through her. "Let's do it, Mack," she said. "Bye, Willis."

"Bye, sweet lips."

The late afternoon was sunny, bright, clear, and cool around the chalet. Van Zandt's body was somewhere down in the crevasse beneath the chalet, lost for all time, Maggie hoped. Even if he were found, the authorities would simply assume he was a victim of the surprising explosion of Hercule Mersot's chalet. And if anyone was still suspicious, she had complete faith in Hamilton's ability to quiet those doubts.

"There's a Jeep Cherokee parked down below the gate," Mack said, his words prosaically normal. The last few minutes of horror and death might never have happened. "Can you stand it?"

"A Jeep Cherokee?" she echoed wearily, matching his coolness. "I haven't recovered from my last ride in one."

"We can always walk to Venice, but it would take a hell of a long time. And I think I've walked enough for one day," Mack said solemnly.

"Venice?" she said, momentarily distracted. "We're going to Venice?"

"If you're amenable. I figure we should give Hamilton and his buddies enough time to clear things up before we go back. And I thought you'd like Venice. You seem to have developed a taste for intrigue, and Venice is the most intrigue-ridden city in history."

She just stood there, looking at him. "Don't you think I might have had my fill of intrigue?"

"That'll only last a day," he said, his voice full of confidence. "Venice is also the most romantic city in history. Seems like a good place to spend our honeymoon. As long as there's not a Holiday Inn on the Grand Canal."

"Honeymoon? Wasn't two times enough?"

Mack grinned, that dear, warm smile that he seemed to reserve just for her. "Not when I kept marrying the wrong women, dear heart. I'd love to get down on one knee and propose, Maggie May, but I think we ought to get away from the chalet before it turns into matchsticks."

"You can get down on one knee in Venice," she said. "I'll

give you my answer then. Are you sure you aren't planning to marry me just to get close to my mother?"

"Screw your mother."

"My point exactly. I want to make sure your intentions are pure—" She was silenced quite effectively by his mouth on hers, a kiss she returned with complete enthusiasm. "You're right," she said when she emerged. "We'd better get out of here while we still can. Lead me to the damned Jeep."

At 5:01 exactly there was a loud rumbling in the valley. Maggie and Mack were already out of sight of the chalet, but they heard the explosion, and their eyes met. "Do you suppose Willis made it out all right?" she asked.

"Do you care?"

She thought about it. "No."

"Neither do I." He leaned back in the driver's seat and shut his eyes.

"Come on, Mack. Drive on. I want to make it to Venice by tomorrow night."

"Maggie May, we have the rest of our lives together," Mack said, his raw voice low and sexy. "What's your hurry?"

"Pulaski, a lifetime isn't long enough for you and me," she said. "Step on it."

And Mack stamped on the accelerator, taking off into the cool evening air with a spurt of gravel. A lifetime wasn't enough to hold them, Maggie thought. But it was a start, and a damned good one. And with their backs turned on the fiery death and destruction that had dogged them for so long, they headed out into the sunset. And into life.

If you liked *Romancing the Stone,* you'll <u>love</u>

THE PEREGRINE CONNECTION

Romantic suspense novels for women who enjoy action, danger, mystery, and intrigue mixed up in their romances.

_____ #1 TALONS OF THE FALCON   18498-3-36

_____ #2 FLIGHT OF THE RAVEN   12560-X-24

_____ #3 IN SEARCH OF THE DOVE   11038-6-12

by Rebecca York   **$2.95 each**